The
IRIS CODE

The
IRIS CODE

Anita Dickason

Mystic Circle Books

Publisher: Mystic Circle Books
Cover Design: Mystic Circle Books & Designs, LLC
Editors:
Lisa Henson: theplainspokenpen.com
Jennie Rosenblum: jennierosenblum.com

ISBN
978-1-958464-05-2: Paperback
978-1-958464-06-9: Hardback
978-1-958464-07-6: eBook

Library of Congress Control Number: 2024910640

Acknowledgments

My daughter
Christy Kay
With her help all things are possible.

My daughter
Julie
for having the patience to listen.

Two amazing editors
Lisa and Jennie
for their expertise and invaluable suggestions.

Chapter 1

Propelled by a sharp jab of anxiety, Riley Phillips bolted to the back of a decrepit barn. A dog's piercing bark and seventy-some-pound body, rigid with tension, stopped her dead in her tracks.

The anxiety morphed into a full-blown state of apprehension, tinged with disbelief. The dog was in the wrong place.

As her gaze swept beyond the animal to the dump site littered with busted trash bags, rusted pieces of metal, broken furniture, and wood, even a refrigerator with the door hanging by one hinge, her sense of wrongness deepened. Had months of training just gone down the tubes? A disheartening thought since there was no reason for Milo to alert.

Earlier, Riley seeded the outside of the abandoned farmhouse with small cadaver-scented decoy bags, not this dump site behind the barn. Not wanting to chance an injury to Milo's paws, she'd steered clear of it. This time, when ordered to find, Milo immediately raced toward the barn instead of heading toward the farmhouse.

When Riley didn't respond, Milo barked again before dropping to the ground in his alert position. His nose pointed toward a pile of trash and wood with a mattress tossed on top. The dog had never alerted over a dead animal. It was a failure for a Human Remains Detection (HRD) certification. Another bark, louder and with a more persistent tone, echoed. With a small sigh of resignation, Riley said,

"Okay, big guy, let's see what you found."

Whatever it was, the incident had to be documented. With a shrug, she slid the backpack off her shoulders. Before setting it on the ground, Riley retrieved her prize possession, a Canon EOS Rebel T7 camera. She was a journalist by trade and a freelance photographer, so the camera was always in the backpack.

After snapping several pictures of the dog, she said, "Milo, sit," before cautiously stepping over the debris. No telling what was living underneath the rubble. It wasn't always a four-legged critter. A gust of wind swirled, raising a faint, nauseating odor.

Deflated by the knowledge of what she was about to find, Riley took pictures of the large pile of debris from different angles, then slung the camera around her neck. Before wrestling the mattress away from the pile, she pulled on leather gloves she'd stuffed in the back pocket of her jeans. Most of the wood was easy to grab and throw. Even so, the stack was large, and it wasn't long before sweat plastered the t-shirt to her back. Unable to escape the noxious odor that was getting stronger, each breath churned her stomach.

Nearby, Milo sat. His tongue dangled out of his mouth as he panted.

Riley shot him a quick look. "I hope you know this isn't good. By now, we should be on our way home," she grumbled, tossing aside the remains of a fence post. Milo woofed.

Once the smaller pieces were out of the way, she stopped to study the large piece of plywood. Too unwieldy to toss, she grabbed it by its edge. In her struggle to lift it, Riley stepped forward to push it upward. When she glanced down, shock rippled through her. "Oh! My! God," she exclaimed. It wasn't an animal. The toes of her boots touched the leg of a corpse. Milo had alerted on the real deal.

With a grunt, Riley shoved. The plywood toppled backward, hitting the ground with a thud. In disbelief, she staggered back. Her fingers trembled as she struggled to strip off the gloves. While gaping at the body, unthinkingly, she slapped them together to remove the dirt before stuffing them back into a pocket. The bitter taste of bile rose in her throat. For cripes' sake, she couldn't puke. What did that say about her ability to handle search and rescue?

Riley gulped, stumbling until she was clear of the debris. As the shock receded, questions flooded her mind. Though for now, they'd have to wait. Milo woofed as he crowded against her legs. His nose nudged her hand.

Riley dropped to one knee, wrapping her arms around the thick ruff. "I didn't believe you. I am so sorry I doubted you." She rubbed his head. "Oh, what a good, good dog you are." Milo gazed at her with adoring eyes and woofed.

Despite her distress at finding a body, praising Milo was necessary. From one of the webbed pockets on the side of the backpack, she pulled out a special treat, a large pepperoni-flavored dog biscuit. The only time he got one was for finding the decoy bag. This time, it was for real.

She waved it in the air. "Good, good dog. Are you ready?" Milo barked, his eyes fixed on her hand. She flipped it in the air for him to catch.

While he chomped on the biscuit, Riley pulled a cellphone from a vest pocket, tapping the speed dial for 911. Even though the dispatcher's voice echoed with disbelief, Riley was assured a deputy sheriff would be on the way.

Pocketing the phone, she moaned, "Great, just great." The county sheriff was the south end of a northbound horse. In the past, she'd had several run-ins with Sheriff Otto Rutherford, *the third*.

From inside the backpack, Riley pulled out a collapsible plastic bowl and punched it open. She filled it with water from a bottle stuck in a mesh pocket. Milo greedily lapped while Riley opened a second bottle, taking a deep swig. Where she stood, the body was out of sight. Still, the image was burned into her mind. There was only one reason it was there. Someone killed him. From what she'd learned about cadavers for the search and rescue program, she didn't believe the body had been there all that long. It wasn't there a few days ago when she and Milo did another training run. After swallowing the last gulp of water, the empty bottles and Milo's dish were stowed in the backpack.

Determined to ignore the churning nausea, Riley moved toward the body. Partially wrapped in a filthy piece of plastic, the body lay in a shallow hole. Not much effort had been put into burying it. It looked like someone started to dig the hole, gave up, dumped the body on its side, and tossed dirt, wood, and trash on top.

Riley carefully stepped around the body, snapping pictures. A flicker of light drew her attention to a ring on a hand. She took advantage of the plywood and knelt on it to get closer. After studying the ring in the viewfinder, intrigued, she zoomed the lens, taking several close-ups before turning to examine the head and face.

For a moment, she considered the dirt scattered across the head. Did she dare? After all, this was a crime scene, but who would know if the dirt was pushed aside to get a clearer picture? Still, she had to be careful. Riley didn't want Rutherford accusing her of messing with the evidence. It wouldn't take much for the sheriff to throw her butt in jail.

Before touching the dirt, she gloved up. As clumps were brushed away, there wasn't a reason to wonder about the cause of death. The bullet hole in the head was a dead giveaway. At the unintentional thought, a grimace crossed Riley's face. What she thought was dirt was dried blood. Dark streaks trailed down the neck.

Continually shifting, she zoomed in on the head and the side of the man's face. Riley wanted to roll the body over, just enough to get a picture of the entire face, but decided moving the body was pushing her luck. Satisfied that she had taken every possible picture, Riley stashed the camera in the backpack. "Come on, Milo. No point hanging around here." They could wait for the deputy in the cool comfort of the truck.

After settling Milo in the backseat, Riley tossed the backpack on the passenger seat before sliding behind the wheel. Since she figured it would take a while for the deputy to arrive, there was time for a call to Susan Hutchin, editor and owner of the *Fredericksburg Register.*

"I didn't expect to hear from you today. I thought you were doing a training run with Milo," Susan said as she answered.

"I did, and it's why I'm calling. I've got a news flash for you. Milo found a body."

Susan chuckled. "Of course he did. After all, you've been training him for months with those bags."

"No. I mean a for … real … body."

"What!" Susan's voice pitched upward.

"Milo alerted on a body buried behind the barn at the old Henning farm. It's where I'm at, waiting for the deputy sheriff to show up."

"Good lord! Hang on. I need to get to my office so I can type."

Rustling noises echoed, then the squeak of a chair before Susan said, "Talk to me."

In concise words, Riley covered the details as Susan typed. When she finished, she added, "I've got pictures, but I'll have to wait until I get home to send them to you."

"I'll get this on the wire as breaking news, then follow up with the pictures and anything else you find out. When do you think you will be home?"

With a wry tone, Riley said, "It all depends on how fast Rutherford kicks me out. I'll keep you posted."

Her boss was still chuckling as the line went dead.

With the air conditioner cranked to full blast, she leaned against the headrest. Her journalistic curiosity tingled. Who had been murdered and why? "Milo, someone sure didn't want anyone finding this guy."

In all the months of using the old, abandoned farm to train Milo, she'd never seen another person. If it hadn't been for Milo, the man would never have been discovered. Milo, his head hanging over the console, woofed.

Her thoughts shifted to when the notion of search and rescue first started. While searching for a hiker at the state park, Riley had been impressed with the search and rescue team. Their dog had swiftly found the man who had tumbled into a ravine. Unconscious, with a broken leg and near death, he might not have been discovered in time if not for the search dog.

The research about search and rescue dogs for her news article sparked an interest. At the time, Milo, an all-white German shepherd, was ten months old. Riley put him through the SAR criteria to see if he qualified, and they began the weekly training curriculum. Today's run was the last before his certification test, though, to her mind, he'd already passed.

The sound of an engine broke her thoughts. A county sheriff's car pulled alongside. Riley hopped out, opening the back door for Milo. While certain he wouldn't be in the way, Riley hooked the leash to be on the safe side. As she walked to the front of the truck, two men dressed in tactical-style uniforms climbed out of the car.

In a loud, demanding voice, one said, "What's this all about? More of your drama to get attention?" Mickey Bennett, a thickly built, dark-haired man with what she always thought were mean eyes, glared at her.

Riley wasn't sure who she disliked more, Mickey or his boss.

They were both cut from the same cloth, arrogant and rude. Like Rutherford, she had locked horns with Mickey on more than one occasion.

"Looks like you have to do some work for a change," she retorted.

Billy Thatcher, a tall, lanky man with long, stringy, blond hair that brushed the collar of his shirt, said, "Hey, don't you two start sniping at each other."

Beside her, Milo tensed. To calm him, she laid her hand on his head. "Billy, I'm not taking any of his guff. Didn't the dispatcher tell you I found a body?"

The two men looked at each other before Billy said, "It's not how the call was worded. It was to meet you about something you found."

She'd been right about the dispatcher not believing her. "Well, for your information, someone stashed a body behind the barn."

Billy turned. "Show us what you found."

At five-three and maybe one hundred and ten pounds dripping wet, and Milo in tow, Riley was hard-pressed to keep up with his long-legged stride. Reaching the back of the barn, Billy stopped, his gaze sweeping piles of debris. "Okay. Where's the body?"

Riley stepped around him, taking a few steps toward the cleared area. She pointed. "There."

Billy walked to where she had gestured. "Son of a gun." He squatted near the edge of the churned-up dirt, studying the body.

Mickey stepped alongside him.

Billy asked, "How did you find it?"

"I didn't. Milo did. I've been using this place for months, training him for search and rescue."

Billy glanced up at her. "I hadn't heard. Was the body like this when you found it?"

"It was covered with the plywood and that pile of trash and

mattress over there." She gestured. "I thought Milo alerted on a dead animal. I had to find out." A shiver raced down her spine. "I didn't expect to find a body."

Mickey's head swiveled. His dark eyes stared at Milo with a disturbing look. She wondered if he had a thing about dogs.

Ignoring Mickey, she asked, "Billy, do you know if a man has been reported missing? I filed a story with Susan and will be doing a follow-up."

Billy stood. "You've already reported this? You sure didn't waste any time. The boss isn't going to like it. As far as telling you anything, no can do."

He pulled out a cellphone. When the call was answered, he said, "Got a body at the Henning farm. Send out the crime scene unit. Might as well go ahead and send the ambulance. Let them know they'll be transporting to Austin." He paused, listened, then added, "You'd better let the boss know."

"Austin! Why Austin?" Riley asked.

He pocketed the phone. "Medical examiner. We don't have one." Billy's gaze shifted across the trash pile, then back to the body.

Riley said, "It doesn't look like he's been here that long." At a questioning look from Billy, she added, "We did another run four days ago. The body wasn't here. It should be easy to identify him."

In a sarcastic tone, Mickey said, "Since when did you become an expert on criminal investigations?"

With a smug look, she said, "You don't have to be an expert. Just look at the ring."

Both men stared down. Billy dropped to one knee, leaning forward to take a closer look.

"I'll save you the trouble," Riley told them. "It's a Texas A&M University class ring."

With a sneer, Mickey said, "So what?"

"His name will be engraved inside. It's a tradition with Aggie class rings."

Billy said, "Something I didn't know." He shot a look at Mickey looming over him. "I guess you didn't either."

Riley said, "If you remove it, you can get his name."

Billy paused, looking down. "No. It would be better to let the M.E. remove it."

Mickey snorted. "Nothing we can do here until the crime scene van arrives." He turned.

As he watched his partner walk away, Billy's eyes narrowed. Once Mickey was out of sight, Billy slowly stepped around the debris, searching the ground.

Riley wondered if Billy was just as disgusted as she was by Mickey's abrasive attitude.

When his phone rang, he stopped. "Thatcher." He listened before saying, "Between the house and the road, there's enough room." After another brief pause, he disconnected, pocketing the phone.

He eyed Riley. "Rutherford's on the way. He's got that fancy new helicopter."

Riley groaned. "That's all I need to really make my day."

With Milo trotting alongside her, Riley followed Billy as he headed to the patrol car. Once Milo was inside the truck, she settled behind the wheel. While she waited, Riley kept an eye on the two deputies in the vehicle. There seemed to be a heated discussion. She wondered what it was all about. Maybe Mickey was getting his comeuppance for his nasty attitude, an uplifting thought.

In the distance, the sound of a helicopter intensified. A few minutes later, it flew overhead, circled, then slowly dropped. The deputies jumped out of their car.

Once it was on the ground, the sheriff climbed out. Attired in dark brown pants, a white shirt, and cowboy boots, his hand clamped down on an oversized cowboy hat that threatened to fly off. His belly, hanging over the gun belt, jiggled as he sidestepped large clumps of weeds.

Riley stood by the truck with Milo alongside her.

In a raucous voice, Rutherford said, "What's she doing here?"

Before the two men could answer, Riley said, "Just so happens, I called about the body. That's why."

"Huh?" Rutherford scowled at her. "How did you know it was here?"

"I didn't," Riley said.

"Then how did you find it? And don't get smart-mouthed with me."

"My dog found it."

With a harsh tone, Rutherford said, "You'd better think twice about lying. You do, and this time, you'll find yourself in jail."

Anger shot through her. "I'm training Milo for search and rescue. Have been for months."

The sheriff stared at Milo sitting next to Riley's legs. His jaw clenched. "You want me to believe that dog found the body?"

"I really don't give a hoot what you believe."

Rutherford's face mottled with anger. "Take your dog and get out of here." He turned to Billy. "Where's this body?"

Mickey's lips twisted in a malicious grin as he walked past her, following the two men.

Angry that she'd let Rutherford push her buttons, Riley opened the back door to let Milo hop inside. But that was usually the case whenever she had the misfortune to encounter the man.

On the way back to town, she passed the crime scene van. Dang, she was hoping to stick around and get a few more pictures. She wanted answers and knew they wouldn't be forthcoming from

Rutherford. She'd just have to go around him. It wouldn't be the first time.

Several months back, she'd discovered the owner of a local bar was dealing drugs. While she'd reported it, Rutherford refused to provide any status on the investigation. When she learned he was planning to search the place, Riley waited until the deputies were inside, then took pictures through the windows. Rutherford had seen her, and there had been a few ugly moments when he threatened to throw her in jail for obstructing an investigation. Since she was in the parking lot, his rants were empty threats. When they didn't find any drugs, Rutherford believed she'd made up the story to get a headline. Though she couldn't prove it, she knew someone had tipped off the owner.

This time, she'd just have to remember not to give Rutherford any reason to follow up on one of his threats.

Chapter 2

As she neared the house, Milo woofed. "I know. It's good to be home." Parked in front of the garage, Riley opened the passenger door. With a sharp bark, Milo jumped out. She grabbed the backpack and strode to the front step while Milo raced around the yard, sometimes stopping to mark a spot along the fence line and trees. Once he finished, she whistled, turning to unlock the front door.

After the morning's traumatic event, Riley desperately wanted a shower. Still, she took a moment to fill Milo's bowls with water and dog chow. While he happily munched, Riley stood under a blast of hot water, hoping to wash away the lingering scent of death. After towel-drying her hair, she donned shorts and a t-shirt before padding to the kitchen. Through the open door leading to the utility room, she checked on Milo. Stretched out on his bed, his tail thumped; otherwise, he didn't move.

Opening the cupboard, she grabbed a glass and filled it with ice, then added tea from the container in the fridge. On the way to her office, she retrieved the camera from the backpack lying on the couch.

When her parents retired, they decided to take to the open road with an RV, giving her the house. Riley moved into the master bedroom and converted her old bedroom into an office. She took a deep swig of tea before setting the glass on a coaster on her desk. Seated, Riley booted the computer and set up a new file folder before transferring the pictures from the camera. As she sipped the tea, she slowly studied each one. The ones with the ring were enlarged to see the date, 2007. Satisfied, she cleared the cache on the camera and saved the file folder to her cloud account.

After taking a moment to gather her thoughts, Riley's fingers flew across the keyboard. Once the article was finished, it and two pictures were attached to an email to Susan. Then she sent a text to alert her boss. A few minutes later, the phone rang. It was Susan.

"Great article and pictures. But you didn't include anything about Milo finding the body."

Riley said, "I didn't think it was necessary to add it."

"I disagree. It adds a great human-interest touch. Any reason why I shouldn't?"

An uneasy feeling rolled over Riley, though she was uncertain why. "I guess not."

"Are these the only pictures you have?"

"I have more, including close-ups of the body. Since we don't know who it is, I didn't think using them would be a good idea."

"If you have one of Milo, send it to me. I'll add a short paragraph about you and Milo, then put it out on the news wire. All the major news outlets have already picked up the first one. What are you doing to follow up?"

"Get an identification."

"Good. I want to stay on top of this." She disconnected.

After sending the pictures to Susan, Riley picked up the glass and phone and strolled back to the kitchen. She couldn't help but wonder what happened after she left. It should be easy to find out. Call the fire department. Even if the crew was still at the scene, she could find out who was on the ambulance run.

She lucked out. One of the medics was Carla Sanchez, a friend from high school. She left word for Carla to call.

Probably because she'd never dealt with murder, she couldn't stop the images of the body rolling in her head. Riley felt like she needed to do something, but what? It was up to the sheriff's department to investigate. There wasn't anything she could do until she had a name.

Riley stuck the phone in her pocket, then refilled the glass. Milo came to life at the sound of the glass door sliding open. He dashed into the backyard.

The patio door led to a covered porch that ran the length of the back of the house. The three-bedroom home wasn't large, about 2200 square feet, with a small dining room, a large open living room, kitchen, and utility room. It sat on two acres, which was a plus for Milo. He had plenty of room to run.

She settled in a chair, propped her feet on the porch rail, and watched him race around the backyard. Milo followed the same trek every time, stopping at the same fence posts. Satisfied that all was well in his world, he trotted toward the porch. His butt hit the grass, while he pointedly stared at the basket next to her chair.

"Oh, you want to play?" She'd swear the dog grinned.

The basket held a variety of toys. His favorite was a chewed-up, ratty-looking baseball. "Milo, fetch." She threw, and he ran. His jaws clamped around the ball. He trotted up the steps and dropped it at her feet. She threw it again, this time higher and further away. His tail whipped as he raced after it. His eyes never left the ball sailing through the air. With a high leap, he caught it in his mouth. Milo pranced back with a distinct "see what I just did" look. The ball dropped in front of her.

Laughing, she said, "Okay. See if you can get this one." She heaved, throwing it deep into the yard. Milo raced after it.

When the phone rang, she quickly tugged it out of a pocket. It was Carla.

"Hey, girlfriend, you had some excitement today."

Riley groaned. "Not the kind I'd want to have every day."

Milo dropped the ball. When Riley ignored him, he woofed. "Okay, okay." She picked it up and threw it, then wiped her hand on her shorts.

"Who are you talking to?"

"Milo. He's playing in the backyard."

"Everyone was talking about him today. The story's already hit the gossip mill, about how he found the body."

"Since I thought he alerted on a dead animal, it was a shock. I'm still trying to get my head around who and why. What was going on when you got there?"

"Typical for our trusty sheriff, Rutherford had his shorts in a wad. Boy, was he ever pissed at you. What set him off this time?"

Outspoken, Carla wasn't the type to back down on any issue. As the only female EMT, surrounded by testosterone-driven males, her bluntness had been honed to a fine point.

"He accused me of lying about Milo finding the body."

"Uh, oh. I bet that didn't go over well."

"I told him I didn't care what he believed."

Milo trotted up. The ball rolled across the porch. With a hand motion, she signaled him to lie down. With a pitiful expression, he dropped, laying his head on his paws.

Carla roared with laughter. "Oh, my gosh! I wish I'd seen that. What did he do?"

"Puffed up like a toad, then kicked me out. It's why I'm curious about what happened after I left."

"Dustin and I had to wait for Henry Caslon to finish taking his pictures. Then we bagged the body along with the plastic wrapped around it. Turned out it was a shower curtain. The dang thing had daisies on it. I'm not sure I will ever look at a daisy in the same way again. Oh, by the way, the guy was shot in the head."

"Did they get a name?"

"Nope. Still a John Doe."

"I'm surprised you got back this fast from Austin."

"We didn't go."

"What!"

Milo's head jerked up. She motioned him back down.

"Yeah. Surprised the heck out of me too. We took the body to the Lombardy funeral home."

"I thought it was supposed to go to the medical examiner."

"So did I. But I'm just a lowly medic. What the heck do I know? Rutherford, Mickey, and Billy got their heads together. The next thing we knew, Rutherford ordered us to take it to the funeral home and let them transport it to Austin in their hearse tomorrow."

"Did he say why?"

"Oh, he mumbled something about not wanting to pull the ambulance out of the county. I thought it was weird. It's not like we've never transferred a patient to an Austin hospital or taken bodies to the M.E.'s office. But hey, it was Rutherford's decision."

"When are they leaving?"

"I guess as soon as the funeral home opens. Why?"

"Susan wants an update. It might be worth a trip to Austin. Once the M.E. gets the body, we'll know his name."

"You sound pretty certain about that."

Riley explained about the ring.

"How odd. I overheard Mickey say something about a ring to Billy. You'd think they'd want to know who this guy was as fast as they could. Why dither around, leaving the body at the funeral home? But then, we're talking about Rutherford here. I've never considered him the brightest bulb on the planet. How he ever got elected is beyond me. I sure didn't vote for him."

In the background, Riley heard alarms going off.

"I've got to go," Carla said. The line went dead.

Riley laid the phone aside. Milo woofed, nudging the ball closer to her foot with his nose. Idly, she picked it up and threw it while pondering what she'd learned. None of it made sense. And it seemed like a flimsy excuse about keeping the ambulance in the county. She tossed the ball a few more times before finally calling a halt.

In the kitchen, Riley pulled out the leftover chicken tortellini casserole from the night before, popping the bowl into the microwave. She'd found from living alone that it was too easy to fall into a routine of sandwiches or frozen pizza. It's why she began experimenting with new recipes. The casserole was a new one, and it was a keeper. The downside was trying to cook small quantities. It was almost impossible, which meant eating leftovers several times.

When the microwave dinged, she grabbed a dishcloth, removed the hot dish, and carried it to the table in the breakfast nook. Seated, she had a broad view of the backyard through the multiple windows.

Milo padded over, laying his head on her thigh. His large, dark eyes looked at her with a woeful expression.

Riley chuckled. "Don't give me that sad look. You've already had your chow."

He whimpered.

"Okay, just one piece, and that's it."

Milo sat back, his body quivering, tail thumping the floor.

"Just who has who trained here?" she muttered, selecting a large piece of chicken. Making sure it was cool, she tossed it over his head.

With one jump, Milo snatched it. He chomped, then sat back down. His gaze locked on her face.

"No, that's all you get. Go back to your bed."

His head drooped as he stood, heading back to the utility room.

Riley chuckled again. Milo acted like he'd just been beaten.

As she ate, her thoughts shifted back to the victim and the questions with no answers, at least not yet. Once the kitchen was squared away, she headed to the office, where she opened the computer folder with the pictures. Riley slowly studied each one. Most were duplicates with only a slight difference. Riley selected the better ones, copying them into a new folder. If she needed any for future articles, she wouldn't have to weed through the entire file.

Before shutting down the computer, she pulled up the newspaper website. Both articles were front and center under breaking news. Susan had used the photo with Milo in his alert position.

Finding Milo had been a blessing in disguise. She'd written a story about the local animal shelter for a drive to adopt animals. When she strolled through the shelter, the sight of a small puppy, his nose pressed against the wire cage, nearly broke her heart. Getting a dog hadn't been part of her plans. But when she walked out, Milo was in her arms, licking her face. She'd never regretted the decision.

According to the vet, white German shepherds were one of the most intelligent breeds in the dog world. They excelled at obedience, canine sports, and jobs like search and rescue. They also got quickly bored, to which she could attest. Milo needed a lot of stimulation.

The subject of her thoughts stood in the doorway and woofed. "Are you telling me it's time to go out?" He woofed again, trotting back to the living room.

She shut down the computer. Her fingers flipped off the light as she walked out. When she slid the glass door open, Milo darted outside. As she waited on the back porch, a light breeze rippled the tips of her hair. In the distance, coyotes yelped. It should have been a pleasant evening, but she couldn't shake the apprehension hovering in the back of her mind.

Chapter 3

With the possibility of a trip to Austin, Riley was up early. The temperature was already rising, promising another hot summer day when she and Milo left. Much to his delight, she lowered the back window to let him stick his nose out. His tail thumped the back of her seat. She had the radio set to her favorite station. The ring of the phone barely registered over Garth Brooks singing *The Dance.* Riley tapped a button, turning off the radio to answer it.

It was Carla. "A call came out on the police radio. It's for the funeral home."

"What for?"

"I don't know. One of those meet-complainant type of calls. I thought you might be interested."

"I sure the heck am. I'm on my way into town. It's now my first stop. Thanks for the heads-up."

Two police cars and a sheriff's car were already parked on the curving driveway in front of the funeral home when Riley pulled to the curb. She hopped out, looking for a place to leave Milo. The water spigot on the wall of the building was her only option. After wrapping the end of the leash around the handle, she headed inside. The woman seated behind a desk gave her a pained look when Riley walked up.

"If you're looking for the rest of the officers, they're in the back."

Giving her a reassuring smile, Riley said, "I'm not a cop. I'm a reporter and want to find out why the police are here." Her hand reached out. "Riley Phillips," she said as they shook hands. "And you are?"

The woman perked up. "Lucy Cannon. What paper?"

"The *Register*. I'd like to ask you some questions."

She hesitated, glancing toward the large double doors that led to the rest of the building. "I'm not sure I should be talking about it."

"Well, at least let me get your picture before I talk to the cops. A picture makes a story much more interesting."

The woman's eyes gleamed. "My picture? Oh, I guess that would be okay. When will it be in the newspaper?"

While Riley removed the camera from the backpack, Lucy hurriedly pulled open a drawer. From the handbag stashed inside, she pulled out a mirror. After adding more lipstick, she fluffed the bangs across her forehead.

"I'm not sure. It will be up to the editor." Riley lifted the camera, snapped a shot, and casually asked, "So, what happened?"

"It's unbelievable." Lucy lowered her voice. "A body is missing. Whoever heard of such a thing?"

Riley's eyes widened. Whatever she expected, it wasn't this. "Oh, my gosh. What do you mean it's missing?"

"It's just gone, disappeared."

"Who was it?"

Lucy's eyes nervously flicked at the doors. "That's what's odd. No one knows. The body was found yesterday at some farm. We were supposed to take it to the medical examiner in Austin today."

Riley's gut tightened. "Someone stole it?" She took another picture.

The woman shrugged her shoulders. "I guess so, though I've got no idea how. When I left last night, all the doors were locked and still locked this morning. All I know is the cops aren't happy about it. There was even an argument between the cops and the sheriff's deputy that showed up."

Riley's fingers itched to take notes, but she was afraid Lucy would stop talking if she stopped taking pictures. "What was the argument about?"

"The sergeant told the sheriff's deputy the body should have immediately gone to the M.E.'s office. Not left here overnight."

"Why was it here?" She shifted to get another angle.

Lucy smiled, waiting for the click of the camera, before saying, "I'm not sure. My boss got a call from Sheriff Rutherford. Then the ambulance showed up and dropped it off."

"Who discovered it was missing?"

"Well, I did. I'm usually the first one to arrive." The phone rang. "Sorry, I have to get this."

Riley thanked her and stowed the camera back in the bag, figuring she had all she would get.

With a quick wiggle of her fingers at Riley, the woman picked up the receiver.

Riley slung the bag over her shoulder and turned toward the double doors. One abruptly opened. Mickey Bennett walked out. A wrathful look flashed in his eyes as he stopped in front of her.

"What the devil are you doing here?" he growled.

She smiled, showing her teeth. "My job. Care to comment on why a murder victim the sheriff left at a funeral home, is missing?"

Mickey's eyes flicked toward the woman on the phone. He stepped closer. "Little girl, it might be wise to keep your nose out of police business. Remember what happened the last time you got involved. You almost landed in jail. This time, it might be worse."

Her jaw tightened in anger. Riley tilted her head to glare up at him. Over six feet tall, the heavy-set deputy towered over her. "First, Deputy Bennett, I'm not a little girl. I'm an accredited reporter and have a right to ask questions. And … don't ever threaten me again."

He snorted with disgust as he stepped around her, heading to the front door. Another officer walked out of the chapel.

"Riley, what are you doing here?"

"Looking for a story. Why is the body Milo found yesterday missing?"

Fredericksburg Police Sergeant Artie Ingram grimaced. "There isn't much I can tell you. Let's walk outside. I need to get back to the office."

She'd known Artie since she was a child. He lived just down the road from Riley's place. Pushing fifty, he'd worked for the police department for as long as she could remember.

"How did you find out so soon?" he asked, holding the front door open for her.

"Aw, now, Sarge. You know I can't reveal my sources."

He chuckled. Spotting Milo, he headed for the dog.

Milo raised his head. His tail thumped the ground in anticipation.

With a flash of her hand, she gave him the release signal, and Milo jumped to his feet with a sharp bark. Artie was a friend.

The sergeant rubbed the dog's head. He glanced at Riley. "I always thought there was something special about this guy. You've done a good job in training him. He's going to be a real asset in search and rescue."

A jolt of pride shot through her. "It was unexpected. Anything you can tell me?"

"Not much. The funeral personnel planned to take the body to the medical examiner's facility this morning. During the night, someone gained access to the building and stole it. That's about all I can tell you. The crime scene unit is on the way, though it's unlikely they'll find anything."

"Who had keys?"

"At this point, I don't know. They may not have needed a key. The lock on the loading dock doors is pretty simple. Easy to jimmy."

"You said they. So you think it was more than one person?"

"Manhandling a corpse isn't easy under the best of conditions. So yes, I think there were at least two."

"Has the man been identified?"

"No."

"Has a man been reported missing?"

"Not that I know about. But I haven't had a chance to check. Since the victim was found in the county, it's Rutherford's jurisdiction."

"Why was the body left here?"

Artie stepped away from the dog. "It was Sheriff Rutherford's decision. You need to ask him."

"Hmm … don't want to rat out a fellow officer." She grinned to take the sting out of the words.

"Not really. I just don't have an answer. I don't like to idly speculate."

"One more, then. Isn't the body of someone murdered supposed to immediately be sent to the medical examiner?"

Artie shrugged his shoulders. "Every case is different. I need to get going." He flashed her an easy smile and headed toward the squad car.

After Riley unhooked Milo's leash from the water fixture, the dog tugged her toward a nearby tree. Unsettled by the conversation, she waited for Milo to finish. Riley had to wonder at Artie's evasiveness. Even during the drive to the newspaper office, she couldn't stop the thoughts rolling in her head. Why steal a body? Was it because the medical examiner would find evidence on the body pointing to the killer? She didn't know much about forensic procedures. Most of what she knew came from cop shows or books. As Riley parked, the questions muddled in her mind.

Inside, old editions of the paper, mounted in frames, covered the walls. Four desks filled the large room, though they were seldom used by any of the reporters. Most filed their reports from home. At the back was Susan's office. After thirty-some years with the *Houston Chronicle*, Susan retired when her husband passed away. She moved to Fredericksburg. When the *Register* came up for sale, bored with retirement, she bought it.

Riley unhooked the leash from Milo's collar. He immediately raced toward Susan's office. The enticing aroma of freshly brewed coffee lured her to the breakroom. With a cup in hand, she stopped in the doorway to watch the byplay between Milo and Susan. Her boss kept a variety of dog treats in a desk drawer. This time, it was a supersized dog biscuit. Milo's body quivered with anticipation as he stared at her hand.

"Have you been a good boy?" Susan said. Milo barked. She waved the biscuit. "So you think you should have this?"

Milo's bark was louder and more insistent. Laughing, Susan held it out where Milo could reach it. He daintily took it before prancing into the outer room.

Still chuckling, she said, "I swear that dog knows what we say."

Riley dropped into a chair. "Did you hear?" She sipped her coffee.

"Well, good morning to you as well. What was I supposed to hear?"

With a smug look at being one up on her boss, she said, "Someone broke into the Lombardy funeral home last night."

A look of puzzlement crossed Susan's face. "Okay. Barely

newsworthy, but I'll bite. What did they steal?"

"The murder victim we found yesterday."

Susan straightened in her chair. "Good lord! What was it doing there?"

"Yesterday, I talked to Carla Sanchez, one of the EMTs on the ambulance run. I wanted to find out what happened after Rutherford told me to take a hike. Rutherford told the medics to take the body to the funeral home. The funeral home's personnel were supposed to transport it to Austin today."

"Why didn't he have the medics take it to the medical examiner's office?"

"According to Carla, the sheriff didn't want the ambulance out of the county. Carla called me this morning when she heard officers had been sent to the funeral home. I stopped on my way into town. The receptionist discovered the body was missing when she got to work this morning. She didn't know why it was there. Just said Rutherford called her boss to make the arrangements. Though she had one interesting tidbit. There was an argument between the city cops and Mickey Bennett about why the body had been left there instead of being sent to the M.E."

"Guess the cops didn't like it either."

"Artie Ingram was there. I asked him about what Rutherford did. Tight-lipped, he told me to ask Rutherford."

Susan's brow furrowed as she thought. "Hmm … why would someone steal the body?"

Riley drank the last swig of coffee. "That question has been rumbling in my head."

"Any answers?"

"The only one that makes any sense to me is there was evidence on the body that would point to the killer. The man was shot. Maybe it's the bullet. That body was in a shallow grave with the debris from an old dump site on top of it. No one would have found it if it hadn't been for Milo. The Henning farm has been abandoned for years. Then, the body gets discovered. You're printing articles. The killer knows his plan has gone awry and has to get rid of it again."

"You could be right. It does make sense. And our highly competent sheriff, and I'm being facetious here, makes it easy for the killer. He stashes it at the funeral home."

Disgusted, Susan slumped in her chair. "The body is gone, and no identification. I hate to say it, but it's a dead end."

Riley leaned forward. "Maybe not. I can call Ted."

"Okay. I know he works for the Dallas Police Department, but what can he do?"

"Even though he was promoted to Major, he's still over the fusion center."

Susan said, "What the devil is a fusion center?"

"I've never fully understood the ins and outs of what he does, but I do know his department has some type of network connecting agencies to share intelligence information. He might be able to run one of the pictures I took of the head through a facial recognition program. I'd bet they have one."

Excitement lit her face. "That's right. You said you took pictures."

"The problem is the body was lying on its side. I could only get the side of the head and part of the face. But you know what? Rutherford should have one. Carla said she had to wait for Henry Caslon to finish taking pictures. Surely, Henry would have taken one of the front of the face."

With a sarcastic tone, Susan said, "But how do we find out? It won't do any good for me to call and ask. The man won't even do me the courtesy of taking my calls. Besides, if it's left up to Rutherford, the guy will never be identified, even if he does have a picture. Since the body has been stolen, I expect Rutherford hopes this all goes away. It certainly doesn't make him look good."

"I'll call Ted when I get home. Tell him what's going on and see if he can help."

Riley rose and walked out. Seated at a desk with Milo at her feet, she quickly typed up an article about the theft of the body, sending it to Susan along with a picture of the receptionist she had downloaded from the camera. Riley looked at Milo. "Ready to go home?" The dog eagerly jumped up. His tail whipped the air. She called out to Susan. "I'm outta here. I'll call if I get anything else."

Susan, back on the computer, waved her hand.

Eager to call Ted, she didn't waste time getting home. Riley zipped into the driveway, braking to a stop. A spurt of fear raced over her at the sight of her front door hanging open.

Not seeing any vehicles, she hesitated, debating whether to go inside. Riley decided staying inside the truck might be the intelligent option and called 911. It was only a few minutes before she heard the distant sound of a siren, though she was surprised at the speedy response. The officer must have been nearby. Her relief quickly faded when she saw the patrol car drive up. "Great, just great," she muttered. Mickey Bennett was behind the wheel.

She hopped out, leaving Milo in the truck while she waited for Mickey to get out of the car. He grinned at her over the steering wheel while talking on a cellphone. Whatever possessed her to call for help? Obviously, whoever broke in was long gone. She might as well check the house herself.

Walking past the squad car, she glared at Bennett, then trotted up the steps. Riley eyed the broken lock before stepping inside to stare at the living room with a sickening feeling. Broken frames and glass from the pictures on the mantel littered the floor. Lamps had been knocked over, seat cushions from the sofa and easy chairs strewn about. In the kitchen, the floor was covered with the contents of the drawers and flour and sugar from the canisters on the counter.

Behind her, a smug voice said, "Sure looks like you pissed someone off."

She gulped back the tears before whipping around. "Is that all you're good for, to make snide remarks? This is a crime scene. Is it possible that's something you don't recognize?"

Mickey's eyes darkened with anger, and his shoulders hunched as he leaned closer.

Fear trickled over her at the dawning awareness she was alone in the house with a man who had already threatened her. Still, Riley held her ground, refusing to give him the satisfaction of knowing he'd rattled her cage.

"Make a list of what's missing or damaged and drop it off at the office. I'll add it to the report." He turned, kicking aside a sofa cushion near the door on his way out.

The emotions drained out of her, leaving her limp. She forced herself to walk into the hallway. None of the rooms had escaped the meaningless havoc. In her office, Riley moaned. "Oh no. Not my computer, too." The laptop had been tossed on the floor, and the screen crushed to bits as if someone had stomped on it.

A faint bark echoed. "Oh, my gosh, Milo." She rushed out to open the truck door. When he jumped out, Riley dropped to her knees. Unable to stop the tears, she buried her face in his fur. Milo wiggled, twisting to lick her face. She swiped the tears with the back of her hand. "It's okay," she said, more to reassure the dog than herself.

Using the remote hooked to the truck's visor, she opened the garage door. The intruders hadn't bothered with the utility room. Milo could stay there until she cleaned up the rest of the house. After Riley filled his bowls with water and food, she walked into the kitchen, closing the door behind her. In dismay, she stared at the mess, overwhelmed by where to begin.

Since the door was the most important, she called Artie at the police department. When he came on the line, she said, "Artie, someone broke into my house and trashed it."

"Did you report it?"

With a bitter tone, she said, "Yes, for all the good it did me. Mickey Bennett has come and gone. Can you recommend a locksmith? I need to get my front door fixed."

"I do. I'll call him. It will get him to your place faster than if you call. Do you need any other help?"

"Not unless you want to wield a broom and mop."

It got a chuckle out of Artie. "I'll pass." Still laughing, he hung up.

Riley headed back outside and grabbed the backpack from the truck. A chill raced down her back at the thought of what might have happened if she'd left the camera in the house. Room by room, she took pictures. Once she finished, she cleaned the kitchen. It didn't take long to get it squared away. As she headed to the living room, dragging the vacuum cleaner, she realized the entire house wasn't as bad as she had first thought. It was just the shock that made it seem worse.

It was like someone rushed through the place, just throwing and dumping what they had quick access to. Maybe because it was broad daylight, and they had no way of knowing how long she would be gone. But why? The only damage was a few broken picture frames, a lamp, and her computer. Nothing was stolen. It just didn't make sense.

Chapter 4

All that was left to clean was the office when the doorbell chimed. Riley hustled into the living room, where the front door still hung open. A tall, lanky man in bib overalls and boots filled the doorway. Seeing Riley loping out of the hallway, he tipped his fingers to his ball cap emblazoned with "John Deere" in bright yellow letters.

"I'm looking for Riley Phillips."

"That's me."

"Ms. Phillips, I'm Frank Tedford. Artie Ingram called. Said you'd had a wee bit of a problem out here and needed a locksmith." He eyed the door. "Ma'am, I'd say you had a heap of trouble. Artie always did have a way of understating something." He grinned. "We go back away."

As they shook hands, she said, "Please, it's Riley, and thank you for getting here so fast. What is it going to take to fix the damage?"

"Make it Frank." He stooped to examine the door, then straightened. "The lock's old. Wasn't hard to jimmy. I'd recommend replacing it with a deadbolt. Much safer. It won't take long. What about your back door?"

"It leads into the garage from the utility room. If you have time, let's replace the lock."

"I do. That way, you won't have to deal with two different keys."

Relieved at knowing she'd soon be able to lock her door, she said, "My dog is in the utility room. Let me introduce you."

He followed her into the kitchen. When she opened the door, Milo rose from his bed, his ears tilted forward.

"Frank, this is Milo. Milo, greet."

The dog sat, lifting a paw.

Frank chuckled as he stepped into the room. His gnarled hand gently closed around Milo's paw. "I heard about what he did, finding that body and all."

"I need to keep him in here until I get all the broken glass cleaned up."

The man nodded. "I'll keep the door closed." Before walking out, he gave Milo's head another pat.

Riley left him to deal with the doors. From the office doorway, she eyed the broken computer. Angered by the loss, Riley tossed pieces into a box. "Dang it all. Why my computer?" she grumbled. If the insurance didn't pay for it, buying a new one would take a big chunk of her budget. With the larger pieces out of the way, Riley made numerous passes with the vacuum cleaner, making sure she had all the bits of glass cleared away.

Satisfied with the results, she stepped into the closet. From the top shelf, Riley pulled down the old laptop she'd saved in case of an emergency and then dug out the electrical cord for it. Hooking it up, Riley turned it on. "Yes," she exclaimed when the login screen popped up. Though it didn't have all the bells and whistles the other one did, it would do until she could get a new one.

She downloaded the pictures she'd taken of the inside of the house. After moving them into a file folder, she sent a copy to the cloud. Next, she typed up the list of damaged items, picture frames, lamp, door, and computer, along with an estimated value for the sheriff's department and the insurance company. She hit print, and it suddenly dawned on her. The printer on a small table in the corner hadn't been touched. Then she eyed the police scanner on top of the file cabinet. More oddities that sparked a sense of disquiet.

From the front of the house, Riley heard Frank call her name. She rushed out to find the front door shut, and Frank testing the lock with a key. He twisted the deadbolt. "Okay, that should do it. The new lock is on the back door." He handed her the key, then pulled two more from the pocket on the front of his bib overalls. "Made some extras."

"How do you want me to pay you?"

"Emma, that's my wife, will send you an invoice."

"Thank you so much."

He flicked his fingers at the bill of his ballcap, opened the door and ambled out.

With the problem of the door out of the way, she still had plenty of time to make a trip into town to drop off her list at the sheriff's office. But first, she needed to call her brother.

With Milo close on her heels, she headed back to the office. Before she made the call, she typed a list of events, starting with Milo alerting on the body. It was a way to organize her thoughts since her brother was a stickler for details. She tapped the speed dial.

"Hey, sis. You must have been reading my mind. I was getting ready to call you."

"You were? Why?"

He laughed. "Do I have to have a reason?"

With a dry tone, she said, "Yes, you usually do."

"I'll have to remedy that. How about I call you each morning just to say rise and shine?"

"Don't you dare. I don't need calls from you at five in the morning." Riley knew that was his usual time to be up. Ted liked to run or cycle around White Rock Lake before getting ready for work.

His laughter rippled over the phone. Before he could come up with another prank, she said, "Why were you going to call?"

His tone sobered. "I saw the news about the body Milo found."

"Oh, my gosh. It hit the news there?"

"Headline news on all four TV networks. Not once, but three times. By the way, kudos to Milo. You put in a lot of hard work training him. Though I had my doubts at the beginning, I don't anymore."

"That body and the pictures I took is why I called."

When she hit the part about the theft, Ted said, "I can't believe Rutherford left the body at the funeral home. That's blatant negligence. What the devil was he thinking? Okay, what else?"

She told him about her theory.

Ted said, "You could be right. Rutherford certainly made it easy for someone to steal it. Who knew the body was at the funeral home?"

"Probably most everyone at the sheriff's office. Then, there are the medics and personnel at the funeral home. You know how news travels in this town. There's another detail I haven't mentioned. The man was wearing an Aggie ring, class of 2007."

"That would have been an instant identification. What's the sheriff doing?"

"I don't know. One of the medics at the scene told me a deputy had taken pictures. They'd probably be better than the ones I took. Since the body lay on its side, I could only get part of the face. Susan doesn't think Rutherford will do anything now that the body is gone. That's not all. While I was in town today, someone broke into the house and trashed it."

"Anything stolen?"

"That's what's so strange. The only damage is a few broken pictures, a lamp, the front door lock, and my computer. It was smashed. The rest was just stuff tossed around or drawers dumped.

I've already had the front door repaired with deadbolt locks on the front and back doors."

There was a pause for several seconds before Ted said, "I saw three of your photos in the article. Did Susan publish more?"

"Just those three."

"So, other than those three, all your photographs were destroyed."

"I still have them. I keep a copy of my photographs in my cloud account."

"Who knew you had taken photos?"

"As far as I know, just Susan. I don't think anyone would have even known I had taken pictures if it hadn't been for what Susan published. The two deputies who showed up didn't know. I had already finished before they arrived."

"Where was your camera when they got there?"

"In my backpack. I never took it out again. What's going on in your cop mind?"

"Exploring possibilities. I'd like to see your photos."

"I was hoping you would. My old laptop still works, so I can email them to you. I told Susan you might be able to help identify the man since both of us believe Rutherford will probably not do anything. I'll know more later today after I stop at the sheriff's office to drop off my list of damages."

"If I can't, I'll try to get a copy of Rutherford's photos."

Riley let out a chuckle. "Boy, I'd really like to be in his office to see his expression when he gets your call."

"What's next on your agenda?" Ted asked.

"Find a name. Since the Aggie yearbooks are online, I might find him."

"Okay, you work that end. I'll see if the facial recognition program comes up with a match." He paused before saying, "One more thing, sis. Don't tell anyone you still have the pictures."

A spark of alarm shot through her. "You think it was my pictures they were after? But that doesn't make sense. What good would it do to destroy my photos when the sheriff also has pictures?"

"A valid point. Your break-in may not be connected to the body. But I don't like the timing. So, let's err on the side of caution. Keep your mouth shut. Talk to you later." He disconnected.

Looking troubled, she slid the phone back into her vest before stashing the camera in the backpack. How could the break-in be connected to the body? Why would someone be worried about her pictures? Still, she'd heed her brother's advice.

****

Ted sat back in his chair, staring at the paper where he'd made notes. Every instinct tingled. He wasn't high on coincidences, and this one smacked him in the face. While Riley had come up with a good theory, another one had jumped into his mind when he factored in her computer and photographs. Did someone not want the body to be identified? Was that why it was stolen? Still, he couldn't ignore Riley's argument. Why go after her pictures when the sheriff had the same? Though his day was already booked with meetings, including one with the police chief, he told his administrative assistant to hold his calls.

He accessed his email account. Riley's email was there. Ted downloaded the pictures to his computer and opened the file. One by one, he studied them. Though it was doubtful he'd get a hit, he selected one.

After initiating the search, Ted settled back in his chair while he thought. Unsettled by his conversation with Riley, he couldn't shake the feeling this was more than some local murder. Whatever it was, his sister had landed in the middle of it, a disturbing thought.

Not long after he was assigned to the fusion center, he became involved with a new FBI unit, the Trackers. They were rather unique, not the typical FBI agents. They'd had phenomenal success in solving several high-profile crimes. The head of the unit was Scott Fleming. Ted had worked on two of their cases, becoming good friends with the unit's computer guru, Nicki Allison. In his list of contacts, he found the number.

A bubbly voice answered on the second ring. "Agent Allison."

"Nicki, it's Ted Phillips."

"Ted, my gosh, how are you doing?"

"I'm good, Nicki. How about you?"

"Being run ragged with a new program we're implementing, but that's nothing new. What can I do for you?"

"I need your help."

"You got it. For what?"

That was typical of Nicki. She never beat about the bush. "Have I caught you at a bad time?"

"No. I just finished teaching a class at the FBI academy and am headed to my car."

Ted hit the highlights of what he'd learned from Riley. "While I don't have anything to base it on, I don't think this is a local homicide. I'm concerned about my sister. If you have the time, I'd like you to look at Riley's photographs and her notes."

"Send them to me. I'll look at them when I get to the office."

Ted said, "I'll have the file to you within the hour."

"I'll call you as soon as I know something."

"Thanks, Nicki. I owe you one."

"No, you don't. Your help on two of our cases was invaluable. We owe you." She clicked off.

Washington, D.C.

Humming, Nicki strolled into the Tracker office. Since the entire team was on other assignments, from Oregon to Georgia to Florida, the place was deserted except for her boss. She dropped the tote bag on the desk as she glanced around. When it came to her office, Nicki had never lost a sense of wonderment. It was a computer geek's dream come true.

When the unit moved into the new office, Scott had an adjoining wall to another office removed to create one large room for her computer equipment. She'd been given carte blanche to order whatever she wanted. With an unlimited budget, she had taken full advantage. A six-by-eight-foot wall-mounted monitor covered most of one wall. With one tap on a keyboard, she could change from one to several pictures on the screen. Facing the giant monitor was a semicircular desk with four smaller monitors, one for each of her systems, spaced across the top. In the center was her chair. Her team members often teased her about being the Trackers' spider-woman, sitting in the middle of her web.

With her obsession with computer games, Nicki thought the comparison was funny and truer than not. Settled into the chair, she tapped the keyboard, pulled up her emails, and searched for Ted's. Nicki wasn't kidding when she told Ted the unit owed him. Whatever she could do to help him, she would.

She opened his email and downloaded a folder labeled "pictures." Before studying them, she read the attached notes. Most were from his sister, but Ted had added his suspicions. The theft of the body was a troubling puzzle. She opened the picture file. Enlarged on the wall monitor, Nicki slowly scrutinized each one. A few she tagged, moving them to a new file. Once she finished, she had a file with several pictures that summed up the case, most of which had different angles of the face and head to show her boss.

When she neared his office door, Scott was on the phone. Since it sounded like he was wrapping up a call with his boss, Director Paul Daykin, she turned toward the breakroom. Considering she and Scott were coffee fanatics, there was always a pot going. One of Scott's contributions to the unit was a top-of-the-line coffee machine with every attachment imaginable. The other was the oversized sofa, which had more than once brought Scott's ire down on her. She tended to spend a lot of time in the office and slept on the couch at night, much to Scott's chagrin. Not only was it convenient, but a way to aggravate him. She poured two cups, carrying them to his office.

At the sight of the brooding look on Scott's face, Nicki paused in the doorway. On the high side of thirty, his six-foot frame was solidly built with an impressive breadth of shoulders. A small scar split an eyebrow, and another curved over his cheekbone, adding a raffish look to his angular, rough-hewn face. A watchful intelligence gleamed in his dark, hooded eyes—at times, with a disturbing intensity that seemed to pierce her very thoughts.

"I take it the director still hasn't approved your request." Scott wanted to set up a new unit located midway between the East and West Coasts. The unit was spread thin, with more cases than they could handle.

His face lightened. "Ah, coffee. Just what I need." His hand extended across the desk to take the cup. He took a deep swig before saying, "He still says he'll take it under advisement. A fancy expression to mean if he can find the money. It always comes down to the budget."

He knew she was late because of a class at the academy. With a resigned sigh, his gaze skimmed over her. Black hair hung in one long braid to her waist. Her dark eyes and high cheekbones bespoke her Native American heritage. While not classically beautiful, Nicki's face was captivating, the type that settled in a man's mind. Nicki gravitated toward leggings and weird, colorful t-shirts that suited her petite frame. The one she sported today had some kind of flying multi-eyed monster on the front against a putrid green background. Probably a creature from one of her computer games.

As an agent, Nicki was an anomaly. Dress code had no meaning, except on rare occasions, though it was partially his fault. When he started the unit, he had relaxed the official FBI edicts on the proper attire. Nicki carried it to the extreme. But no one cared. As the top computer expert in the Bureau, her eccentricity was ignored. She was a genius, graduating from MIT at the top of her class. Scott had always suspected her IQ was off the charts.

He had fended off numerous offers from other SACs, Special Agent in Charge, wanting to steal her. Scott had even mildly threatened his boss with his resignation if he allowed Nicki to be transferred.

"Please tell me you didn't appear at the academy in that outfit."

Her lips twisted with a taunting smile. "Now, boss man, you should know better. I did change my shirt before I started the class. I didn't think an overly large monster with an agent dangling from his mouth was quite the thing for all those recruits."

He groaned.

Relenting, she laughed before assuring him she had been appropriately dressed in approved FBI attire, dark pants, a white shirt, and a suit coat. "I changed downstairs." The agents had permanent lockers in the gym located on the first floor.

Only slightly reassured, he knew something was up by the gleam in her eye. A sense of optimism rejuvenated him.

"As I was leaving the academy, I got a call from Ted Phillips. He needs our help with a problem in Fredericksburg, Texas. It involves his sister. If you've got a few minutes, I want to show you what he sent me."

Scott shoved his chair back. Once he was seated alongside her, Nicki tapped the keyboard, bringing up Riley's notes on the wall monitor. "This is from his sister, Riley. She's a reporter and photographer."

Focused on the document, Scott leaned forward. "Intriguing," he mused. "What else?"

The document disappeared and was replaced by the photographs. "These are exceptionally good," Nicki said. She slowly clicked through them, stopping when Scott held up a hand to take a closer look.

When she brought up the last picture, he steepled his fingers, resting his chin on the fingertips as he thought. As a kid, he'd always excelled in games requiring an analysis of each move. The first time he picked up a Rubik's cube, he'd solved the enigma of the colored blocks in minutes. Scott soon learned he could apply his uncanny talents to unravel the twists and turns of criminal behavior. What he always referred to as connecting the dots in an investigation had led to many arrests. It was why he was tagged to head the new team, the Tracker Unit.

"Go back to the first one."

Nicki started over.

"Stop. Magnify that one." It was one where Riley had zoomed in to get as much of the face as possible. He intently scrutinized the image before saying, "It would be good if we had one of the sheriff's pictures, but can you do anything with this one?"

"Interesting you should ask. This would be a good test for the new software program."

"Did you finish it?"

"Ran the last set of tests last night." If the new AI software she'd written worked, it would transform facial recognition. She should be able to reconstruct missing pieces of a face. The tests on creating an image from a skull had been surprisingly accurate when compared to the actual image of the person.

He glared at her. "Nicki. Did you sleep on that dang couch again? One of these days, I swear, it's going out the door."

She laughed, knowing it was an idle threat. "No, I didn't. I finished in time to go home." She didn't think he needed to know the only reason she'd gone home was because she had to teach a class at the academy that morning. Her apartment was closer than the office.

Scott went back to studying the image of the face. The longer he stared at it, the more uneasy he became. Something about the image was off, but Scott couldn't pinpoint what.

He finally said, "I agree with Ted. What is disturbing is how fast someone reacted to the discovery of the body. A body that should never have been found gets conveniently left at a funeral home, where it's stolen, then a reporter's computer becomes a target after three pictures she took were published." He rose. "I don't like coincidences either."

Seated at his desk, Scott opened the personnel file on his computer. His gaze scanned the current list of Trackers. His team was extraordinary. Despite their growing reputation within the Bureau, he was probably the only person who knew just how special they were. Scott had applied the same methods to the initial selection process for his new team as he did his investigations. He'd spent months evaluating agent profiles, their case closure rates, and conducting interviews. In a select few, Scott had found anomalies in their investigations, unexplained gaps hinting at unidentified abilities. He was always on the hunt for new candidates.

Scott studied the names he planned to tap for a second unit. He already had tentative approval to transfer the agents, even though his boss was dragging his feet over the budget. Scott didn't figure he'd have a problem if he went ahead with at least one transfer. He picked up the phone and tapped the number of the Special Agent in Charge of the Nevada office.

Chapter 5

Texas

Riley turned into the parking lot for the sheriff's department, stopping in a visitor's space. She grabbed the backpack from the front passenger seat and climbed out. What to do with Milo was a problem. She glanced around and spotted a bench on a small section of grass next to the building. It would have to do. After she wrapped the end of the leash around the leg of the bench, she said, "Don't give me that sad look. You can't go inside."

With a whimper, Milo dropped to the ground, still gazing at her with a forlorn look.

Inside, a man in a sheriff's uniform manned a desk near the door. Since she didn't recognize him, she figured he must be new. Riley stepped up and asked to see the sheriff. Before asking her name, he gave her one of those up-and-down looks cops did.

"Riley Phillips, and it's about a break-in to my house."

He picked up the receiver on the desk phone and punched a button. "There is a Riley Phillips here to see Sheriff Rutherford." He listened, then hung up. "I'm sorry, but the sheriff is in a conference and can't be disturbed."

So, he wanted to play hardball. Well, she could, too. She reached inside the backpack and pulled out the press pass, waving it in front of the deputy's nose. "I'm a reporter with the *Fredericksburg Register*. I'm about to file an article on the body that was stolen from the funeral home. It might behoove the sheriff to talk to me. I suggest you call and tell him."

Glaring at her, he picked up the phone. "She says she's doing a story for the newspaper." He listened, then hung up. "Have a seat. Someone will be with you in a minute."

While she waited, she looked around. Several deputies walked past her, each giving her the once-over. A couple of them she knew, but they didn't stop to greet her. Billy walked up. With a somber look, he said, "Riley, the sheriff said he would give you a few minutes."

She followed Billy to an office at the back of the building. The door was open.

"Go on in," Billy told her.

As she strolled inside, Rutherford, seated behind a large desk, said, "Now, what's so gall-darn important that you just had to talk to me?"

Riley crossed the room and sat. Rutherford's lips thinned.

Before dropping the backpack on the floor, she pulled out a notepad, the list of damaged items, and a pen.

"I don't have all day. Whatever you want, get to it," Rutherford growled.

Riley leaned forward, dropping the list of damages on the desk. "What's this?"

"The damage to my house when someone broke in. Your deputy, Mickey Bennett, said to drop it off. What's the status of your investigation?"

He tossed the paper aside. "There's nothing to investigate. I figure it was just kids."

"I'm not surprised since all Bennett did was walk in and walk out of my house. Bennett didn't investigate diddly-squat. My editor wants an update on the body found at the farm."

"The body's gone, case closed."

Stunned, Riley stared at him. "My god. A man was murdered and buried in a remote section of the county. After one day, all you can say is the case is closed. What about trying to identify the man from the pictures you took? Or is that something that's not important to you, the identification of a murdered victim?"

"I don't have to justify myself or the actions of this department to you or your editor."

"You may not have to justify it to my boss or me, but you do to the people living in this county. The people who elected you. And that's what will get reported."

His face red with anger, Rutherford shouted, "Billy."

When Billy appeared in the doorway, Rutherford said, "Escort her out of the building."

Riley grabbed her backpack, stuffing the notepad and pen inside. She rose. "I can promise you this. You may be done, but I'm not, and neither is the newspaper's editor."

Billy said as they walked to the front door, "Geez, Riley. What the heck were you thinking? Getting into a pissing contest with the sheriff isn't getting you any brownie points."

"Billy, I hate to tell you, but I'm not looking for brownie points. I'm looking for justice for a murdered man." She brushed past him, heading out the door. She untied Milo. Fuming, she stomped to the truck.

When she pulled into the newspaper's parking lot, she still hadn't cooled down. Another reporter, Ben Fremont, seated at a desk, looked up as she tromped inside. Seeing Riley's angry expression, he said, "Whoa. Whatever happened, I hope the other guy is still standing."

A tall, gangly man, Ben had worked on and off for the newspaper for several years. When Riley started, he'd taken her under his wing, giving her tips that helped boost her confidence.

Milo tugged on the leash. Riley unclipped it, and Milo charged toward Ben.

Ben pushed his chair back. "What a good boy you are, finding that body." He gave Milo's head a robust rub. "Heck of a job you did, Riley. Looks like the county has a new search and rescue dog."

"Not until we do the certification run. I still have to schedule it."

"Sorry to hear about your house." Still rubbing on Milo's head, Ben shot her a sympathetic glance.

At her questioning look, he added, "I heard the call come out on the police scanner. I followed up."

Riley grinned. "Of course you did."

Susan walked up. Milo eased away from Ben and trotted over to her, where he plunked down on his butt, staring up at her with a worshipful gaze.

"You know I've got something, don't you?" He woofed. The hand she'd hidden behind her back reached out, holding a large dog biscuit. Milo daintily took it, laid down, and happily began to chew.

"So, how bad was the damage?" Ben asked.

"Not as bad as it first looked. The house was trashed, drawers dumped. The worst was my computer. It was destroyed."

Ben asked, "Does the sheriff's department have any idea who did it?"

Riley shot him a disbelieving look.

Ben threw up his hands. "Okay. Forgot for a moment who you had to deal with."

"Come on back to my office. Let's talk," Susan said.

"Would you mind if I take Milo for a walk?" Ben asked. Milo's head shot up. He scrambled to his feet, the dog biscuit forgotten.

Riley laughed as she handed Ben the leash. They headed out the door with Milo trotting alongside Ben, his tail waving.

Once the two settled in chairs, Susan asked, "Why didn't you send me a write-up about your house?"

Riley shrugged. "I didn't think it would be newsworthy."

"For future reference, it is. You're a reporter for this newspaper, which makes it newsworthy. Now, about your break-in. What happened?"

Riley briefly explained, ending with, "I stopped by Rutherford's office on my way into town and dropped off my list of damaged items. I asked about his investigation. There's none. Said it was likely kids."

Susan grunted. "Typical. I've heard other complaints along the same lines. What I don't like is your house gets broken into the day after you find a mysterious body. Though it could just be a coincidence."

Riley stirred uneasily in her chair, remembering similar comments from Ted.

"Did you ask Rutherford about the body? Is he going to be able to identify the man?"

"You're not going to believe his answer."

"Do I need to hold my breath?" Susan asked.

"Body is gone, case closed."

"What!"

Riley held up a hand, palm out. "I swear, that was the man's answer."

"Good lord. Rutherford's got pebbles for brain cells. He knows the man was murdered. He's got pictures. Why isn't he trying to identify the man?"

"I was just as outraged as you. When I asked, Rutherford said he didn't have to account for his actions or his department's to you or me."

"What did you tell him?"

"He did to the people who voted for him. I told him that was how we would report it."

"Good for you. We will, though it doesn't help us." Glumly, she mused, "A missing body, no identification. Rutherford shuts down the case, no identification. Your computer is destroyed, bye-bye pictures and no chance of identification. I hate to say it, but it's a dead end for us."

"Maybe not." A smug look settled on Riley's face.

Susan shot her a sharp look. "Okay, don't keep me in suspense here."

"I've still got the pictures. They weren't destroyed."

"How?"

"I always back up my computer to my cloud account. I still have every single one."

"Oh. My. Gosh. Does anyone know you still have them?"

"Just you and Ted. I sent him the file. By the way, this is on the QT. He doesn't want anyone to know that I still have the pictures. He told me to keep my mouth shut."

A belly laugh rolled out of Susan. "I can't imagine anyone other than Ted could tell you that and not get cut off at the knees."

"What can I say? The man's my brother. I have to put up with him. We also have one other lead, the ring."

"Ring! What ring? You've never mentioned a ring."

"At the time, it wasn't important. The man had a 2007 Texas A&M class ring on his hand. I told Billy Thatcher the man's name would be engraved inside. Billy wanted to wait and let the medical examiner remove the ring. A&M's yearbooks are online. Even though I've only got one side of the face, it might be enough. Plus, Ted's running it through his facial recognition program."

"Dang, keep going with this. Have you checked with the PD to see if they came up with anything on the theft of the body?"

"I'll stop by there on my way out of town. Artie was going to check missing persons. You'd think somebody would have reported him missing."

"I'm going to run another article to activate the Crime Stoppers program, offering a reward for information about the victim. I'll mention the ring."

"That's a good idea. When I talk to Artie, I'll let him know." A malicious grin crossed her face. "I'd like to see Rutherford's face when he finds out his case isn't closed after all."

"If we keep stirring the pot, no telling what we'll get."

With a determined look, she strode outside looking for Milo. Ben and the dog stood on the sidewalk where Ben talked to a woman. As Riley approached, he said, "I'll call you." The woman gave him a cozy look as she walked away.

"New girlfriend?"

He shrugged. "I just met her. She asked about Milo. She's new in town, moved here from Austin." He handed over the leash. "You should let me keep Milo more often. He's a chick magnet. The women love him."

Riley laughed. "I'll keep that in mind, but I don't think you really need any help with your love life."

Riley drove the short distance to the police department. This time, she could take Milo with her. When she started training Milo, she talked to the officers in the K-9 unit, getting their input on training methods.

Artie stood by the front desk as she and Milo entered the front door. At the sight of Artie, Milo woofed. His head swiveled, a smile crossing his face. He walked over, giving the dog a rub.

"Didn't expect to see the two of you today. What's up?"

"If you've got a minute, I have a few questions."

"Sure, come on back to my office." Once settled, Artie said,

"Okay, what can I help you with?"

"Have you made any progress on the theft of the body?"

Artie shook his head. "Not much I can tell you that you don't already know. The only prints we found at the funeral home belonged to the employees."

"How about missing persons? Has anyone been reported in the county?"

"No. But it could be he didn't live here."

"Dang, we sure need to identify him. The sheriff has bailed, already closed the case."

A troubled look crossed his face. "I hadn't heard. How'd you find out?"

She explained about her visit, then added, "Since the sheriff isn't doing anything, Susan is activating Crime Stoppers. Offering a reward for information. She's including the ring."

"I hate to ask, but what ring?"

"The man was wearing a Texas A&M University class ring for 2007. When I saw it, I told Mickey and Billy the man's name would be engraved inside the ring."

Artie's lips thinned as anger sparked in his eyes. "Funny, they didn't tell us."

"Billy Thatcher said he'd let the medical examiner remove it."

"I'll let the chief know what's going on."

As they walked out, Artie turned toward the police chief's office at the end of the hall, his face grim. Riley smiled. She'd like to be a fly on the wall when the police chief called Rutherford, wanting to know why his department didn't get notified of a critical piece of evidence.

By the time she left, it was too late to stop and buy a new computer. Instead, she headed home. While Milo raced around the backyard, chasing the crows sitting on the fence, she pulled a pepperoni pizza out of the freezer. After she popped it into the microwave, she refilled Milo's bowls with water and dog chow. Once he was back inside, she slid the pizza on a plate and set it on the table, along with a glass of iced tea.

When she sat, Milo plunked down beside her, his gaze fixed on her plate. "Oh, you think you'll get some, do you?" He woofed. With a smile, she picked up a piece of pepperoni and tossed it into the air. Milo's jaws latched onto it. With a gulp, it was gone, and he was back for another piece. "Nope, that's it. Go to your bed." He turned, shooting her a sad look over his shoulder.

As much as Riley wanted to dwell on pleasant topics while she ate, her thoughts kept twisting to the mystery man. Before she realized it, the plate was empty, and she had no memory of eating.

After cleaning up, she headed to her office, where she pulled up the Texas A&M website. She downloaded the 2007 yearbook and began studying the pictures. It was more difficult than she imagined. Even working with a split screen, a yearbook page on one side and the photo of the victim's face on the other side for reference, she couldn't find a single one that came close. So much for that clue.

Frustrated, she exited the site. Her gaze shifted toward the window. An eerie chill raced over her. The darkness of the night pressed against the glass. Someone could stand outside the window, watching. She'd never see them.

Rising, she closed the drapes on the double windows facing the front yard. Having lived in the house most of her life, she'd never been unnerved by the lack of close neighbors. Today, her home had been violated by intruders. Anger stirred inside her at what had been stolen, her peace of mind. Mentally, she shook herself. All she could do was take steps to ensure her safety. Still, Riley couldn't get rid of the niggly feeling of trepidation. As she turned to walk out, a call came over the police scanner. A fire. Her heart leaped into her throat when she heard the address. It was the newspaper office.

Chapter 6

Riley grabbed her phone and rushed into her bedroom. She tugged on thick socks and hiking boots. Despite the trembling of her fingers, she managed to lace them. The phone went into the pocket of the vest she slipped on.

As she raced toward the living room, she shouted for Milo. The dog darted out of the kitchen. Not bothering to turn off the lights, she checked the patio door before grabbing the backpack's strap. With it slung over one shoulder, she threw open the front door. Milo dashed around her, charging outside.

When she turned out of her driveway, fear rode with her. Susan often worked late. She tried calling, but the call rolled to voice mail, increasing the panic clawing through her body. As she neared town, she saw the flames shooting high in the sky. Within minutes, she turned onto the street leading to the newspaper office. Fire trucks, police cars, and barricades blocked the street.

She pulled to the curb. Even from a distance, it was a fearsome sight. Flames whipped and twisted, casting a hellish glow over the street and buildings. The extension ladder on a fire truck was in the air, with a fireman at the top, wielding the end of a hose, spraying water onto the rooftop.

Riley pulled the camera out of the backpack and hung it around her neck, then hopped out. Milo whined. "Stay," Riley said as she hit the remote lock on her ignition key.

The police officer, occupied with gawkers on the sidewalk, didn't see her dart around the squad car. As she edged closer to the front of the building, two firefighters pulled a hose through the front door. In the thick haze of smoke and soot, they were barely visible. Another on a second truck spewed water on the adjacent building.

She raced up to the firefighter operating the controls for the ladder. She screamed at him. "Was anyone in the building?"

He gave her a quick glance. "We don't know. Get out of here." He turned his eyes back to the man on top of the long ladder.

Despite her debilitating terror for Susan, she couldn't stand by and do nothing. Riley lifted her camera, taking pictures as she stepped over hoses. Their attention on the burning building, the firefighters ignored her. More people had arrived, gathering in the street on the other side of the barricades. The officers were busy keeping them back. No one stopped her as she moved around the fire truck, taking pictures at different angles and positions. She even dropped to one knee, shooting upward. Through the camera's lens, the fire was a breathing, living entity as it consumed its prey.

The smoke and soot made it difficult to breathe. Despite the sharp pricks of pain in her lungs, she darted into the parking lot, snapping pictures of the side of the building. A shout rang out. "The roof is going!" A deafening roar echoed. Smoke, burning ashes, and debris flew into the air. Coughing, she charged across the alley and headed to a side street. As the air cleared, she gulped deep breaths. When she spotted Susan standing behind the barricades, her legs wobbled with relief.

"Was anyone in the building when the roof went?" she hollered.

Susan reached across the barricade, grabbing Riley's hands and tugging her. "They got out just in time. For cripes' sake, what have you been doing? You're covered with smoke and ash."

Riley wiggled the camera before crawling over the barricade.

"Young lady, I should kick your butt from here to wherever and back again for such a foolish stunt. You could have been hurt or killed. Pictures aren't worth your life."

"I wasn't in any danger. I didn't get that close." It was probably best that she didn't mention her mad dash through the flying ashes and debris.

Susan turned her gaze back to the fire. "All that history gone, just gone." Her voice choked with tears. "What a horrible, senseless loss."

Ben pushed his way through the crowd. "Was anyone hurt? I heard it on the police scanner."

Susan answered, "No, thank god."

"What started it? Do you know?" Ben asked.

"I'll see if I can find out." Riley climbed back over the barricade. When a police officer started toward her, she raised the camera hanging around her neck. He nodded and moved away.

She headed toward the cluster of firefighters standing beside the fire truck. It appeared they had the fire under control.

"Ah, excuse me."

They turned to look at her. She recognized most of them.

Matt Taylor, the fire chief, stepped forward. "Riley. Might have expected to see you here."

"Do you know what started the fire?"

"Could be arson. Until I get a fire inspector out here, I won't know for certain. It looks like it started in the back office."

Her heart lurched. A sickening feeling crushed her chest.

"I'll know more tomorrow if you want to check back with me. Now, you need to get out of here. Go home."

"I need just a few more pictures, then I will."

Riley moved across the front of the building, taking pictures before moving around the side and back. Satisfied, she walked toward Susan and Ben. Not wanting Ben to know what she had learned, she said, "Matt said to go home. He'd know more tomorrow. Susan, where is your car?"

Susan motioned toward where Riley had parked. "Back there a couple of blocks."

Ben's car was in the opposite direction. After assuring Susan he'd do anything to help, Ben left.

Riley climbed over the barricade. "Come on. We can talk while we walk."

As they edged out of the crowd, Riley, concerned by the pale look on the older woman's face, held onto her arm. "Do you want me to follow you home?"

"Oh, no, my dear. I'm okay. It's just the shock."

Once they were out of earshot of the bystanders, Susan said, "Now, what did Matt really say?"

Riley didn't sugarcoat it. "Could be arson and likely started in your office."

A muffled curse echoed. "We can be thankful for one thing."

"I can't imagine what."

"They didn't burn down your house."

Stunned, Riley was speechless as the horrifying thought flashed in her mind. "Oh. My. God."

In a harsh voice, Susan said, "I don't like coincidences. This one stinks to high heaven." She squared her shoulders. "First thing in the morning, I'll look for a temporary location. In the meantime, I can run the website from my home. Since you risked life and limb, send me an article with pictures when you get home. The building may be gone, but the *Fredericksburg Register* isn't. It's alive and well. Nobody, and I mean nobody, is going to shut me down."

When they reached Susan's car, Riley said, "Are you sure you're all right?"

"Yes." Susan hugged her. "I'll talk to you tomorrow." With a return of her dry humor, she added, "I'd also recommend a shower before you do anything else." She brushed her hands down her clothes before climbing into the car.

Dismayed by the idea the fire and break-in were connected, Riley headed toward her truck. Milo's nose pressed against the window. Sharp barks echoed. Instead of running to do his business when he hopped out, Milo pushed against her leg, his nose nuzzling her hand.

"What's wrong?"

The dog whimpered, his body quivering with tension.

She knelt on one knee. Hugging his neck, she could feel his body relax. A wet tongue lapped at her ear. Laughing, she said, "Okay, okay. That's enough. Let's go home."

He barked and jumped back into the truck. As Riley drove off, she wondered about his behavior. She'd never seen him act the way he just did.

During the drive home, the fear she'd felt since hearing the call come out, mixed with an adrenaline rush, ebbed, leaving her exhausted. Too tired to mess with parking in the garage, she pulled in front of the house. When she opened the backdoor, Milo jumped out and took off running, circling and barking until she whistled. Inside, Riley pulled a bottle of water from the fridge. The cold water eased the rawness in her throat. Once Milo was settled, she headed to her bedroom.

In the bathroom, Riley looked at herself in the mirror and yelped. It was worse than she realized. Soot covered her clothes, and her hair was thick with it. Streaks of soot ran down her face and neck. No wonder Susan mentioned a shower.

She headed back to the utility room, stripped down, then chunked the clothes into the washing machine. By the time she stepped out of the shower, she'd copiously washed her hair and skin several times. To make sure the smell of the fire was gone, Riley slathered on the lotion. Dressed in a pair of sweatpants and t-shirt, she began to feel somewhat normal.

Before starting on the article, she snagged another bottle of water. Seated at the desk, she sipped and typed. It took several rewrites before she was satisfied. Riley pulled the camera from her bag. She transferred the pictures to her computer, then studied each one. Even to her critical eye, several were exceptional, showing the incredible, destructive power of the fire. Riley attached four to her article before sending it to Susan. Then, she moved the picture file to the cloud. Tired, she started to close down the computer when it dinged, indicating an incoming email. It was an answer from Susan. "Awesome article and even more awesome pictures. Kudos to you. Sending it out now."

Susan was right. Nothing would stop her.

Chapter 7

Riley groaned. She knew the bark. Groggy and blurry-eyed, she rolled over. Milo stood beside her bed with his "need to go outside" look. He whined, then trotted to the door, where he looked back at her. He barked again, this time louder.

"Okay, okay. I got the message."

After letting him out the patio door, she started the coffee pot before getting dressed. When she strolled back, Milo's nose was pushed against the glass, his signal to come back inside. Once he was settled with a bowl of fresh water and dog chow, Riley wandered to the office to check her article on the newspaper's website. It was front and center with the photos.

She took a sip of her coffee as she studied each one. Satisfied she couldn't have done any better, she reached for the phone. She was surprised Ted hadn't already called. As the thought crossed her mind, the phone chimed.

When she answered, he didn't waste any time on greetings. "You made the headlines again. What happened?"

"Someone burned down the newspaper office. It may have started in Susan's office."

"You're certain?"

"Not one hundred percent. The fire chief thinks so, though he won't know until the fire inspector gets inside."

"Is Matt Taylor still the fire chief?"

"Yeah."

"Good man. If he thinks arson, it is. I don't like the pattern I'm seeing. The break-in, your computer destroyed, now the newspaper office."

"Susan had the same thought."

"She's a smart lady. Send me the pictures you took and call once you have an update."

"Anything new on your search?"

"Not yet. I've got another call." He disconnected.

She set up the email and attached the file folder of pictures. Before shutting down the computer, she looked at them on the small screen one last time. She really had to get a new computer. Eager to get to town, she skipped breakfast. She gathered up her gear and Milo, and they headed out.

Riley turned onto the street leading to the burned building and spotted Susan's car. She parked behind it. Ahead, two men stood on the sidewalk. One was the fire chief, Matt Taylor. She didn't recognize the other, and she didn't see Susan. Before hopping out, she dropped her camera around her neck. With all the debris still on the sidewalk and street, Riley didn't want Milo walking across it. She hooked his leash around the limb of a nearby tree.

As she approached, her gaze swept over what was left of the building gutted by the fire. In the daylight, the sight was devastating. Wanton destruction for what reason? A slow burn of anger bit into her. There was an answer. She just had to find it.

Matt greeted her. "Back for more pictures?"

She nodded. "Have you seen Susan?"

"Yes, we talked to her earlier. She's down the street in the realtor's office. She said something about finding a temporary location for the paper. Riley, this is Ken Stapleton, a fire inspector with the Austin Fire Department. I called and asked if he could take a look at the building. Ken, this is Riley Phillips, one of our up-and-coming reporters. I would also add photographer." He motioned toward her camera. "I saw your article this morning. Amazing pictures you took."

Riley felt the heat from the blush on her face from the compliments.

"Nice to meet you," the fire inspector said as they shook hands. "I'm sure you want to know my findings. The fire was deliberately set. I found traces of accelerants in a room at the back of the building. According to your editor, it was her office." He paused before adding, "This was a pro."

Matt asked, "Do you know of any reason someone would set fire to the place? I asked Susan the same question."

Not ready to voice her suspicions, she said, "No, I don't. You know the type of stuff we report. The only significant event lately was the body Milo and I found."

"Hmm … Susan said the same. Though, I don't know how it could connect. If anything occurs to you, let me know."

"Will I cause a problem if I take a few pictures?"

"Not at all. We're done here."

Glad she'd worn her boots, Riley sloshed through the water and debris, snapping pictures of the gutted interior. From across the street, she heard a shout. Susan was on the sidewalk, waving to her. Riley took a couple more shots before loping over.

"Did you find a place to rent?"

"Yes, it's on the outskirts of town. A two-room office, but I think it will do until we can rebuild. Did you talk to Matt?"

"Yes. And the fire inspector. Susan, the fire inspector said the arsonist was a pro."

"I know. I still think it has something to do with the body you found, but I didn't say so. No proof."

"I didn't say anything about it either."

A sheen of tears glistened in Susan's eyes. "This is still unbelievable. It defies my comprehension. What matters now is making sure we keep the paper going. I'll let you know as soon as I have the keys to the new office. Let's do one more article with the pictures you just took."

On the way out of town, Riley stopped and bought a new computer. The dent in her checking account reminded her to file an insurance claim. When she and Milo arrived home, Riley carried the new computer to the office before letting Milo out the patio door. By the time she tossed the clothes from the night before into the dryer and fixed a glass of iced tea, Milo's nose pressed against the glass. He charged inside, heading to his bowls.

With the glass in her hand, Riley strode into the office, where she unboxed the computer. Once it was up and running, she stashed the old one in the closet. After downloading her files from the cloud, she sent Ted a quick note about the fire chief's report.

The growling of her stomach reminded her she'd skipped breakfast, and now lunch was in jeopardy. In the kitchen, she quickly made a turkey and cheese sandwich. From the cupboard, she grabbed a bag of chips and a can of soda from the fridge. Milo trotted to the patio door, and she opened it. At the breakfast nook table, Riley watched him chase a butterfly. The butterfly was winning the race.

After cleaning up the dishes, she opened the patio door for Milo, then strode to the office. Seated at the desk, Riley pulled up the form to file a claim, only to discover she needed a copy of the police report. She groaned. It meant another trip to the sheriff's office.

She accessed the list she'd made for Ted, adding the new details about the fire. It was a good way to keep track of the investigation. The only problem was that she didn't know where to investigate next. As she studied the details of the Henning farm, the location suddenly struck her as odd.

It would be highly unlikely a stranger would know about the place. Even many of the locals probably didn't know about the farm. Located on a remote county road with little to no traffic, why would anyone go there? Why would the victim have been there in the first place? Of course, she surmised, a killer would want just such a location. A place where the body would never be found.

Whoa, back up, she thought. Was the farm just the dump site for the body? She'd never given a thought to where he was killed. The dang shower curtain should have told her. "Some hotshot investigator you are," she muttered. Riley tapped the folder with the crime scene photos, zooming on one of the close-ups of the head. Head wounds bled copiously. Yet there was no blood around the head. What was on the body had dried. The man was killed at another location and then hauled to the farm. It did indicate the killer had prior knowledge of the place. She couldn't imagine he'd just drive around with a corpse in the car, looking for a place to bury it.

There might be a connection between the farm and the killer. She had no idea who owned the property or even the legal address. As far back as she could remember, the place had been abandoned and was always referred to as the old Henning place.

Another thought struck—the county tax records. Without an address, Riley had to use the county road number. Two pages containing eight addresses popped up. Methodically, she clicked on each one. She found it on the second page. "Bingo," she muttered. After writing down the address, she scrolled, looking for the owner. Near the bottom of the form, she found it—Abel Walter.

Next, she turned her attention to other homeowners and addresses on the county road where the farm was located. She added them to her list, planning to contact each one. They might have seen something. A sense of eagerness buoyed her thoughts. She still hadn't given up on the yearbooks, and now she had another lead. *Case closed, my ass*, she thought.

****

Ted read Riley's latest email. The confirmation the fire was arson was troubling. It was time to get some answers. He pulled up the sheriff's department's website for the phone number. When a voice answered, he said, "I would like to speak with Sheriff Rutherford."

"Who is calling?"

"Major Ted Phillips with the Dallas Police Department."

"Hold the line, please."

A few clicks echoed, and a gravelly voice answered, "Sheriff Rutherford. What can I do for you, Major Phillips?"

"I appreciate your taking my call. I am Riley Phillips' brother. I am interested in the status of the investigation into the burglary of her home."

There was a short silence before Rutherford cleared his throat. "I'm afraid I can't tell you much. I have a meeting scheduled later today with my staff to discuss current investigations. I would be able to tell you more after that meeting."

"I would appreciate a callback. Before I get off the line, I'll leave you my number. I am also interested in the body that Riley and her dog found. Do you have any leads as to his identity?"

"Uh, no, we haven't. What is your interest in a local homicide?"

"I manage Dallas PD's Fusion Center. I might be able to help."

"What could you possibly do?"

"Are you familiar with fusion centers?"

Rutherford cleared his throat. "Ah, yes."

From the tone of his voice, Ted wondered if he'd ever heard of a fusion center. "Then you are aware, we can input the details about the body and the crime scene to look for a match to similar details

[62]

from multiple agencies, federal, state, and local. I can also run a picture of the victim's face through our facial recognition software."

Rutherford cleared his throat again. "There's no reason to involve your department with extra work."

"I can assure you it isn't a problem with my department. We routinely assist other agencies. I can have one of my personnel contact your lead detective, if for nothing else than to obtain a picture of the victim. It could speed up your investigation."

Ted could hear the irritation in the man's voice as he said, "I have very few details since the body was stolen. Quite frankly, we're at a standstill. As far as my department is concerned, the case is closed."

Ted knew a stonewall when he heard it. Rutherford wanted this case to be closed. "Still, there are the pictures of the crime scene and victim. Even though you've closed the case, using my program to analyze the images would benefit your agency."

"My crime scene technician experienced a malfunction with the department's camera that affected the pictures. While I appreciate your offer, as I said, the case is closed."

"I have to say you certainly experienced a strange series of events for a local homicide."

"What are you implying?"

"I'm not implying anything. I'm just looking at the facts. A murder victim's body is stolen. My sister's house was broken into. Her computer destroyed along with the pictures she took. Last night, someone torched the newspaper building. The same newspaper that printed articles about the discovery of the murdered man along with pictures my sister took."

"I fail to see any connection. No offense to your sister, but she has a way of stirring up trouble. As I said, my office closed the case for lack of evidence."

"If it changes, my offer is still open."

"Leave your number with my secretary. I'll contact you if anything new comes up." He clicked off.

After talking to the secretary, Ted hung up. He leaned back in his chair. Now, that was enlightening. Rutherford never conducted an investigation. He never mentioned the ring, a telling omission. Then there was the issue with his pictures. Ted's cop instinct wasn't just tingling, it was clanging.

His sergeant stepped into the doorway. "Line two, a Scott Fleming. I told him you were on a call. He said he'd hold."

Ted reached for the receiver. "Hello, Scott. I'm hoping you've got good news. Did you identify this guy?"

"Not yet. Nicki is still working on it. She'll find him. I'm calling to tell you one of my agents, Cody Lightfoot, is headed to Fredericksburg."

"Unexpected, but decidedly warranted. That phone call I was on was with the local sheriff. I offered the services of my department to help identify the victim. Rutherford turned me down. Said he had no evidence, never mentioned the ring, and had no pictures. He's already closed the case."

Scott's voice deepened with intensity. "No pictures. An interesting twist. Did he say why?"

"A technical malfunction with the camera."

There was a pause. "How convenient."

"I thought so. Considering how tight-lipped he was, I'd like to know what happened to those pictures. Scott, that's not all. Last night, the newspaper office burned down. It was arson, and according to the fire inspector, the arsonist was a pro. It started in the editor's office."

"They went after the pictures." It wasn't a question.

"It was my first thought. My second was, why burn down the building? An over-the-top crime to get rid of whatever pictures the editor, Susan Hutchin, had. Whoever is behind this could have easily broken in and destroyed the computer. Here's my take. If they had, there was a chance someone would snap to the similarity to what happened to Riley's computer. Burning down the building, a different type of crime, put a different spin on it. The fire could have been intended to put the newspaper out of business, stop the articles, and keep anyone from identifying the victim. It adds up to one reason, to buy time. But why?"

"And then there was the ring," Scott mused. "Without it, the body would ultimately have been identified, though it would have taken time, especially if the victim's fingerprints or DNA were not in the system. But that ring, instant identification. Any chance Rutherford is involved?"

"Maybe. He parked the body at the funeral home, where it could conveniently be stolen before reaching the M.E.'s office. That tells me something else. Someone has boots on the ground in Fredericksburg. I'm concerned about what will happen when it's discovered my sister still has pictures and Susan is still printing articles."

Scott was impressed by Ted's reasoning. "I agree. Whatever is going down is about to happen. But what or where?"

"How soon will your agent get there?" Ted asked.

"No later than tomorrow. He's going undercover. I don't want to advertise that the FBI is in town, and that includes your sister, even though she is his primary assignment."

As Ted hung up the phone, he felt the weight lift from his shoulders. Riley would have someone keeping an eye on her, a bodyguard. Knowing his sister, though, he was sure she wouldn't see it quite that way if she found out.

Chapter 8

The first stop of the day was the sheriff's office to get a copy of her report. After explaining why she was there, the deputy at the front desk told her to take a seat.

A few minutes later, Billy walked up and greeted her.

"The clerk is printing the report." He crossed his arms and leaned against the counter in front of her. "Too bad about what happened to the newspaper office. Is Susan shutting down the paper?"

"No. She's got a temporary office. The *Register* is up and running."

"Surprising. I figured the fire would put the paper out of business. I'm glad to hear that's not the case."

She eyed him. He seemed sincere.

"Those pictures you took of the fire were good. I think you surprised more than a few people. I've heard several comments about them."

Stunned by his compliment, she wasn't sure what to say. "Uh, well, thank you."

Taking advantage of his goodwill, she asked, "Did you ever find out anything more about the missing victim?"

"No, we haven't. There's nothing for us to investigate. It's why Rutherford closed the case. Are you still digging into it?"

Something told her to keep her ideas to herself. "What can I do?"

"Well, nothing. With the fire and all, I expect you have enough to worry about. I heard your brother called the sheriff. I didn't know he was with Dallas PD. He asked about our pictures of the crime scene. He even offered to help identify the man."

She leaned forward, eagerly asking, "Does that mean you'll reopen the case? Are you going to send your photos to my brother?"

He shook his head. "The sheriff isn't reopening the case."

It didn't escape her attention that Billy dodged the question about sending Ted a picture. Her senses tingled. Why?

Billy said, "Didn't you take pictures after you found the body? I'd have thought your brother could have used one of them."

Was this why Billy was out here? Did the sheriff put him up to pumping her for information?

With an angry tone, she said, "If you recall, my computer was destroyed when someone broke into my house. It's why I'm sitting here, waiting for a report about a crime your department didn't investigate."

A sheepish look crossed Billy's face. "Riley, I didn't mean to get you all stirred up. There wasn't anything to investigate. That's too bad you lost them. How about Susan? Didn't she have pictures?"

"The fire destroyed her office and the few pictures she had." She paused as if gathering her thoughts. It was time to turn the tables. "The pictures. I hadn't thought about it, but it seems to me there is a definite connection between someone breaking into my house and burning down the newspaper office. In both, pictures of a missing body were destroyed." She waited to see what Billy would come up with.

"I doubt it. It's too far-fetched to think the two incidents are connected. These were completely different crimes. Is your brother investigating?"

"He's just concerned that I found the body, and then someone broke into my home. As you said, what is there to investigate?"

A woman walked up with papers in her hand.

"Ah, here's your report. If you need anything else, give me a call."

Riley took the papers the woman handed her. "Thanks, I will."

She turned and walked out. Outside, Milo waited. She'd leashed him to the same bench. Riley climbed into her truck and muttered, "Now that was odd."

Her next stop was the new office in one of the older strip malls. When she walked in, Ben and another reporter, Ruby Parker, were seated at two small desks along one wall. Ruby wrote the food, craft, and entertainment articles.

At the back was an enclosed office next to the bathroom. On the opposite wall, two long tables were set up. A few office supplies were stacked on them.

Milo eagerly trotted toward the reporters. Ben rubbed his head before Milo twisted toward Ruby. She dutifully did the same while laughing. "He knows how to get attention."

"Were you planning on working here today?" Ben said. "With only two desks, we may have to set up a schedule."

"No, I'm good. I want to talk to Susan."

"Be warned. She's in a grumpy mood. The insurance company has bowed up over the claim. That's who she's talking to."

From where she stood, Riley could see Susan seated in an office half the size of the one that burned down. She had a phone stuck to her ear and angrily gestured as she talked.

Susan wasn't a large woman, only an inch or so taller than Riley and a few pounds heavier. Despite her pushing sixty, Susan was a force to be reckoned with when she got on a roll. Riley could almost feel sorry for the insurance agent.

Ben stood. "We've got a long list of supplies to purchase. We'll be back later this afternoon."

Belatedly, Riley realized they had to rebuild the business from the ground up, even purchasing something as simple as a stapler. "If you need help, let me know."

With a wave of her hand, Ruby said, "We got it covered."

Milo wistfully watched them walk out. "Expected them to take you for a walk, did you?" Milo woofed before dropping to the floor with his head dejectedly on his paws.

At the sound, Susan turned her head. When she spotted Riley, she waved her into the office.

Riley strolled in, dropping into the only chair in front of the desk.

Once Susan hung up, she grimaced. "It's not much, but it's home until we get a new building."

"Ben said you had some problems with the insurance company."

"They won't pay the claim until they get the full report from the fire inspector, which means I can't start construction." Her gaze focused on Riley. In a sharp tone, she said, "What's happened?"

"Nothing gets by you, does it?"

"Hey, I've been a newshound for thirty-some years. You don't survive in this business if you don't have the nose."

"I stopped by the sheriff's office to pick up my report for my insurance claim. I had an odd conversation with Billy. He wanted to know if I was still digging into the disappearance of the body. He also made an odd comment about the fire keeping us occupied."

Susan leaned back. Her eyes narrowed with speculation. "I wonder why he would be asking."

"He asked about my pictures and yours, wanting to know if they'd been destroyed. I suspect the sheriff put him up to it."

Susan leaned forward. Her nails tapped the desk. "You're right. It is odd. Why would the sheriff be interested in our pictures?"

"Maybe because Ted called Rutherford, asking for a picture to run through the facial recognition program. When I asked if Rutherford was sending a picture, Billy sidestepped the question."

"What did Ted have to say?"

"Haven't talked to him yet. But I'm going to call him. Last night, I had another idea. Someone had to know about the farm. That man was killed somewhere else, and his body dumped there. My next stop is the courthouse. I want to research the Henning farm. I don't even know why it's called the Henning farm. According to the tax assessor's records, Abel Walter owns the place. There must be a reason why the killer used the farm, a connection there somewhere."

Susan nodded her head. "Never heard of him, but that's heads-up investigating."

"Is it all right if I leave Milo here? I can't leave him in the truck, and I sure didn't want to leave him at home."

"Absolutely. He and I will get along just fine."

On her way out, she told Milo to stay. Even though Milo gave her a pitiful look, he laid back down.

Seated in the truck, she pulled out her cellphone and tapped the speed dial. When Ted answered, she said, "I heard you called Rutherford. What happened?"

"How did you find out?" Ted asked.

Riley gave him a quick rundown on her conversation with Billy.

"So, Rutherford was curious about your pictures and Susan's?"

"That's how Susan and I figured it. Otherwise, why would Billy be quizzing me? I bet Rutherford put him up to it."

"He doesn't have any pictures. Rutherford told me the tech's camera malfunctioned."

"Good lord. No wonder he closed the case so fast. He doesn't want to have to admit to another glitch in his investigation. But it doesn't make sense. I talked to Carla Sanchez, the medic who was there to pick up the body. She said they had to wait until the deputy finished taking pictures. Carla would have known if there was a problem with the camera."

"It could have happened at the sheriff's office. I need to be sure about one point. You never told this deputy you still had your pictures?"

"No. I didn't." As the implication of Ted's question sunk in, a chill raced over her. "That means the break-in, the fire, and the sheriff's pictures are all connected. Someone doesn't want the body identified."

"That's how I figure it."

"But why?"

"That's the sixty-four-million-dollar question. I'll talk to you later."

She pocketed the phone and started the engine, pulling out of the parking lot. Troubled by the conversation, she didn't see the truck that tailed her to the courthouse. Riley parked in the lot next to the building.

Inside, she had to walk through a metal detector before being directed to the records office down the hallway. She stopped at the front desk, explaining she needed to search the history of a property. The woman directed her to a computer and showed Riley how to pull up the information and where the books with the titles and deeds were kept if the document wasn't online.

From the backpack, she pulled out a notepad and pen. For each new reference she found, Riley jotted down the information. She discovered Abel Walter bought the property from Jesse Henning in 1971. The Hennings acquired the land in the late 1800s. No wonder it was still known as the Henning farm.

She also searched the history of the other homes on the same county road. Though she was unsure whether the information would help, she was still looking for a connection.

By the time she finished, it was late afternoon. She packed up her materials and the documents she printed, then paid for her printed copies at the front desk.

As she pulled into the parking lot in front of the office, Ben and Ruby walked out.

"We were wondering when you'd get back," Ben said. "Milo is showing signs of distress."

Inside, she was greeted by a very enthusiastic animal, jumping and barking. "Quiet," Riley said. The dog immediately stopped barking but leaned against her legs, refusing to move.

Susan walked up. "I'm not sure why, but after you left, he got restless, whining and pacing to the door and back. He finally stopped, then started up again just before you got here. He's never done that before. Any idea what was wrong?"

"I don't have a clue. Maybe it's because I didn't take him with me."

Milo, still huddled against Riley's legs, whimpered. She rubbed his head to reassure him before she followed Susan to her office.

"What did you find out?" Susan asked.

"Before I get into what I found, I talked to Ted. Rutherford doesn't have any pictures. He told Ted the camera malfunctioned."

"You're the camera expert. How could that happen?"

"I'm not sure. But it sounds suspicious."

Susan's brow wrinkled with a worried look. "That means someone may believe all the pictures have been destroyed. What happens if they find out you still have them? Riley, I don't like this one darn bit. And you're all alone with no close neighbors. I've got plenty of room. Why don't you stay with me for a few days?"

Despite the anxiety she felt, she gave a reassuring laugh. "Hey, I'll be just fine. I've got the best alarm system I could have—Milo. I'll be okay."

With a reluctant air, Susan said, "My offer's open if you change your mind. Now, what did you find out at the courthouse?"

Riley told her about the farm's purchase history. "I wonder if Abel Walter still lives around here."

"I bet Ruby might know."

"I'll give her a call. Any other assignments?"

"No. I want you to stay on this case. Any stories, I'll give to Ben."

"Okay. I'll check in tomorrow." She looked down. Milo still hovered next to her as if he was afraid to let her out of his sight. She clipped the leash on his collar and picked up the backpack, slinging it over her shoulder.

Outside, as she strolled toward the truck, Milo gave a sharp bark, stopping in the middle of the sidewalk. When Riley looked down, the dog gazed toward a group of buildings across the street. He barked again before slipping into his deep growl.

Chapter 9

Riley slowly scanned the buildings and parking lots. Nothing she could see explained Milo's strange behavior. The dog suddenly relaxed, giving her one of his woofs.

As she pulled out, she kept an eye on the rearview mirror. A white car pulled out of a parking lot. Her body tensed, hands tightening on the steering wheel. When the car turned onto another street, she looked at Milo. As usual, his head hung over the console. "You've got me jumping at shadows now."

Still, she kept watching, making sure she wasn't followed. It wasn't until the garage door closed behind her that she finally relaxed. Once inside, she opened the patio door. Milo raced outside, making his trek around the fence. She plunked into a chair on the patio, figuring she'd throw his baseball a few times when he was done. Suddenly, he stopped, his nose sniffing a reddish mound on the grass near the fence.

His unexpected behavior triggered a frightening thought. "Milo, leave it," she screamed as she ran. Milo's head snapped up to look at her as she raced toward him. She skidded to a stop, horrified at what she saw. A large pile of raw hamburger had been dropped over the fence. Certain it had been poisoned, she grabbed Milo by the collar, pulling him away from the meat. "Heel." Riley hung on to his collar as he trotted alongside her.

Inside, she closed the sliding glass door. She grabbed a trash bag, rubber gloves, and a bottle of disinfectant from the utility room. It would be a waste of time to make another report. Rutherford wouldn't do anything. And there was no point in getting the meat tested since she knew it was poisoned. It was the only reason someone put the meat in her backyard. As an afterthought, Riley retrieved the camera from her bag, hanging it around her neck. At least she'd have pictures.

"Stay," she said as she opened the patio door just far enough to slip outside. Before she gloved up, Riley took several pictures. Then she dropped large handfuls of the raw meat into the trash bag, making sure she picked up every speck of meat. Once the area was clean, she stripped off the gloves, tossing them inside the bag. She poured disinfectant over the meat before tightly tying the bag with a plastic tie. Then Riley sprinkled the disinfectant over the grass to keep Milo away from the spot. The bag went into the large bin at the side of the house.

It wasn't until she was back inside that the fear hit her with all the speed of an oncoming train. Riley collapsed on a chair. Milo's nose nuzzled her cheek as she bent over to keep from passing out. He softly whimpered. She slowly straightened, though her hand trembled as she stroked his back. Shudders rippled over Riley at the thought of what would have happened if she hadn't been watching. Milo would have eaten the meat. From now on, before she let him out, she'd walk the backyard, making sure another present hadn't been left.

Milo whimpered again.

"It's okay. No one is going to hurt you." As the fear faded, anger built, and she headed to her bedroom. Growing up in a rural area, her dad made sure she and Ted knew how to shoot. From inside the closet, she pulled out her dad's shotgun and grabbed a box of shells from the top shelf. After loading the shotgun, she hauled it to the kitchen, leaning it in a corner.

Though her appetite had fled, she still needed to eat. She checked Milo's bowls, refilled them, then looked in the freezer. Nothing appealed, so she opened a can of soup and made a sandwich. While the soup heated in the microwave, she flipped on the front porch and backyard lights.

Once she finished and had the kitchen squared away, it was back on the computer. To her list of case notes, she added the poisoned meat, then typed up the notes on her research. The part about Abel Walter reminded her to call Ruby. She tapped the number.

When Ruby answered, Riley said, "Have I caught you at a bad time?"

Ruby snorted. "Are you kidding? At my age, the most exciting thing I do in the evening is watch forty-year-old reruns on the old folks' TV channel. What's up?"

"Do you know Abel Walter? He owns the Henning farm."

"Researching that, are you?"

"Just wondering why someone would use the place to dump a body. I looked it up at the courthouse today."

"I know him. Have for years. I think he bought the place back, I don't know, maybe the sixties, seventies, time frame. Didn't live there long. Probably why it's still referred to as the Henning farm."

"Why didn't he live there?"

"His son was killed in Vietnam. The sun rose and set on that boy. It devastated Abel and his wife. She passed away a year or so after the boy was killed. I think she died of a broken heart. Abel couldn't abide being out there by himself, so he upped and moved into town. Just let the place go."

"How sad. Is he still alive?"

"Sure, he gets around pretty good for his age. He's out at that apartment complex for seniors."

"Did he have any relatives?"

"Not that I know about."

"What about the Hennings?"

"Now there's a family that goes way back. They were originally from Germany. Jesse Henning was the last one to own the place. He died not long after he sold it to Abel."

"Any family members still live around here?"

"The kids all left. If some relative has moved back, I don't know about it."

"Someone has to know about the place. Why else would they have used it?"

Ruby cackled. "You just stay with it, young lady. You got the kind of mind that will find the answers. Give me a holler if you have any other questions."

"I will. Thanks."

Pondering what she'd learned, she laid the phone aside. Tomorrow, she would stop by the senior center. Maybe Abel Walter could shed some light on the mystery. Milo's toenails clicked on the floor. He was headed to her office, a sure sign he wanted to go outside. From the doorway, he woofed.

"Okay, let's go."

Tail whipping, he turned, racing toward the glass doors.

She grabbed the shotgun and eased out the door, ordering Milo to stay. Riley wasn't letting him out until she checked the yard, even though it was doubtful there was any danger. If anyone was watching, she wanted to make dang sure he knew she was ready for him.

****

Cody Lightfoot pulled into the service station on the edge of town. He started the gas pump, then raised his arms, stretching his back. It had been a long drive from Las Vegas to Fredericksburg. It would have been quicker to fly, but he had gear he couldn't get on a plane.

He was now officially a Tracker agent. Cody wasn't sure just yet whether this was a good career move or not. He liked working in the FBI office in Vegas. Had felt comfortable there, which said a lot. Since getting out of the military, there weren't too many places where he felt comfortable.

Before he left Vegas, Scott sent a case summary of his new assignment and a large file of pictures. Since the reporter was his reason for heading to Texas, he'd taken the time to study the pictures the woman took. On the long drive, he'd had plenty of time to think about it. At first, it seemed an odd assignment for an FBI agent, undercover as a bodyguard because of a local homicide. Still, the more he mulled over the details, the more he agreed with Scott that it didn't fit the profile of a local crime.

He'd made reservations at a hotel, but before he checked in, Cody wanted to drive by the home of his new assignment. The pump clicked off. He waited for the receipt to print before sliding behind the wheel. During one of his stops, he pulled up a map of the area on his laptop. Cody had a rare ability, a photographic memory. Once he saw a map, he could recall every detail.

His ability had proved invaluable during his stint in the military, even more so as an agent, since he could remember the smallest detail of a crime scene or written documents. Unerringly, he turned onto the road that led to Riley Phillips' house. Cody didn't have difficulty seeing it. The place was lit up like a Christmas tree. As he drove past, his lights reflected off a truck parked under a stand of trees on the opposite side of the road. His senses spiked. Cody didn't back off his speed, ignoring the vehicle as if he hadn't seen it. Ahead was a crossroads. He turned and pulled to the side once he was certain his truck was out of sight. His hand brushed the Glock riding on his hip as he slid out. The sound of an engine broke the silence. *Must have spooked him*, he thought.

Nicknamed "The Ghost" by his army buddies, Cody silently worked his way back. As he suspected, the truck was gone. Using the small flashlight he'd stuck in his vest pocket, he flashed the beam over the ground. By the number of tracks, a vehicle had parked there several times. He looked toward the house. A dog barked, running along the fence. A young woman stood in the middle of the yard, holding a shotgun.

With the lights and shotgun, his new assignment sent a strong message. Don't mess with Riley Phillips. Intrigued, he watched until she and the dog were back inside. This should prove interesting.

He pulled out his phone and tapped the number he added to his speed dial hours earlier. His new boss said to call once he had a chance to evaluate the situation, no matter what time of day or night. Not wanting to get off on the wrong foot, Cody hoped Scott meant it.

Scott answered on the second ring. He'd already come across as a man of few words. Not wasting time on niceties, he asked, "Are you in Fredericksburg?"

"Yes. Something else may have happened. Riley Phillips lives in a house outside of town. The front and back are lit up like a football stadium. She was in the backyard with her dog and a shotgun. Someone was watching her. I spooked him out of his hiding hole tonight, but I'm betting he'll be back. We need to change our game plan. Instead of staying undercover, I need to be upfront and visible."

"Do you need to stay in the house?"

Cody hesitated before answering, considering the pros and cons. "No. I need the flexibility to move around. I won't have it if I'm in the house."

"I'll call her brother in the morning and set it up."

Chapter 10

Between bites of a cinnamon bagel and blueberry yogurt, Riley studied her list. At the top was a visit to the senior center. Next were the names and addresses of the other homes on the road where the farm was located.

Another thought had occurred to her the night before. If the victim was a visitor, where was he living? A local would surely have been reported missing, but not a visitor. She ruled out hotels and B&Bs. If an occupant disappeared, the police would have been notified. Rental houses, maybe not.

There were a few realtors in town who handled rentals. Not wanting to use a picture of the hand with the ring, Riley had found a picture online. She printed it. Being a graduate and daughter of an Aggie graduate, Riley knew it didn't take long for Aggies to recognize each other, especially by their class ring. The ring was distinctive and might have drawn the attention of a realtor.

Riley cleaned the kitchen before gathering her documents and notes. Stuffed inside a file folder, she slid them into the backpack. Since she planned on spending most of the day in a remote part of the county, she had wrapped the shotgun in a sheet. It was on the backseat, away from Milo's feet.

During the drive into town, Riley kept an eye on the rearview mirror, though with the early morning traffic it was nearly impossible to tell if someone was tailing her.

When she walked into the office, Susan was the only occupant. After greeting Milo and giving him the obligatory head rub, Susan said, "Ben's out on a traffic accident. Ruby's already come and gone. She mentioned your phone call."

Riley nodded. "My first stop today is the senior center where Abel Walter lives. I have a list of other stops as well." After explaining, she added, "Would you mind if I left Milo here again?"

"Of course, you can. I'm not planning to go anywhere."

For a moment, Riley hesitated about mentioning the meat, then decided Susan needed to know, if for no other reason than to keep a close eye on Milo. "Last night, someone left Milo a present in the backyard, raw hamburger meat."

A look of horror crossed Susan's face. "Poisoned?"

"I'm sure it was. I got to him before he started chomping on it." The memory still sent chills racing down Riley's back. "Don't let anyone give him any food."

"I'll be careful."

Riley's phone chimed. She glanced at the screen. "My brother," she told Susan.

"Hey, sis," he said after she answered. "I've got news for you. Where are you?"

"At the newspaper office with Susan."

"What office?"

"She rented temporary office space."

"Anyone else there?"

"Uh … no. What's going on?"

"An FBI agent is in Fredericksburg. He's there on the QT. His boss thought it would help if I called you and explained."

Riley squealed, "FBI! What the devil is the FBI doing here?"

Susan's brows disappeared under her bangs.

Milo whined, restlessly pushing against her leg. Riley patted his head. "It's okay."

Ted said, "I know it is."

"Not you, you idiot. I was talking to Milo."

"Riley, calm down. He's there because I contacted the head of the Trackers', a special unit in the FBI. I've worked with them on other cases."

That diverted her attention. "You've been working with the FBI? Wow, you never mentioned it."

"Didn't see a reason to talk about it. It's just part of what I do. But we're getting off track here. He's in Fredericksburg because I asked for help in identifying the body. If anyone can identify your murder victim, it's the unit's computer guru, Nicki Allison."

"Okay, you asked for help to identify the victim. Still doesn't explain why an agent is in town. I know enough to realize the FBI doesn't get involved in a local murder. So, what else is going on here? Please tell me you didn't ask the FBI to babysit me."

"It's not just about you. This isn't some local homicide. Someone has a serious agenda. You and Susan got in the way. After Scott Fleming, the head of the unit, looked at your write-up and pictures, he decided to send an agent to Fredericksburg. He arrived last night and has already discovered someone has you under surveillance."

That shook her up more than she wanted to admit.

"Quite frankly, Riley, he needs your help. He doesn't know the area or the people. You do. Local law enforcement hasn't asked the FBI to assist in the investigation, so he can't officially get involved."

'Oh." Ted always knew how to spike her guns. An annoying habit. "You really sent that list I wrote and my photos to the FBI?"

"I did. Here's what I suggest. He's a cousin on Mom's side. Mom has that whole offshoot of relatives out on the West Coast. He's not working undercover, just doesn't want to advertise he's FBI. He'll be there in a few minutes. I texted him your location."

Before Riley could protest, Ted disconnected. Muttering an oath, she pocketed the phone.

"Before I bust a gut with curiosity, you'd better fill me in. I take it we've got an FBI agent in town."

Riley grunted. "We do. Ted called an FBI agent he knows for help in identifying the victim. So now, we've got an agent here. He's on the way. Ted seems to think I can help him. What do I know about working with the FBI?"

"Calm down. Grab a cup of coffee, and let's wait in my office. You know this could be good."

Riley shot her a grumpy look as she poured a cup. "How? I don't want an agent bird-dogging my every step. I still think this is a sneaky plot to make sure I have a bodyguard." She followed Susan into her office.

"Look at it this way. The FBI has access to information that mere mortals like us don't. It will help in any articles we write. A good way to get your byline recognized."

Seated in the chair, Riley perked up. "Okay, you've got a point. After all, it shouldn't be too bad. I guess I can put up with one of the men-in-black, the MIBs, for a few days. I expect he's bald, pot-bellied, and married with several kids."

Milo woofed as the front door opened.

Susan muttered, "I don't *think* so. Not if this is your agent."

Riley twisted in her chair to look.

A man, around six feet tall, with broad shoulders and narrow hips, strode in. No black suit with a white shirt or wing-tipped shoes. Instead, it was cowboy boots, crisply pressed blue jeans, a white shirt and vest. While his physique was riveting, it failed to compare to his face. Waves of raven black hair framed the sharp edges of his cheekbones and decidedly craggy jaw. Dark eyes under heavy black brows added to his rakish look. Riley had no problem envisioning him on the bow of a ship, sword in hand.

Milo trotted toward him, stopping in front. His butt hit the floor, and he stared up at the man. Riley watched in amazement. She'd never seen Milo greet a stranger without giving him a command.

The man looked down and, in a slow, low drawl, said, "I bet you're Milo."

Milo woofed.

"I thought so. Nice to meet you, Milo."

Milo woofed again, lifting his paw. The man reached, lightly gripped it, then brushed his hand across the top of the dog's head before straightening.

Susan rose, striding into the outer room. Still befuddled by Milo's behavior, Riley followed.

"I'm Susan Hutchin, owner and editor of the *Register*. May I help you?"

A slow smile lit his face. "Yes, ma'am," he said with an old-fashioned tone of courtesy. "I'm looking for Riley Phillips."

Riley stepped forward. "I'm Riley Phillips."

"Pleased to meet you. I'm FBI Special Agent Cody Lightfoot."

Riley should have immediately recognized his Native American heritage. A bit grumpily, she thought, *should have put him on a horse with a bow and arrows.* "My brother called and said you were in town."

"Is there somewhere we can talk? I have several questions I'm hoping you can answer." Whether intentional or by happenstance, Cody's comments instantly overcame Riley's reluctance.

Susan said, "Agent Lightfoot, you're welcome to use my office."

"Why don't we sit at one of these desks? It might be more comfortable than her office. She needs to hear this," Riley said.

"I'm fine with it if you are. And, if you don't mind, let's make it first names all the way around. I have a feeling we'll see a lot of each other." He grabbed another chair, pulling it around the desk.

Once they were seated, Riley said, "Tell me why you're here. I got an abbreviated version from my brother."

"I'm assigned to a specialized unit, Trackers, based in Washington, D.C. Your brother contacted one of our agents about the body you and Milo found. After my boss examined the documents and pictures your brother sent, he believed what's happened goes beyond a local homicide. It was enough of a concern to send me here. The initial idea was to stay in the background while I investigated." What he didn't say was that in Ted's text message, he was told to avoid the word "bodyguard."

"What changed?" Susan asked.

Cody grimly said, "After I arrived last night, I drove by your house. I spotted a truck backed into a stand of trees. By the time I circled back on foot, the truck was gone. But someone was watching you. I didn't like it, and neither did my boss. That's why the change in plans. I need it known I'm visiting you, just not that I'm FBI."

Susan crossed her arms across her chest. With a determined look, she said, "Well, I, for one, am glad to hear it. Someone tried to poison Milo last night."

A dark look crossed his face. After Riley explained, Cody asked, "Is that why you were in the backyard with your shotgun?"

At her surprised look, he said, "Where the truck was parked, whoever was watching had a clear view of your backyard. Of course, all the lights helped."

"Good! I hope he saw the shotgun. That was my plan."

"While I have a general idea of what's been going on, if you don't mind, I'd like to hear it in your words."

Susan said, "That will take time. Would you like a cup of coffee, water, or a soda?"

"Coffee would be good. Just black."

"Riley?"

"Water, please." She started with Milo alerting to the body. By the time she finished, Cody had drunk two cups of coffee, and Riley had polished off a bottle of water.

"Susan, do you have the arson investigator's report on the fire?" Cody asked.

"Not yet. He said it would take a few days."

"Please, follow up on it. I need that report. I'm curious about the farm where you found the body. Who owns it?" Cody asked.

Riley shot him a surprised look. "It's interesting you should ask. I spent several hours yesterday at the courthouse researching the property's history. It was purchased from the original owners in 1971 and is owned by Abel Walter. I plan to contact him today. He lives in an apartment complex on the edge of town."

"Good idea. I want to go with you. Before we leave, we have one more piece of business. What story can we use to explain why I'm here?"

"Uh … well, Ted, my brother suggested you could be a cousin."

"Would it be believable?"

"Yes. My mom is one of five children, three sisters and a brother. It would be possible. In California, there's quite a clan of relatives."

"Okay, cousin it is. What else do you have planned for the day?"

"There are a few residences on the road where the farm is located. I planned to stop at each one. I thought there could be a link. Who would know about the property unless you were a local? Also, they might have seen a car or other activity at the farm. My other idea was to check with realtors and find out about rental houses in the area. I even have a picture of the ring. It's odd there isn't a missing person report unless the man was a visitor."

He looked at her with a new respect in his eyes.

Chapter 11

When he arrived, Cody was uncertain as to what to expect. Riley's diminutive frame, attired in blue jeans, t-shirt, and vest, her russet hair pulled through the back of a ball cap, didn't fit his idea of a hard-hitting investigative reporter. Until he got to her face. Despite her stunning good looks, the suspicion on her heart-shaped face and in her hazel eyes told a different story.

He said, "Which is why you eliminated hotels and other places that rent rooms. Those facilities would likely have reported a man was missing. I'd like to see the farm. Get a feel for the place."

He glanced down at Milo, lying near his feet. "Is Milo going with us?" The dog's head snapped up.

"He's staying here. I don't want to leave him at home, and I can't leave him in the truck."

"I have a suggestion. First, let's hit the places in town where he could be a problem. Then come back and pick him up. I'd like to have him with us when we go to the farm."

A somber look crossed his face. "One other item. I need your cellphone numbers, and I'll give you mine. Put it on your speed dial. Do not hesitate to call, no matter what time, day or night."

After everyone had exchanged numbers, Riley retrieved the backpack from Susan's office. Milo gave them a look of reproach when he was told to stay.

"Your vehicle or mine?" Cody asked as he held the door open for Riley.

"Let's take mine. It's easier to talk if I'm not giving you directions."

Cody didn't bother to tell her it wasn't necessary.

Before she backed out of the parking space, she pulled her file folder from the backpack and handed it to him. "The results of my research at the courthouse and a list of places to stop."

While Riley drove, Cody studied each page before replacing them in the file folder. "Tell me about the sheriff. From what I gather from the material my boss sent and your earlier comments, there are issues. My boss, by the way, is Scott Fleming. He was quite impressed with your documentation and the photographs we received from your brother."

Riley couldn't stop the twinge of satisfaction at the comment. In a casual tone, though, she said, "So, you're not here just to be my bodyguard?"

Giving her a sharp look, he said, "After what I saw last night, I'd say you're capable of protecting yourself. Still, my boss and your brother are concerned about you and Susan's safety, and rightfully so. It would be foolhardy not to take precautions. But no, it's not the only reason I'm here."

Somewhat reassured, she explained about the issues with the sheriff.

"It's interesting he closed the case, though I'm stymied by his decision to leave the body at the funeral home."

With a grim tone, Riley said, "I thought it was strange. It certainly made it easy for someone to steal the body. It's why I don't trust him or anyone who works for the man."

Riley pulled into a visitor's parking space in front of the main entrance to the recreation center at the senior citizen complex.

"Nice facility," Cody said as he exited, looking around at the well-manicured lawns and flower beds.

Inside, Riley approached the office window. After identifying herself, she asked for the apartment number. The elderly receptionist directed them to a building near the rear of the complex.

The apartment was located on the ground floor. As they approached, sounds of an argument radiated into the hallway. Riley cocked an eyebrow at Cody before tapping on the door.

It swung open, and the voices intensified. A small man in bib overalls peered at her over the top of his glasses. Then his gaze shifted to Cody standing behind her.

"Humph," he grunted. "Whatever you're selling, not interested." He took a step back to close the door.

"Mr. Walter, we're not selling. We want to speak with you."

He stopped, though he still held onto the door. Rheumy, bird-like eyes sparked with suspicion. "About what?"

"I'm Riley Phillips. I work for the *Register*. This is Cody Lightfoot. We have a few questions about the Henning farm."

"You Hank Phillips' daughter?"

"Yes, sir. You know him?"

"Lived here all my life. Of course, I know him. I used to be on the school board. Though I'd left before your dad became the high school principal." He looked at Cody. "Don't know you. You work for the paper?"

"They had a fire, so I'm helping out."

"Might as well come on in. No point standing here where all the neighbors can hear. Bunch of nosy busybodies as it is."

He turned, shuffling toward a big easy chair in front of a wall-mounted TV, the source of the loud voices. Behind him, Cody closed the door as they walked in.

Walter motioned toward a small couch. "Have a seat. Throw

those magazines on the floor."

He picked up the remote lying on the chair seat, clicking off the TV. The sudden quiet brought new meaning to the phrase "deafening silence."

"I bet you're here about that body you found at my place." He settled into the chair.

Riley gathered the magazines, lying them on an end table before sitting. Cody dropped next to her. She raised an eyebrow.

"I'm old, but I'm not blind and deaf yet. Saw the story on the news. About how you and that dog of yours found the body. Smart mutt you got there. So, who was it?"

"Sheriff Rutherford hasn't identified the victim," Riley said.

A raspy chuckle erupted. "Not surprising. Rutherford's a sorry lot. Always has been. He couldn't even hang onto a dead body. Got stolen right out from under his nose."

Riley leaned forward. "Mr. Walter. Has anyone expressed an interest in the property?"

"I've had it for sale for years. A couple of calls, but nothing recent."

"Do you have any idea why someone would use your property to bury a body?"

"Don't have a clue."

"Do you know if any of the Henning family live here?"

"They packed up and moved. Ain't seen hide nor hair of them for years. Another bunch that's a sorry lot."

"How so?" Cody asked.

"The boy, can't remember his name, was always in trouble, stealing, drinking. Old man Henning never did anything. Whenever the boy got crossways with the law, the old man had a way of making the charges go away."

"Do you know where they moved to?"

He thought, scratching his jaw. "Seems I heard Arizona, or was that the Bradfords that moved there? They lived down the road a piece."

Riley remembered seeing the name from her research at the courthouse.

"Do you have any relatives here?"

A look of sadness crossed his face. "If you're thinking some kin of mine is involved, hate to disappoint you, but there isn't anyone."

Riley cast a glance at Cody. He gave a quick, negative shake of his head. Riley reached inside the backpack for a business card. She laid it on the table. "If you happen to remember anything that might help, please call me." She rose. "Thank you for talking to us."

"Sorry I can't be more help. Just close the door behind you." He picked up the remote, clicking on the TV. The sound followed them out the door.

"Well, we didn't get much out of that," Riley grumped.

"You never know. Investigations are all about gathering trivia. Where to next?"

"The first real estate office on the list."

On the way into town, she noticed Cody kept glancing at the side mirror. "Anyone following us?"

"Caught me." Cody grinned.

"Hard to miss. How long have you worked for the FBI?"

"A little over two years."

At her look of surprise, he added, "I did a stint in the Army after college."

"Oh, where did you graduate?"

"Colorado University. My family still lives outside of Denver."

"I went to Texas A&M."

"That's how you knew about the ring."

"Yep, I've got one. So do my dad and my brother. I've been going through the 2007 yearbook to see if I could find a match. So far, no luck. It's difficult with only a partial view."

Riley pulled into the parking lot of an old house, renovated into office space. A sign read *Gentz Real Estate.*

When they walked inside, a woman rose from behind a desk, saying, "I'm Barbara Gentz. How may I help you?"

Riley introduced herself and Cody, then added, "We're with the *Register.* We are interested in rental homes. Do you handle any?"

"Please have a seat. I do have several. What type of place are you looking for?" Her interested look scanned their faces.

Riley quickly said, "It's not to rent. I'm doing a follow-up on a story to locate a person. He might have rented a house in the area. How many rentals do you manage?"

"At the moment, three. Who is it you are looking for?"

"Well, that's the problem. I don't have a name." She pulled the picture of the ring she printed from the backpack. "He would have been wearing an Aggie class ring. It's quite distinctive."

The woman studied the ring with a look of astonishment. "Is this the ring mentioned in the newspaper's crime-stopper article? Now I know why your name seemed familiar. You're the reporter who found the body in the county."

"Yes, though it was actually my dog. So far, the sheriff's department hasn't identified the victim."

"Well, I'm afraid I can't be of much help. All three of my properties are rented to families." She passed the paper back to Riley. "While I can check, it's doubtful someone is missing."

Before leaving, they thanked her for her time. Riley left a business card.

It was the same at the next two stops. By the time they walked out, Riley was getting discouraged.

Cody said, "Why don't we take a break and grab a bite of lunch?

Do you have any recommendations?"

"Umm …" She glanced at her watch. "I do, and we still have time to get there. The Sunset Grill is only open for breakfast and lunch. They close at two."

"Lead on, then."

A sheriff's car pulled into the parking lot as Riley pulled out. She glanced in her rearview mirror. "Wonder what he's doing here?"

"Who?" Cody asked, craning his neck to look out the back window.

"Mickey Bennett. If we cross paths, I should warn you. I'm not one of his favorite people."

Chapter 12

Riley parked under the shade of a large tree at the edge of the parking lot. As they walked toward the attractive white building with red trim and rockers on the front porch, Cody said, "This looks quaint."

Laughter bubbled from Riley.

Cody glanced at her, cocking an eyebrow.

Still laughing, Riley said, "Somehow, you and the word quaint don't compute."

"I have my softer moments," he said, shooting her a mischievous grin.

Riley's breath caught at the back of her throat. The man was drop-dead gorgeous. She wondered if he was married.

Once they were seated, each ordered iced tea. After studying the menu, Cody opted for the Baja fish tacos, and Riley decided on the Southwestern turkey melt.

"Where are you staying?"

"At the La Quinta." Cody leaned back, letting the waitress set glasses of tea and a basket of chips and salsa on the table. "Have you always lived here?"

"Yep. As you found out earlier, Dad was the high school principal, and Mom is an accountant. They retired a couple of years ago and bought an RV. The last time I talked to them, they were headed into the wilds of Montana. Told me not to expect a call for a few weeks." She picked up a chip. "How about you? Where'd you grow up?"

"Colorado. I don't get home often. The FBI has a way of keeping me busy." He took a deep swallow of the tea before picking up a chip and scooping it into the salsa.

Does that mean he isn't married? Riley thought. With a casual tone, she said, "I would imagine it's hard on your family."

"Probably a good reason why I'm still single."

Not wanting to examine her tingling sense of relief, she said, "Where does Lightfoot come from?"

He grinned. "Apache, full-blooded great-grandparents on my dad's side. Some of my ancestors supposedly served as scouts for the U.S. Army."

"Seems like a good match for an FBI Tracker. So what kind of unit is it?"

Cody laughed. "I hadn't thought about it from that viewpoint. The unit's fairly new. The original purpose was to track down peripatetic serial killers. The nomads who move around, staying under law enforcement's radar. A new tracking software program was developed to link law enforcement agencies."

She nibbled on a chip. "You said original."

"The team has caught some unusual cases not connected to serial killers." He grabbed another chip.

"My brother mentioned getting help to identify the victim. What can your unit do that Ted can't?"

"The unit's facial recognition software surpasses anything currently in use by other agencies. Since I'm the new kid on the block, I don't know a lot about it yet. I do know the genius behind the program is Nicki Allison. She's rated as the top computer expert in the Bureau. I'm looking forward to meeting her and the rest of the team."

Surprised, she said, "You don't know them?"

He swallowed. "Not yet. I've been assigned to the Las Vegas office since getting out of the academy. That's why Scott sent me here. A stopover on my way to Washington."

The waitress walked up with plates of food, then refilled the tea glasses.

Conversation lagged over the next several minutes as they dug into the food. After swallowing the last bite of a taco, Cody said, "That was good."

The waitress walked up. "Anything else? We have an excellent selection of desserts," she said.

Cody looked at Riley.

She waved a hand in the air. "Not a speck of room left. I'll pass."

After the waitress laid the bill on the table, Riley and Cody each made a grab for it. Cody was faster. "My treat, or should I say the FBI."

"I didn't mean for you to pick up the tab. But thank you."

As they walked out, Riley said, "One more realtor, and then we can head back to the newspaper office and get Milo." She abruptly stopped.

A sheriff's car was parked next to her truck.

Her eyes narrowed as the deputy strutted toward them. "Mickey, what are you doing here?"

Mickey's gaze flickered over Cody, then shifted back to Riley. "Finding out what the hell you're up to."

"What I do is none of your business." She started to walk past him. Mickey grabbed her arm.

Cody stepped forward. His face tightened with a hard look. "Unless you have a legal right to lay hands on the lady, I suggest you back off."

"Cowboy, you stay out of this," Mickey sneered, though he let go of her arm. "Riley, you're interfering in a police investigation. I could charge you with obstruction."

"What police investigation?"

"You've been talking to realtors about the body you found. I told you before to keep your nose out of police business."

"I guess you didn't get the sheriff's memo."

"What memo?"

"The one that said," her hands flashed in the air, two fingers on each curling to mimic quotation marks, "case closed." With a smug look, she added, "There is no investigation. I can't obstruct something that doesn't exist."

Anger flushed his face. "Keep on, and you're going to find out it could be unhealthy."

Riley's hands fisted. Her chin thrust forward. "Is that a threat? If it is, then I'm warning you. Anything happens, I'll come looking for you. Now, get out of my face."

"You heard the lady," Cody said.

Mickey's head snapped around. "Just who the hell are you?"

"Someone you don't want to know. Riley, let's go."

His body rigid with anger, Mickey watched them drive out of the lot.

"You're right."

Her thoughts on Mickey, she didn't immediately pick up on Cody's meaning. "What?"

"You said you weren't one of his favorite people."

"Ever since he hit town, he's been a jerk." The anger faded, leaving her with an unsettled feeling. "Why would he be interested in what I'm doing?"

"Something I've been asking myself," Cody said.

At the last realtor's office, they struck out. As they strode into the newspaper office, Milo stood by the door. He jumped with a sharp bark of excitement. His nose nuzzled her hand.

"Hey, big guy. You'd think I had been gone for days, not just a few hours."

Susan walked up. "He's been fine until about an hour ago when he started getting restless. Like he did yesterday. I thought he needed a pit stop and took him out back, but that wasn't it. Did something happen?"

Riley thought about the encounter with the deputy sheriff. The time frame matched. "A run-in with Mickey Bennett, being his typical, obnoxious self. But it wasn't any big deal."

For a moment, all three looked down at Milo.

With a shake of her head, Susan asked, "Any luck on our missing victim?"

"Nope. Abel Walter didn't have any clue why the body was dumped on his property. None of the realtors we contacted rented a house to the victim."

"Dang. I guess it couldn't have been that simple. So, where next?"

"The farm. And I want to visit some of the homeowners in the area."

"Call if you learn anything."

"Will do. See you tomorrow."

Milo woofed.

Riley smiled. "Yes, you're going."

The dog raced toward the door.

Susan grumped. "Ungrateful creature. I've been giving him treats all day, and this is what I get for a thank you." She raised her voice. "Bye, Milo."

The dog raced back, licked her hand, then headed back to the front door.

Susan laughed, "How about that."

As Riley pulled out, Milo's head hung over the console between the seats.

"Does he always do that?" Cody asked.

"It's his favorite position."

"I've noticed he's very well trained. Seems to easily understand your commands."

"He always has, even when he was a puppy."

"How did you get him?"

Riley explained about her article and finding Milo at the dog shelter. She laughed. "There wasn't any way I was leaving without him."

Milo woofed as if in agreement.

During the drive, Cody queried Riley about the farm. "From your pictures, the man wasn't killed there. Someone dumped him there, which would indicate prior knowledge."

"That finally dawned on me, and it's why I spent several hours at the courthouse."

"How many times did you use the place?"

"A lot over the last year. At least four or five times a month, and more these last few weeks."

"How did you find the place?"

"Headed out one day, driving the backroads. It was just by chance. I can't see someone doing that with a body."

Cody shifted in his seat, glancing at the side mirror. A car had been behind them too long for comfort.

"The black car?"

"Maybe. I'll have to be careful around you. You see too much."

"Guess it comes from being a nosy reporter. I spotted it a few miles back. Just in case, my shotgun is on the backseat, one in the chamber, safety on."

She turned onto the road leading to the farm. She watched the rearview mirror, but the car kept going. "I guess not."

Cody, who had also been watching, said, "Or the driver knows where you're going and doesn't need to follow. When was the last time you used the farm before you found the body?"

"Four days. I'd stepped up the training runs." Riley turned into the long driveway, pulling to a stop near the front of the old house.

"Desolate looking place," Cody said as he stepped out of the truck. He stood wide-legged while his dark eyes slowly scanned the limestone hills, trees, and brush. His gaze skimmed over multiple buildings in a state of collapse. Gusts of wind kicked up dust swirls in the hot, dry air.

Riley said, "We found the body behind the barn." She led the way with Milo trotting alongside her.

From the tracks, it was apparent where the body had lain. Cody envisioned every detail from Riley's pictures before she moved the wood. It had been a substantial stack on top of the body. His mind's eye shifted to Riley's photo of the body lying in a partial grave. For a moment, it was as if the body lay before him. He studied its position and the dirt covering it.

Fascinated by his intense look, Riley wondered what was going through his mind. Whatever it was had his total concentration.

Still looking at the ground, he slowly circled the area, scrutinizing each scrap of wood, debris, and other junk that filled the dump site. He stopped, waving his hand. "None of this debris is recent. It's not a place people use to get rid of their junk." Then he headed to the front of the barn, where he stopped again, thinking as he stared at the road.

"It was daylight when the killer dumped the body."

"What makes you think that?" Riley asked.

"At night, it would be darker than a lump of coal out here. While car lights would light up the front, the light wouldn't reach the back of the barn." Cody twisted, pointing to the growth of weeds and bushes on the side of the property. "With how the trees and bushes have grown up, you can't get a vehicle back there. The killer would need light to dig a grave, move the body, and pile wood on top. The killer would also need both hands. Assuming there was a second man with a flashlight, the risk was still too great. This wasn't a quick dump and leave. It took time."

He turned, looking toward the road. "Anyone driving along the road would instantly be suspicious of a car with its lights on or seeing any light. Would probably call the sheriff's department and report it. In the daylight, no. A vehicle wouldn't be as suspicious. After all, you've been using this place for your training runs. Has anyone ever stopped to find out what you were up to?"

For a moment, she thought. "You're right. Sometimes, a vehicle drove by, but the driver never stopped to ask what I was doing here."

With his hands on his hips, Cody slowly turned, taking one last look. "Do you still want to contact the other residents?"

"It might be better to wait until tomorrow." Riley loaded Milo in the truck, where he took up his usual position with his butt pushed against the backseat, and his head stuck between the front seats.

Cody slid inside. "Before we go tomorrow, I need to finish the paperwork on a couple of cases from Vegas. I'll give you a call."

When they arrived at the newspaper office, Susan was gone. Knowing she'd want all the gritty details, Riley planned to call her when she got home.

Before he got out of the truck, Cody said, "I'm going to follow you."

"You don't have to. It's only a few miles. I'll be fine."

"Maybe so, but I'd prefer to make sure."

She took one look at his tight-jawed face and figured arguing was a waste of breath. As she pulled out, his truck behind her, Riley muttered, "Cripes, just what I don't need, a dang bodyguard."

A sharp bark echoed. Grumpily, she said, "What! You think I need one?" Milo woofed as if he agreed.

****

Settled at the small desk in his hotel room, Cody opened the bag with two double meat cheeseburgers and a double order of fries he'd picked up on his way to the hotel. Not exactly healthy, but he had plans for tonight, and sitting in some restaurant wasn't one of them.

He opened his laptop, accessing a blank page. While he chewed on a bite of the hamburger, Cody typed a list of his activities since arriving in town, including a footnote about the confrontation with Bennett. Unsure about what Scott expected, Cody didn't add his impressions or opinion. By the time he finished, he'd polished off both sandwiches, the fries, and a supersized container of Dr Pepper.

Cody attached the report to an email and sent it to Scott. After a glance at his watch, he decided it was too early to leave. The chime of his phone was a surprise since he figured his boss had already left the office. "Lightfoot," he answered.

"Got your report. What's your take?"

He had his answer about what Scott expected. "Something's in the wind, and it's more than a homicide. The disposal of the body was a methodical, well-thought-out plan. It was only a fluke it was discovered. Once I get the arson investigator's report, I expect to see a similar pattern. The investigator told Riley the arsonist was a pro."

"How are you getting it without identifying you're FBI?"

"Through the editor, Susan Hutchin. She owned the building."

Scott said, "Send me a copy as soon as you get it."

"How are you coming with the identification?" Cody asked.

"Nothing yet, but Nicki is working full-time on it."

"His identity is the key to this. It's my belief the killer thinks the pictures of the body were destroyed. I'd sure like to find out what really happened to the ones the sheriff's personnel took. Finding out, though, will put me front and center with the sheriff. From Ted Phillips' notes and what Riley told me, I doubt I'll get his cooperation. I do have another request. I need a rundown of Mickey Bennett, a deputy sheriff. He's borderline with his threats to Riley. Way too interested in what she's doing."

"I'll have Nicki do a dungeon sweep. See what pops up."

"A what?" Cody exclaimed.

"Sorry, forgot you aren't tuned into her terminology yet. A dungeon sweep is what she calls a deep background check, beyond anything a local agency can do."

Cody's laugh rumbled. "Okay. I'm looking forward to meeting her." They disconnected.

From his large suitcase, Cody pulled out black tactical pants and a shirt. He locked the suitcase, then quickly changed, slipping into his combat boots. His Glock 19 went into the holster strapped to his belt. In his truck bed, under a locked cover, was a locked container bolted to the floor with the rest of his weapons, ammunition, and tactical gear.

With the laptop tucked under his arm, Cody eased open the door, checking to ensure the hallway was empty before he strode to the stairs at the end of the hall. At the foot of the stairs, he opened the door but didn't step out until he had scanned the parking lot. Not seeing any signs of surveillance, he headed toward his truck.

As he pulled out, Cody kept an eye on the rearview mirror, watching for a vehicle pulling onto the street behind him. After a few evasive maneuvers, turning onto side streets, waiting until the last second to zip through an intersection, he hadn't spotted a tail. Cody sped up, turning onto a road that would take him to Riley's home from a different direction. This time, he wasn't driving by his target.

About two miles from Riley's house, he pulled off the road onto a dirt track winding its way into the hills. From the road, the truck was nearly invisible. Inside the console was a container of black grease. With a quick motion, Cody swiped a few streaks across his face. After muting his phone, he slid out of the truck. For a moment, he paused, absorbing the sounds and smells of the night. A light breeze tickled the hair on his neck. The moon, covered by drifting clouds, hung low on the horizon. Nearby an owl's hoot softly echoed, and in the distance, coyotes yipped. This was his turf, the night. Cody slowly moved forward, working his way through the brush and trees to where he had seen the truck. Not a single sound marked his passage. He stopped a short distance away. Crouched in the shadow of a large tree, he waited. In the distance, lights from Riley's house lit up the sky. She had left all the outside lights on.

It wasn't until a faint haze of sunlight gleamed on the horizon that Cody stirred. He rose, stretching his tight muscles. At a half trot, he covered the return trip in far less time than earlier.

He figured Riley probably spooked the man with the lights and shotgun. A pro would consider the odds and wouldn't make another attempt at her home, especially since his effort to take out Milo failed. Though a new worry had reared its ugly head. Would the next time the killer tried be different? Was there enough motivation to murder Riley? He didn't have an answer.

Chapter 13

Washington, D.C.

Troubled by Cody's report, Scott spent a restless night. When he arrived at his office, it was early, even for him. The silence of empty rooms greeted him. No coffee. No sounds in Nicki's office. He dropped his briefcase on his desk before walking to the breakroom. The couch was empty. Wonder of wonders, she'd actually followed one of his edicts and gone home.

Nicki wasn't happy when he ordered her out of the office last night. Though he wouldn't put it past her to sneak back. When she had a problem, she was like a dog with a bone. Wouldn't let go until she had a hole to bury it in.

The Fredericksburg victim had caused not just a ripple but a tsunami in her computer world. Nicki didn't have a name, and she wasn't a happy camper when she left. Scott wasn't sure why but knew he'd find out. Rarely could Nicki keep any problems under wraps. He punched the buttons on the coffee machine. While he waited, the outer door slammed shut.

When the machine beeped, he filled two cups. He stopped in the doorway of Nicki's office. She was perched on the edge of her chair. Her eyes were locked on images flashing across the wall monitor while her fingers danced on the keyboard. Stopping alongside her, he set a cup down within easy reach. A quick flick of the eyes was the only acknowledgment. She was in the zone. Hoping that whatever epiphany had struck solved the problem, Scott strolled to his office.

Seated behind his desk, he sipped the rich brew before setting the cup aside. He booted his computer and pulled up Cody's report. While he studied the details, his fingers idly tapped a pen on the desk. A habit he had acquired long ago. One that annoyed the hell out of his team.

What was so important about the victim that it would motivate a systematic scheme to eradicate any evidence of the crime? Tap, tap, tap. Not only steal the body but destroy the pictures, even burning down the office of the newspaper that reported it. Tap, tap, tap. No one goes to such lengths unless there is a good reason behind it.

A rap on the door broke into his musings. With a scowl, Nicki flounced in, dropping onto a chair.

Scott leaned back, eyeing her t-shirt, a telling indicator of her mood. Today's epitaph read, "Don't mess with me," above a fire-breathing dragon.

Suppressing a grin, he said, "Ready to tell me what's wrong?"

"My new facial reconstruction program, that's what's wrong. There must be a bug somewhere, but I'll be danged if I can find it. How many times what's left of a body are a few bones and the skull? Identifying the victim is a time-consuming and expensive reconstruction. Tissue depth markers are first attached to the skull, building a clay model. From there, either a 2D or 3D image can be created. My program works on the same theory, except the AI algorithms I designed add digital tissue depth markers."

Energized by the topic, she leaned forward, her hands flapping as she spoke. "I've tested the software with skulls identified by other means and have a corresponding picture of the person. The images from my software are amazingly accurate. The same algorithms should work for an image like the Fredericksburg victim. Even though it's a side view of the face, the program should be able to replicate the face by using the depth analysis scan and a reversal of the image to create the other half of the face for a full-frontal view. I've run the face through the facial recognition software."

Disgusted, Nicki flopped back in the chair. "Cripes, by now, I should have a name. I don't. I've loaded the 2007 yearbook for Texas A&M. In addition to class pictures, the yearbook is loaded with photographs of events with pictures of students. Nada, nothing, not a single match. Which tells me something is wrong with the reconstruction."

"Have you sent it to me?"

"It's in your case file on your computer."

Scott tapped the keyboard, opening the file folder labeled "Fredericksburg." All the documents and photographs Ted Phillips had sent were in it. He tapped a new image, and a face appeared on the screen. Short, dark hair framed a round face with flat cheekbones, a broad nose, thin lips, and a jutting chin.

Nicki stood, walking around the desk to look over his shoulder at the computer. "Adding 3D was the next step." She reached to tap the keyboard. The image slowly turned. It was a reconstruction of the entire head. "I still have to add emotion."

"Nicki, it's possible there's not a picture of him to be found, though it's hard to believe."

"Maybe, but I still feel there's something wrong. I just can't put my finger on it. Back to the drawing board. I'm loading the 2006 yearbook." Muttering to herself, Nicki strolled out.

Her comment reminded him of his initial take the first time he saw Riley's photo of the head, a sense of wrongness. As he studied the slow movement of the head on the screen, his senses twitched. But why? The image was astounding even without emotion, which would be difficult since the eyelids were closed. Nicki had placed Riley's photo next to the new image for comparison. Nicki's reconstruction had picked up the smallest of details.

In the side view of Riley's picture, the hairline was hidden by the top of the ear. In Nicki's image, the hairline was in the same position. The slope of the forehead matched the slope in the side view of the original photo. Even how the eyebrows tapered on the forehead matched the side view of the face.

His hand reached for the cup, and he took a deep swig. Abruptly, Scott set the cup aside to lean closer to the screen. His sharp gaze scrutinized the image. Slowly, he rotated the face to one side, then back to the other side.

Was it possible? He magnified Riley's picture. His eyes shifted from one image to the other. "Not only possible but highly likely," he muttered.

Scott searched his list of contacts for the number he needed. Calling it, he impatiently waited for someone to answer.

After several rings, a man said, "Logan County Medical Examiner. How may I direct your call?"

"This is FBI Special Agent Scott Fleming. I'd like to speak with Dr. Cole. It's urgent."

"Hold, please."

The next voice on the line said, "Okay, Scott. What's got your detective senses in a tight wad this time?"

Scott chuckled. "I need your expertise."

He had first met David Cole while hunting a serial killer in Kentucky before he formed the Tracker Unit. He'd discovered that David was one of the most knowledgeable and insightful medical examiners he'd ever dealt with. They'd become good friends, and David was one of Scott's most valuable resources.

"How can I help?"

"I'm sending you several photos. The body was found buried on an abandoned farm in Texas. I need your best estimate on how long the man has been dead. I want to see if your opinion confirms my hypothesis."

"Why can't the local medical examiner tell you?"

"The body disappeared before it reached the M.E.'s office."

A whistle echoed. "Interesting. That's a new wrinkle. How did someone lose it?"

"The sheriff left it at a funeral home. Someone broke in and stole it."

"The sheriff needs a lesson on the chain of custody for evidence. Or was it intentional?"

"The jury is still out on that one. All I have are pictures taken by the woman who found the body. She's a reporter and photographer with the local newspaper. She was on a SAR training run with her dog. The dog alerted on the body."

"Sounds as if the dog just qualified for SAR. Why do I get a feeling this is more than wanting to know a time frame on death? Are you going to tell me what you're looking for?"

"No. I don't want to influence you. If I'm right, you'll spot it."

"Working from a photograph is iffy at best. It depends on the quality, and even then, it's a judgment call."

"I think you'll be surprised."

While they talked, Scott had typed an email, selecting several of Riley's pictures with closeups of the upper torso. He hit send.

"I just sent the email."

"How soon do you need an answer?"

"As soon as you can give me one."

"I don't know why I bothered to ask. You're going to owe me, especially since I've got four autopsies waiting."

"I think I can come up with a case of your favorite Scotch whisky."

After disconnecting, he picked up his cup and walked out. His gut tightened in a familiar feeling as every instinct tingled. In the breakroom, he refilled his cup as he considered the appalling consequences. From the beginning, he'd sensed the murder didn't fit the profile of a local homicide. The speed and efficiency of the reaction to the discovery of the body said otherwise.

If he was right, the case had taken an ominous turn. The list of possible targets was endless. Nuclear power plants, law enforcement agencies, military installations, and financial institutions immediately came to mind. And not just the physical locations but also the computer networks.

He filled his cup and strode back to his office. When his phone rang, he quickly set the cup down and reached across the desk to get his phone.

"Fleming," he said, settling in his chair.

David Cole didn't waste time. "I'd like to hire the woman who took those photos. They're as good as, if not better than, any I've seen. My team couldn't have done as well. I'd say, with about ninety percent certainty, the man had been dead from 24 to 36 hours, probably on the low side rather than higher. The eye is missing. I suspect that's what you spotted."

"Yes. That's why the timeframe is so critical. I couldn't be sure if the flat eyelid was part of the normal decomposition or if the eye had been removed."

"I'd say you've got a major problem."

"That's an understatement. Thanks, David. Be looking for a package."

He hung up the phone. "Nicki," he roared.

"What!" she exclaimed when she came rushing through the doorway.

"I found one of your problems, though it may not be why you haven't found a match. You know the old computer adage, garbage in, garbage out. In this case, your program gave you back exactly what you input. It's not a problem with the software. It's the original picture."

She stepped around the desk to look at his monitor.

He motioned toward her reconstruction. "Look at the eyes. There are no eyeballs. Those eyelids are flat, even slightly concave. I had David Cole in Kentucky verify it. I sent him the pictures Riley took."

"Oh, my gosh, boss man. You're right."

"Look at Phillips' picture. From the side, the eyelid has sunk into the eye socket."

"No wonder the reconstruction looked strange. It replicated the missing eye for the other side of the face."

He said, "The iris of the eye is as unique as fingerprints, even more so. There's only one reason to remove it. Wherever this man worked, it's high security with eye scans to access the facility or a computer program."

She slid off the desk. "It answers one question. Why isn't there a missing person report? No one knows he's missing. If they did, the eye would be useless. I'll rerun the reconstruction, adding eyes."

Knowing she was knee-deep in the reconstruction, he hadn't mentioned Cody's request yet. Now, time was of the essence. "Nicki, run a sweep on the sheriff and one of his deputies, Mickey Bennett."

She waggled her fingers in the air as she loped out.

Scott's eyes shifted to the computer, where the head still slowly turned. The pieces started to fall into place. He had one of the answers. He knew why the body was so important its discovery triggered a systematic, organized operation to eradicate any chance of identifying the body.

Nicki had nailed it—the eye would be useless. From the beginning, he'd sensed this wasn't a local murder. Learning the why added to his deepening sense of apprehension. The extraction of the eye would require a precise surgical operation. That meant money. The same for the equipment to stop the deterioration. Varying studies had the viability time factor at about three weeks under optimum conditions.

Whoever was roaming Fredericksburg was the puppet, not the mastermind. Someone else was yanking the strings with an unnerving single-mindedness to stop anyone from getting in the way. Cody and Riley were still in the crosshairs of a killer. Until he could discover the where, he was powerless. The clock was ticking down.

Chapter 14

Texas

Cody was about to leave his room when his phone rang. "Hi, Riley. I was just about to call you and let you know I was on my way." With the phone tucked between his ear and shoulder, he closed down his computer.

"If you wouldn't mind, please stop at the newspaper office. Susan has the report on the fire."

"Will do."

With a quick glance to ensure the suitcase was locked, he picked up the room key card, his laptop and headed out the door.

During the drive, he kept an eye on the rearview mirror, but none of the vehicles appeared suspicious. Still, after parking, he surveyed the parking lot and street before walking inside.

A man seated at a desk looked up at the sound of the door. "May I help you?" he asked.

Before he could answer, Susan hustled out of her office. "Cody, this is Ben Fremont, another reporter. Ben, this is Cody Lightfoot, Riley's cousin."

A wide smile split his face as Ben rose, hand extended. "Nice to meet you. Where are you from?"

Evidently, Ben was unaware of Cody's real identity, so he played along. "California, just passing through. Nice town you've got here."

"We like it. I've got to run. Today is the monthly meeting of the city council. Hope I see you again, Cody."

Once Ben was out the door, Susan said, "I don't like keeping him in the dark."

"Tell him I insisted on it."

With a wry smile, she said, "Thank you, but I don't need to make you the culprit. It is what it is. Riley called and said you would be by to pick up the fire report. Would you like a cup of coffee?"

"I sure would. The coffee at the hotel isn't the best."

He poured a cup and followed her into the small office.

With a grimace, she looked around. "It's not much, but home for now. It will take eight to ten months before the new building will be ready. I met with a contractor this morning to get construction started." She picked up a stapled document and handed it to him. "No doubt it was arson."

Cody glanced over it, noting the descriptions of the traces of accelerants found in the office at the back of the building. None were found anywhere else. "Your office was the target." He swallowed a swig of coffee. "Do you have this on your computer?"

"Yes."

"Would you email it to me? I don't have a way of getting it on my computer. I don't want to use the hotel's office services."

"Give me your email address." She typed as he dictated. "Have you had any luck on the victim's identification?" She attached the report and hit send.

"Not yet. An agent in my unit is working on it. If anyone can find out, she can."

Her face was somber as Susan leaned forward, her arms on the desk. "You're the expert here, but I'm about to throw in my two cents' worth, which may be all that it's worth. I'm an old news hound, and this stinks to high heaven. Whoever this guy was, he's damn important to someone. What bothers me is why there's no missing person report. Is it because no one knows he's missing?"

Respect sparked in Cody's eyes. "Highly likely. This was a concerted effort to keep him from being identified. Let me ask you something. Did you know Rutherford doesn't have any photos of the body or crime scene?"

"Yes. Ted talked to Rutherford and found out."

"Do you have any contacts in the sheriff's department? I'd like to know more about what happened to the pictures from the crime scene."

"So you're not buying our trusty sheriff's story about a malfunctioning camera, either. I'll see what I can find out. I've got a couple of favors I can call in."

He finished the last of the coffee and rose.

"Where are you headed?" she asked.

"Riley's place. From there, we plan on talking to some of the residents that live around the farm where the body was found."

"Keep me posted." Her lips twisted in a wry smile. "Don't worry. Nothing gets printed until you give me the okay. I want this S.O.B. as bad as you do."

****

From the front of the house, Milo barked. When he didn't get a response, his next one was more insistent.

"I'm coming," she muttered as she walked out of the hallway. Milo stood by the front door; his tail whipped the air. She checked the peephole, then opened the door. Milo charged out. "Milo, hold." The dog stopped, though his body quivered with anticipation. Riley hoped the same tingle of eagerness she felt wasn't as evident. Not often did she meet someone who set her pulse to racing.

Cody stepped out of the truck, and Riley released the dog. He bounded forward, clearing the front steps with a single leap. Dashing toward Cody, he barked, then sat. His head tilted to stare at the man.

Cody greeted him, rubbing his head before walking up the steps. "I do believe that dog has different barks."

Riley grinned. "Oh, he does. Two levels to get your attention and several levels of the soft woof depending on what he wants. Milo has a way of making his wishes known. Come on in."

They stepped inside with Milo trailing behind them.

"Coffee?"

"I'll pass. I had a cup at Susan's office. That's stout stuff she brews."

Her eyes twinkled with amusement. "She's famous, or maybe I should say infamous, for her coffee. It's hardcore and not for the faint of heart."

He glanced around. "Nice house, comfortable looking."

"I grew up here."

She added at his look of interest, "Mom and Dad turned it over to me when they decided to become nomads. Ted wasn't interested. He's got his life in Dallas. I doubt he'll ever come back here to live."

Cody pulled out the report he had folded and stuck in his vest pocket. "The report on the fire. Definitely arson."

Her face turned grim as she reached for it. She quickly scanned it. "I'll drop this in my office and take a closer look when we get back. I just need to grab my backpack."

As they walked out, Cody said, "Let's go in my truck today."

"You sure you want dog hair?"

He laughed. "I've had a lot worse."

Once Milo was settled in the back, Riley slid into the passenger seat. From the backpack she set at her feet, she pulled out the file folder with the list of residents.

As Cody started the engine, she said, "Let's see who's up first."

Cody idly said, "Wesley Hollingworth. His place is about two miles west of the farm. He's first on the list."

Surprised, she flipped open the folder. "You're right. How do you know that?"

"You showed me the list yesterday."

"Some memory you've got."

Cody just grinned as he pulled onto the highway.

The traffic was light and non-existent when they turned onto the road leading to the Henning farm. Cody pulled into a driveway where two men stood in front of a barn on the far side of the two-story house. They immediately headed toward the truck.

Riley and Cody exited, leaving Milo inside.

The older man's gaze assessed Cody and Riley before saying, "Can I help you?"

"Hello. I'm Riley Phillips. I work for the *Register*, and this is Cody Lightfoot."

At hearing Cody's name, interest sparked in the men's eyes.

"I'm Wesley Hollingworth. This is my son, Jacob." He glanced at Cody. "Navajo or Apache?"

"Apache," Cody said.

"We've got a bit of Navajo." Then he looked at Riley. "You're the reporter who found the body at the Henning place." He glanced at the truck, where Milo had his face plastered against the passenger window. "That the dog?"

"Yes. Would you like to meet him?"

"Sure would."

Cody said, "I'll let him out."

"His leash is on the backseat."

Wesley said, "Ma'am, you don't need a leash. He's not going to get into any trouble here."

As soon as the truck door opened, Milo eagerly jumped out.

"Milo, here." She patted her leg. He trotted toward Riley. "Sit."

The dog sat, though his head stretched forward, his dark eyes alert as he watched the two men.

"Milo, greet." The dog raised his paw.

"Well, I'll be danged," Wesley said as he leaned over to grip Milo's paw. "You've got a right fine dog here." He rubbed the dog's head before stepping back. "What can I do for you?"

Cody spoke up. "Have you seen any vehicles at the Henning place?"

A thoughtful look crossed his face. "I've seen a white truck there several times."

"That would probably be mine. I've used the place to train Milo. Any others?" Riley said.

The younger man, a spitting image of his dad, said, "There was another. Remember, Dad? We saw it the last time we went to the feed store."

Not wanting to appear overly anxious, Riley casually asked, "Can you describe it?"

Wesley answered, "A black truck, newer model. It was backed in near that old barn."

"Did you see anyone?"

"I didn't, but then I was driving. Did you, Jacob?"

"Yeah, I did," his son said. "I was curious who it was. It wasn't a farm truck. As we passed, I looked back. A man stood by the passenger door, but I didn't get a good look at him."

"Tell us what you can," Cody said.

"On the hefty side, wearing a ballcap. I only got a glimpse before he headed around the back of the truck."

"About what time was that?"

Wesley said, "Mid-afternoon, three or so."

"Is that the only time you saw the vehicle there?" Cody asked.

"Yes. The place has been deserted for a long time. Abel Walter moved out years ago."

"We talked to Abel yesterday," Riley said.

"Haven't seen him for a while. How's he doing?" Wesley asked.

"Seemed to be in good spirits," Riley said.

A barking laugh erupted. "What you mean is he was cantankerous as usual. He's a crusty old coot."

Riley just shook her head, though she grinned in agreement.

Cody asked, "What day did you see the truck?"

Wesley hesitated as he scratched his chin.

His son jumped in, saying, "The day before you found the body."

A glimmer of understanding lit Wesley's face. "By golly, do you think that's when the body was buried? Somehow, I got the notion it had been there a long time."

Not wanting to encourage the idea it was the killer's truck, Cody said, "Jacob, you said the truck wasn't a farm truck. What did you mean?"

The young man said, "The truck had a cover like yours. At the time, I thought it was odd."

"Why?" Cody asked.

Jacob grinned. "Ever work a ranch?"

Cody suddenly had an idea where the man was going. "No, I haven't."

"A cover is a royal pain in the …," He looked at Riley. "Uh, let's just say it gets in the way. I've generally found people who put covers on the truck's bed want to hide something." Jacob shot a humorous look at the bed of Cody's truck.

"I get your point," Cody said.

Riley stepped back to the truck, where she pulled out a business card from the backpack. After handing it to Wesley, she said, "If you think of anything else, please call me."

Wesley asked, "Did they ever find out the dead man's name?"

"Not yet," she said.

As Riley pulled onto the highway, she observed, "It does confirm your theory the body was dumped during the day." She shot him a smug look. "Who's next?"

"Smithers place, four miles down the road."

She opened the file folder she had laid atop the dashboard. "Son of a gun. You're right. What do you have, some kind of photographic memory or something?"

"Just an eye for details."

At each place, they went through the same routine, but none of the other residents had seen any vehicles other than Riley's truck.

As they pulled out of the last location, Riley said, "This is a bit discouraging."

"It's how investigations go. A lot of talking, mostly useless details. Where to now?"

"I guess back to the house. I've run out of ideas."

"Well, I have one. Food. I haven't eaten since early this morning."

"Let's head to town then. There's a German restaurant that has an outside patio. I won't have to leave Milo in the truck. And, right now, I'm not taking a chance on leaving him at home."

Riley's phone chimed. Not recognizing the number, she said, "Riley Phillips."

On the other end, a woman's voice said, "Riley, this is Barbara Gentz. You stopped by my office yesterday. I happened to think of something that might interest you."

Riley hit the speakerphone.

Chapter 15

The woman's voice echoed in the truck. "I'm sorry I didn't think about this sooner. There are several homes available for short-term rentals in the county. Typically, they're rented by families on vacation or frat houses from the University of Texas. It's much cheaper than staying in a hotel. It's why it didn't come to mind when we talked. It's not the usual type of rental for one person."

Excitement surged through Riley. "How do I get a list?"

"I have a short list with contact information, though I don't know how complete it is. I would imagine most realtors have one. We work off commission for the referral, though it doesn't often happen. Vacation rentals are usually booked well in advance. I can email it to you if you like."

"Please do. My email address is on the business card. I sure appreciate your letting me know."

"I'll be curious to know if it helps."

"If it does, you'll read about it in the *Register*. Thank you again." She disconnected. "Let's go to my house. I'd rather use my computer to check the addresses than my phone. I can fix a quick meal, sandwiches and soup."

"How about we order a pizza instead?"

"Even better."

"What do you like? A girlie one with vegetables?"

She scoffed. "Are you kidding? The meat lover's special."

He grinned. "A woman after my own heart."

She refused to consider why a buzz lifted her spirits. "I wonder how many are on the list. Dang, I should have asked." She tapped her phone. "No email yet."

"I can help with the research. I've got my laptop with me."

It wasn't until Cody pulled into the driveway that Riley's phone dinged. She quickly tapped the screen. "Got it. Eight places."

Cody pulled up to the front of the house. In the back, Milo wiggled. When Riley opened the door, he shot out, heading toward the nearest tree. After taking care of his business, he raced around the yard, sniffing and marking more spots.

With the backpack slung over a shoulder, Riley stood on the porch and watched. Before turning to unlock the door, she whistled. Milo charged through the doorway when it opened.

Cody followed, carrying his laptop. "That's an impressive whistle."

"I had to learn. Got tired of shouting. There's enough room in my office to set up your computer."

Dumping the pack on the couch, she followed Milo into the kitchen and refilled his bowls. From the office, Cody's voice rumbled.

"Pizza will be here in about thirty minutes," he said when she walked in. On a corner of the desk, he'd set up his laptop. On the screen was a map of the county.

Riley opened the realtor's email, printing off two copies. She handed one to Cody.

His gaze quickly scanned the list of addresses and contact information. "Are you familiar with any of these?"

After looking them over, she said, "Five are in the county. The rest are in Fredericksburg. We could call the contact number."

"I doubt calling will do any good. No one is going to release information about the renter. It means we have to check each one. To expedite the process, I suggest we lay out a route." He went back to the map. "You've got the list on your computer. Let's rearrange it, and I want to find out who owns the houses."

"You've already got it figured out, haven't you? How could you do it that fast?"

With a wry twist to his lips, he said, "Experience from moving troops around the Afghanistan countryside."

Riley had just finished retyping the list, adding the owners' information from the tax office, when Milo's toenails clicked in the hallway. He came to a stop in the doorway and woofed. The doorbell chimed.

Cody rose, setting his laptop on the desk. "I bet that's the pizza. I'll get it. Milo, I'd say you are better than any alarm system." Milo woofed and followed him down the hallway.

While Cody went to the door, Riley headed to the kitchen. The aroma of pepperoni wafted ahead of Cody when he walked in, carrying three extra-large boxes. Milo was right on his heels.

"Wow! Three. That's a lot."

"Hmm … not really. I figured you for close to one. That leaves two for me and Milo." He looked down at the dog. "Right, Milo?"

Milo had already plunked down near the table. He woofed as his tail swept the floor.

"Pizza isn't on his list of foods. One piece of pepperoni is all I ever let him have." She glanced at Milo. "That's all you get."

Milo barked, a quick, sharp sound.

Cody laughed. "I think he's protesting. Surely, as a treat, he could have two."

Milo woofed. She'd swear the dog grinned.

As they loaded their plates, Riley said, "I wasn't sure what you'd want to drink. I've got diet Dr Pepper or iced tea."

A wounded look settled on his face. "Diet?"

"I'm sorry. I know. Girlie, right?"

"Yep. I'll have the tea."

Once Cody was seated, the dog plopped next to his chair and stared up at him with a worshipful gaze.

Riley muttered, "Traitor." Milo woofed. "Well, you don't have to agree with me."

Cody chuckled. "You two are quite the pair."

Throughout the lighthearted conversation about likes and dislikes for movies, books, and sporting events, she kept an eye on Milo. Riley suppressed a smile as she ignored the byplay. Cody kept slipping him a piece of meat or a small piece of crust under the table.

When Cody's phone chimed, his face turned somber. "My boss. I need to take this." As he answered, he rose, walking into the living room.

Scott said, "We have a new development. Where are you?"

"At Riley's house."

"She needs to hear this."

Cody stepped back to the doorway. "Scott wants you on the call."

Her hands in soapy water, she stared at him with a wide-eyed look. "Uh … okay."

She quickly rinsed and dried her hands, then scurried into the living room, dropping onto the couch next to Cody.

He tapped the speakerphone. "Scott, she's listening."

"Nice to meet you, Riley, even if it's on the phone."

"Uh, thank you, Mr. Fleming, or I guess it should be Agent Fleming."

"No, it's Scott. Here's what we discovered today."

Scott explained Nicki's reconstruction process. When he started talking about the missing eye, Cody felt Riley's shudder. He glanced at her. Though her face paled, her expression was resolute.

Cody said, "Eye scans are high-tech security, which tells me big bucks are behind this."

Scott said, "You're right. Based on the pictures Riley took, this was a professional extraction. The eyelid wasn't damaged. That kind of expertise doesn't come cheap."

"Any thoughts on what's going down?"

"None. Too many variables, but I would say it's in Texas since that's where the body was found."

"How much time do you think we have?" Cody asked.

"Depends on the condition of the eye and how well it's preserved. Maybe three weeks at the most. I sent Riley's pictures to a medical examiner I've worked with. He estimated the man had been dead about 24 to 36 hours when Riley found him."

Riley spoke up. "It fits with what we found out from a nearby neighbor. He and his son were on the way back from town when they saw a truck parked in front of the barn around three in the afternoon. Milo found the body the next morning."

Scott said, "Then I'd say we're looking at days. Any other developments on your end?"

Cody said, "Still trying to find if the man was living in the area. A local realtor sent Riley a list of vacation rentals. We're heading out to check each one. I also want to know more about the sheriff's pictures. Since I don't have any grounds for asking, I asked Susan Hutchin, the editor, to see what she could dig up. We also got the arson report. You should have received it."

"I did. Check your email. I sent you what we believe is a picture of the victim. It might help in your identification."

"Can I publish it?" Riley asked. "Someone might recognize him."

"Run the story. We don't have time to mess around with this."

Riley asked, "Am I going to have a problem with the sheriff?"

"I doubt it, but we'll handle it if there is. Cody, anything else?"

When the call ended, Riley exclaimed, "Dang it. Scott doesn't know Rutherford. He'll use any excuse to come after me."

"I wouldn't worry. You've got a bigger stick than he does."

"Okay, I'll bite. What stick?"

"Scott. He's not someone Rutherford wants to tangle with. Scuttlebutt is that he's in line as the next director of the FBI when the current director retires. I need to check my computer for the picture. I want to take a copy with us."

He stood, holding out his hand to help her up. When they touched, she felt an unsettling tingle. Mentally, she chastised herself. They were in the middle of a murder investigation. Bad timing all the way around.

The email was waiting. Cody opened the attachment, and a man's face appeared.

Riley said, "Oh, my, gosh. How did the agent do this? It even has eyes. It's amazing. I wonder how accurate it is."

"From what I have heard about Nicki, it'll be dang accurate."

Riley moved the photo from Cody's computer to hers to print the copies.

"Before we go, I want to get this to Susan." She picked up her phone and called. When Susan answered, Riley exclaimed, "You're not going to believe this, but I've got a picture of the dead guy. I'm sending it to you."

"What! How?"

"From Cody's boss, Scott Fleming. It's a reconstruction, but Cody's boss said to release it."

"What about Rutherford?"

"Cody's here. I'm putting this on the speakerphone."

Cody, leaning closer to the phone on the desk, said, "What's your question?"

With a grim tone, Susan said, "As soon as this goes out, I expect I'll have Rutherford front and center in my office, wanting to know where I got it. What do I tell him?"

"Tell him it came from the FBI. Give him Scott's number if he wants to know more." He rattled off a number.

A gleeful chuckle erupted. "Oh, I'm going to enjoy this." Susan was still laughing as she disconnected.

Riley, sliding the phone back into her pocket, was laughing as well. "Rutherford doesn't stand a chance." Rising, she asked, "Do you want to go in my truck?"

"I'd prefer to use mine. I've got my gear with me."

She smiled. "Stuff you want to hide."

His lips twitched. "You could say that."

Milo was waiting at the door.

"I don't know how he does it. He can sense when I'm about to leave. I guess he wants to make sure he doesn't get left behind."

Milo's head was between the seats as they pulled out of the driveway. Riley had the list and was giving Cody directions. He didn't have the heart to tell her it wasn't necessary.

Chapter 16

Two kids were playing in the yard at the first place on their list. Leaving Milo in the truck, they walked to the front door. Before they could knock, the door opened, and a man stepped out.

They'd already agreed to let Riley do the talking since she was the local. After Riley identified herself, she showed him the picture. The man shook his head, telling them he'd never seen the man.

In the truck, Riley drew a line through the address. Each place they stopped was the same story as they weaved through the hills. By the time they were down to the last two, it was dark.

Cody slowed to make the turn into the next driveway. Even then, he almost missed it. Under large trees, the dark, ranch-style house was nearly invisible. He pulled to a stop on the driveway. A tingle tickled his senses.

"Why don't you wait in the truck while I check it out?"

Riley, slightly incensed at the suggestion, said, "Are you kidding? I'm not staying here." She opened the door and hopped out. Milo woofed. "No, you can't go."

With a sigh of resignation, Cody opened the console and removed a large flashlight. He didn't want to use his headlights—too much backlight.

Riley followed him to the front door. A realtor's combination lock box for the key hung on the doorknob. Windows overlooked the front yard. He moved to one, shining his light into the room.

Riley, peering over his shoulder, said, "It looks rather barren. Not much furniture." They circled the house, looking through the windows not covered with drapes. Even the garage was empty.

Stymied, they headed to the truck, where Milo enthusiastically greeted them as if they had been gone for days.

Buckling her seatbelt, she asked, "What do you think?"

"I think this one is a good bet. Since a company in Oklahoma City owns the house, we'll have to wait until tomorrow to contact them."

Not wanting to back out on the highway, Cody turned the truck around. As he pulled to a stop at the end of the driveway, he motioned toward a house across the road. Welcoming lights gleamed through the front windows of an attractive two-story house. "Let's talk to them. They might have seen something."

"What a pretty house," Riley said as Cody stopped. She hopped out, admiring the lush front yard and rose bushes along the front edge of the wrap-around porch. "Someone has spent a lot of time gardening." She walked up the steps and rang the doorbell. The porch light came on, and an attractive woman, mid-forties, opened the door.

She glanced over Riley's shoulder at Cody standing behind her. "May I help you?"

Behind her, a man stepped into view. "Who is it, Helen?"

"I don't know yet," the woman said.

"Ma'am, I'm Riley Phillips, a reporter for the *Fredericksburg Register*. This is my associate Cody Lightfoot. May we have a few minutes of your time to answer a couple of questions?"

With a troubled look, she said, "Well, I suppose so. I hope nothing is wrong."

Uncertain how to answer, Riley ignored the comment as she

stepped inside. The couple introduced themselves as Helen and Charles Reynolds. They led the way into the living room. In the tidy room, a couch faced the fireplace. Several chairs and small tables made for an attractive seating arrangement. Pictures of Texas bluebonnets adorned the walls.

At Riley's gasp of pleasure, Helen said, "I'm an artist, and one of my favorite subjects is bluebonnets."

Riley strode forward to take a closer look. "These are stunning."

"Why, thank you. Please, have a seat." She gestured toward the chairs.

Reluctantly, Riley moved away from the pictures. "We have a few questions about the house across the road."

A grimace crossed Helen's face as she glanced at her husband, who had settled beside his wife on the couch.

"Are you here about the complaints?" she asked.

"What complaints?"

"I guess not then. The house is a rental. There's been problems with some of the renters. I've called the sheriff's office several times."

"What kind of problems?"

"Loud music, underage drinking parties, stuff like that."

"Has anyone rented it lately?" Riley asked.

"A man, which was nice for a change," Charles said. "A single person isn't the typical renter. The group before this guy was a bunch of college kids."

"When did he arrive?" Cody asked.

"Four, five weeks ago?" Helen looked at her husband.

Charles said, "Thereabouts."

"What type of car was he driving?"

"It was blue, though I don't know the make," Charles said.

"Was this the man?" Riley pulled the picture from the backpack, handing it to Charles, the closer of the two.

He studied it for a few seconds. "I'm not sure. I saw him drive out a couple of times. It might be him." Then he handed it to his wife.

She shook her head. "I only saw him once, the day he arrived. He was getting out of his car, so I never saw his face." Her eyes widened. "This is a reconstruction."

"How do you know?" Riley asked.

"One of my art classes in college was reconstruction of faces from a skull. This has some amazing details." Helen straightened. "My gosh, now I know why your name is familiar. Your dog, the one you're training for search and rescue, found a body. Is this a picture of the man?"

"Yes," Riley said.

"Why would you believe he was renting the house across the street?" She passed the picture back to Riley.

Cody spoke up. "We're checking all the vacation rentals. Did you ever see anyone else there?"

Charles said, "A couple of vehicles. They usually didn't stay long."

"What type?"

Charles answered, "There was a black Ford pickup with one of those covers over the bed and a maroon car. It was parked in front of the black truck, and I didn't get a good look at it."

"Do you know when the man left?" Cody asked.

"No, I don't."

Cody leaned forward. "When was the last time you saw the blue car there?"

Charles said, "A week or so ago. After that, I saw the black truck over for most of a day or two before the cleaning crew showed up."

"Cleaning crew?" Riley said.

"The company sends out a crew to clean the house before the next group moves in."

"When did they arrive?"

"Three or four days ago," Charles told him. "That's when I knew for sure the man was gone."

"I don't suppose you know the name of the service?" Riley asked.

"Clean and Shine, something like that. They have a van."

Riley reached into the backpack to remove a business card. Handing it to Helen, she said, "If you think of anything else, please call. We sure appreciate your help."

Helen said, "Sometime, I'd like to know more about your dog. I have a friend in Michigan who has a SAR dog. I've learned a lot just from talking to her. I'm going to let her know about what's happened. She will be interested."

"He's in the truck."

Her face lit up. "Charles, get the camera. I want to get a picture."

Before walking out, Helen flipped a switch by the front door. When they stepped outside, the front yard was brightly lit.

Riley walked to the truck. Milo's nose was pushed against the passenger window. A sharp bark echoed when he saw her.

She opened the door, and he hopped out. "Milo, sit."

Helen and Charles walked up. "Oh, my gosh, he is all white. How unusual."

Riley said, "The color is rare, but I don't have any details on his pedigree. I found him at the dog pound."

"May I pet him?" Helen asked.

"Of course. Milo, greet."

Milo lifted his paw.

"Charles, get a picture of this." He snapped several while his wife oohed and aahed over Milo.

When Cody drove out, the couple enthusiastically waved.

Cody said, "You made a couple of friends there."

Riley, rubbing Milo's head hanging over the console, said, "Not me, Milo." The dog woofed.

"In the morning, I'll call the rental company. If they don't release the information about who rented the house, Scott can send a local agent for a personal visit."

Riley asked, "What's your take on this?"

"We found the house. The description of the truck dovetails with what Hollingsworth told us. I'd say someone sanitized the place before the cleaning crew showed up, making sure there wasn't any evidence."

"The extraction of the eye."

With a grim tone in his voice, Cody said, "Not only the eye but also the murder. I'll bet the shower curtain came from that house."

Riley hunkered down in the seat. She couldn't stop the chill racing through her or the growing sense of trepidation.

Chapter 17

Before heading to the breakfast buffet, Cody called his boss. When Scott answered, Cody said, "We found the house where the victim was living. It's a vacation rental."

He went on to explain what they learned after they visited the Reynolds. "I plan to contact the company this morning, but I expect they will refuse to release any information."

"Let me handle it from this end. I can get an agent from the Oklahoma City office to make an unannounced visit. Email me the details. What else?"

"Riley and I plan to show the victim's picture around town before heading to Austin. I located the cleaning service the rental company uses. Any progress on the identity of the victim?"

"Not yet. Run up the red flag if you encounter any difficulties with the sheriff." He paused, then said, "On second thought, let's hit this head-on. Stop by his office, introduce yourself, give him a copy of the picture."

"Susan Hutchin was concerned about Rutherford's reaction. It would take the pressure off her. How much do you want me to tell him?"

"No more than you have to. I think someone in his office is in the thick of this. The question is, who?"

"I've had the same thought."

Once they disconnected, Cody set up the email and sent it, then headed downstairs. With a plateful of bacon, eggs, and potatoes in one hand and a coffee cup in the other, he looked around the room before heading to an empty table against one wall. He had tucked his laptop under his arm. While he ate, he pulled up a city map, looking for stores where the victim might have shopped.

The boisterous activity of two small children and their parents at a nearby table suddenly died away. Cody looked up to see two deputies in the doorway. One he'd already met. When Bennett's eyes locked onto Cody, the man swaggered toward the table. Cody casually closed the computer.

Bennett grabbed a chair, flipping it around to straddle it. His buddy leaned against the wall with one hand resting on the butt of his gun.

Cody gave Bennett a hard look. "You want something?"

Bennett sneered. "Yeah. ID."

The man at the other table quickly gathered their possessions while the woman hustled their two children out of the room.

Cody leaned back, where he could see the second deputy in the corner of his eye. "There's no legal reason why I should."

Bennett looked around the now empty room. "I say there is. Refusing to identify, looks like a clear-cut case of resisting arrest to me."

"That would be a bad … very bad mistake."

Bennett snorted. "You're on my turf now. Nothing you can do about it."

"That's where you're wrong."

With two deputies just looking for a reason to slap cuffs on him, Cody lifted both hands in the air. With two fingers, he pulled his ID case from his front pocket, tossing it on the table. When it landed, it flipped open. Light glinted on his FBI badge. "I don't think your boss wants a contingent of FBI agents invading his office."

Stunned, Bennett looked at the badge, then pushed off from the chair. Anger flashed in his eyes before he nodded toward his companion. He turned to walk away.

In a menacing, though even tone, Cody said, "Tell your boss I'll be by later to talk to him."

****

Before letting Milo outside, Riley trotted around the yard. Satisfied it was safe, she opened the door for Milo. Energized by the whiff of the cool, refreshing, early morning smell, she poured a cup of coffee and wandered onto the porch. Settled into one of the rocking chairs, she called her brother.

Ted answered on the first ring.

"What were you doing, sitting on the dang thing?" she laughingly asked.

"No. Just happened to have it in my hand because I was getting ready to call you. You're awfully chipper for this early in the morning." His sister wasn't an early-morning person. At least not until she had a couple of cups of coffee under her belt. "What's up?"

The reason for the call was a sobering thought. "Just touching base with you on what's happening."

"How's it going with Lightfoot?"

"He's not exactly what I picture as an MIB. In fact, not even close. Which I guess has helped. So far, no one knows who he is. But it's about to change. I expect I'll have a problem with Rutherford. Cody received a reconstruction of the victim from his boss."

"Nicki sent me a copy. I'm running it through my systems, even though we're linked into the Tracker network."

"Did she tell you about the eye?"

"Yeah, she did."

"I've seen it in movies, but thought it was just a gimmick. So, how does it work?"

"It's all about biometrics, a technology using a person's unique physical characteristics for identification. Facial recognition, DNA, and fingerprints are the more commonly known. The iris of the eye is just as unique. During the initial setup phase, the software takes a picture of the person's eye and creates an algorithm for future comparison. It's called the Iris Code. To gain entry to a facility or computer program, the eye scan, which is another picture, is compared to the Iris Code on file. If they match, entry is allowed. It's similar to using your fingerprint to access your phone. The phone's software compares the imprint of your finger to the imprint on file."

"Wow, it is super high-tech, then."

"Somewhat, but gaining in popularity as a deterrent to hackers. What do you plan to do with the reconstruction?"

"Show it around town. Cody talked to his boss yesterday, and he said to release it. Susan has already broadcast it. She's concerned about what Rutherford will do. And so am I."

"You think he's going to blame you?"

"Big time. We have an image that won't look good for him, and I'm the one he can blame. It wouldn't be the first time he's threatened to arrest me."

A muttered oath echoed over the line before Ted said, "You've never mentioned any problems before."

"No reason to. I handled it. Rutherford is a bully and blowhard. They were empty threats. This time, maybe not, though Cody didn't seem worried."

"Why is that?"

"He said I had a bigger stick than Rutherford. I've got Scott. Cody said Scott may be the next director of the FBI, and Rutherford wouldn't want to tangle with him."

Laughter rippled over the phone. "I hadn't heard that rumor. I think I am going to like Lightfoot. Keep me posted, sis."

"Will do."

She whistled, and Milo came running. After cleaning up the kitchen, she gathered up her gear. Before she headed out with Cody, she wanted to talk to Susan.

On the way into town, her phone chimed. It was Cody. After learning she was going to the office, he asked, "Are you up for a trip to Austin? I found the cleaning service."

"Yes, when?"

"I need to make a stop, then I'll come by and pick you up. We'll check out where our victim might have shopped before we head to Austin."

As she disconnected, she wondered what that was all about. What stop?

An enticing aroma tickled Riley's nose when she strode into the office. "Cinnamon donuts," Riley exclaimed, dropping the backpack on the desk.

"Fresh from the oven. Picked them up at the donut shop across the street. There are some raspberry and lemon-filled ones, too." Susan leaned over to greet Milo. Rubbing his head, she glanced toward Riley. "I was going to call you. I've got news."

Riley filled her coffee cup before grabbing a cinnamon-crusted donut. Mumbling around a bite of the donut, she said, "I've got some for you too."

"Good. I can't wait to hear it. Milo, treat?" The dog woofed.

Seated in her chair, Susan set her cup on the desk. From a drawer, she removed a large chew bone. Milo scooted closer, his gaze fixated on the bone until Susan gave it to him. With it crossways in his mouth, his tail flying in the air, he pranced into the main room, collapsing onto the floor.

"You know you're spoiling him." Riley waved the last piece of donut in the air before popping it in her mouth. "He expects a treat every time he comes in here."

"I don't have kids, so I get my kicks spoiling a dog. Okay, start talking."

Riley brought her up to date on the house they'd found.

"I know the place. It's usually rented out to the college crowd."

"We talked to the neighbors. They said they've complained about the noise and parties. Not that it did much good."

"So how sure are you this guy rented it?"

"Cody's certain." She explained about the black truck, then added, "We're headed to Austin to talk to the people who cleaned the place. Did you find out what happened to the pictures from the crime scene?"

"I did." Susan took a sip of coffee. "I talked to Henry Caslon. At first, he didn't want to answer my questions until I reassured him his answers wouldn't appear in the newspaper. He said someone sabotaged his camera. Henry left it in his office overnight, planning to download the pictures the next morning. By then, they had disappeared. There wasn't a malfunction as Rutherford claimed."

"Who sabotaged the camera?"

"Rutherford is blaming Henry. He doesn't believe anyone tampered with it, that Henry screwed up."

Riley said, "If there was some hanky-panky to get rid of the pictures, our good sheriff isn't going to like it when he sees the reconstruction. There's something else I waited to tell you." Riley told Susan about the missing eye and the suspected reason for it.

Susan's face turned grim. "I can't think of a single business around here that would require that level of security. Any clues from your new partner?"

"He's as stymied as we are. Since I'm not sure how soon I'll be back, can I park Milo here again?"

"Sure can, and if you get back late, don't worry. He can go home with me." She hollered, "Right, Milo?" The dog woofed. "I swear that dog understands what we say. So, when is Cody getting here?"

"I'm not sure. He had to stop somewhere."

****

The subject of their conversation was striding into the sheriff's department with a briefcase. Seated behind a front counter, a uniformed officer greeted him. Cody removed his ID, flipping it open. "FBI Special Agent Cody Lightfoot. I need to speak to the sheriff."

Slightly flustered, the officer hesitated, then said, "Uh … uh, just a moment, Agent Lightfoot." She picked up the phone and tapped a number. "There is an FBI agent here. He wants to talk to the sheriff."

After disconnecting, she said, "Someone will be right with you. Please have a seat."

Cody sat, his gaze sweeping the nearby desks and officers. From the hushed tones and sideways looks, his presence seemed to create quite a stir. At a desk on the far side, Bennett caught his eye. The man sported a smug smile. Something was up.

An officer strode toward him. His tone brusque, he said, "Homicide detective Billy Thatcher." He didn't offer to shake hands. "Follow me."

Thatcher opened the door to an office overlooking the parking lot at the back of the building. Cody stepped into the room.

Seated at a large desk, a heavyset man glowered at him. "Lightfoot, don't bother sitting down. The only reason I agreed to see you is to tell you to stay out of county business. Now, get out, or I'll have my deputy physically remove you."

Cody glanced over his shoulder at Thatcher standing in the doorway. With a thin-lipped smile he walked across the room. "As I said to your other deputy this morning when he illegally tried to roust me, that would be a bad … very bad mistake." Before sitting, he moved the chair to let him keep an eye on Thatcher.

Rutherford leaned forward, his sizeable belly scrunched against the desk. "You don't have jurisdiction here, and I never invited the FBI to stick your noses into county business. I plan to lodge a formal complaint with the Texas Attorney General for interfering in a local investigation."

"Another bad … very bad mistake. It will make you look like a fool." He was tempted to say an even bigger fool. He clicked open the briefcase on his lap.

A streak of red blossomed across his cheeks. Rutherford snarled, "You can't talk to me that way. I'll have your badge for it."

Cody ignored the threat. "You parked a homicide victim at a funeral home where it was stolen instead of transporting it to the medical examiner. You don't have an investigation, never attempted to investigate, and closed the case. When those facts become known, your credibility will be flushed down the toilet. As a courtesy, I'm here to provide a copy of the victim's face."

Cody removed the picture from the briefcase and tossed it on Rutherford's desk.

The man stared at it like it was a snake about to strike. "I saw Hutchin's news article. This picture has no credibility. Hutchin and Phillips made it up. I've already taken steps to retract its publication. Even as we speak, I've got personnel typing up an arrest warrant. Once the judge signs it, I'm arresting them." He picked up the paper and flipped it back at Cody. It floated in the air before drifting to the floor.

Cody leaned down, retrieved it, and stuck it back in his briefcase. So, this was the reason for Bennett's smug look. "You do, and it will be another bad … very bad mistake that will cost you your job. You failed to check your facts. This picture came from an FBI agent in my unit in Washington, D.C. The FBI authorized its release to the news media. If you arrest them, you'll be looking at a lawsuit for false arrest. I can guarantee you the federal government will back their defense. You won't like what is printed when you and whoever else is involved are hauled into court."

He shot a hard look at Thatcher before turning back to look at Rutherford. "You can kiss your career goodbye." His lips twisted with a sardonic grin.

Though his face paled, Rutherford tried to brazen it out. He snorted. "I know Phillips is involved in this, and before I'm through, I'll prove she obstructed my investigation. I demand to know where you got the original picture."

"Rutherford, you're not in a position to demand anything."

"This is blatant interference. I want the name of your supervisor."

"Scott Fleming. His boss is the Director of the FBI. I'm sure Scott would like to talk to you." He locked the briefcase and rose. Cody's voice deepened with a menacing harshness. "If you, or any of your guard dogs, ever again threaten me or anyone associated with this case, you will regret it."

Cody stepped toward Thatcher. His body rigid with tension, Thatcher eyed him momentarily before stepping aside. Cody strode past him. Bennett stood by the front desk, talking to the officer. As Cody passed by, he said, "I think your boss might like to speak with you."

Seated in his truck, Cody debated whether to call Scott and give him a heads up, then decided it was a waste of time. If Rutherford was stupid enough to call, Scott didn't need any help. Traffic was light, and it only took a few minutes to reach the newspaper office.

He strolled inside to be greeted with an energetic bark. Milo jumped up from a mammoth chew bone covered with teeth marks. Cody rubbed his head. "That's some bone you got there." Milo, his body wiggling with delight, woofed.

"Susan is spoiling him," Riley said. She stepped out of Susan's office.

Behind her, Susan loudly exclaimed, "And I'm going to keep on doing it. Grab a cup of coffee. It's a fresh pot. And there are donuts."

Cody walked over to the table, poured a cup, and picked up a jelly-filled donut.

Susan sat at one of the desks. "Grab a chair. From the glint in your eyes, I suspect you have news."

He sat, took a bite of donut, followed with a swig of coffee before saying, "I had a meeting with Rutherford."

Susan leaned forward, an avid look on her face. "Oh, do tell. Keep no secrets."

After swallowing another large bite, Cody said, "I gave him a copy of the picture. You won't have a problem."

Both Susan and Riley eyed him in disbelief.

Riley said, "I can't imagine that Rutherford just went quietly into the night."

"He didn't. I just trumped what he believed was a winning hand."

"Now, you do have me curious," Susan said. "What did you do?"

"Told him he could be out of a job." He'd already decided not to mention the arrest warrant. The less said about it, the better for everyone. It would only cause unnecessary anxiety for the two women.

Susan went into whoops, followed by Riley.

Wiping the tears that threatened to roll down her cheeks, Susan said, "Oh, my gosh. I wish I could have seen his face."

Cody said, "Riley, you shouldn't have any more problems, but if anyone at the sheriff's office even looks cross-eyed at you, I want to know it."

Still trying to control her laughter, all Riley could do was nod.

Once the laughter died, Susan's face took on a somber look. "I did find out about the sheriff's pictures." After listening to her explanation, Cody said, "From what I saw of the place today, it would seem difficult for a stranger to get his hands on the camera. We need to get going." He swallowed the last of the coffee, then pitched the paper cup into a nearby trash can.

"Susan is going to take care of Milo. I thought it would be easier to get around if he wasn't with us."

"Dang, I kinda like having him in the truck. But you're right."

Riley picked up the backpack, then bent to hug Milo. He looked at her with a dejected look. "I know. You can't go, not today. You be good for Susan." Milo woofed.

As they walked out the door, she said, "I don't know if a child could do any better at putting me on a guilt trip."

Chapter 18

Riley snapped her seat belt into place. "How did you find the cleaning service?"

"It wasn't difficult, not with the description we had. I've already made arrangements to meet the crew that cleaned the house. It's later this afternoon."

"Okay, what's first on the list?"

"A gas station. The one closest to the rental property."

"I do have one request. I want to stop by the PD and introduce you to one of their sergeants." After telling him about Artie Ingram, she added, "I'd like to give him a copy of the reconstruction."

The morning turned into a fruitless effort to find someone who recognized the picture. Before heading out of town, they stopped at the police department.

When Riley walked in, the officer behind the desk said, "Where's Milo?"

"He's with Susan at the newspaper office. Is Artie in?"

"In his office. Go on back."

Cody followed Riley along a hallway until they reached a large room with multiple desks. Most were empty. She walked to an open doorway, rapping on the doorjamb.

"Riley, come on in." He rose to greet her. "What are you doing here?" Then he spotted Cody. The smile faded, replaced by an assessing look.

Cody stepped forward. "FBI Special Agent Cody Lightfoot." He extended a hand.

"Sergeant Artie Ingram."

His eyebrow cocked up as he looked at Riley. "Why do you have an FBI agent in tow?" He waved them toward the chairs.

"It's all about that body Milo found."

Artie settled back in his chair with a definite look of interest.

Though it was an abbreviated explanation, Cody hit the high points.

"I should have figured Ted had something to do with it. Known that boy since he was a kid. Tenacious is how I would describe him. I saw Susan's article with a picture. You have something to do with that?"

Cody said, "It came from another agent in my unit."

Riley pulled a copy from her backpack and handed it to Artie.

He studied it for a few seconds before asking, "How accurate do you think this is?"

"Knowing who came up with it, I'd say it's on the money. The agent is the top computer expert in the Bureau," Cody told him.

"I bet this made our sheriff unhappy, considering he closed the case."

"I gave him a copy this morning."

Artie chuckled. "Now, that is one conversation I'd like to have been privy to. If I can keep this, I'll give a copy to our patrol officers. They can show it around town. If you need any help, let me know."

Cody rose, thanking him.

Riley waited until they were out of town to ask, "Did you talk to Scott today?"

"This morning. He's sending an Oklahoma City agent to talk to the personnel at the rental company. I expect a call from him sometime today with an update. Nicki still hasn't identified the corpse."

Cody signaled to change lanes, passing a truck. "Until we do, we're at a standstill. His identity has been key all along. Still, what Nicki has done so far is amazing. I'm looking forward to meeting her."

"Do you think you'll like living in Washington, D.C.?" For some reason she didn't want to examine, the thought was depressing.

"I don't know. I passed through the airport a few times when I was in the military but never had a chance to see the city. From what I've been told, the Tracker agents are on the road a lot. Right now, the entire team is on assignment in other states."

"Is that an occupational hazard in the FBI, always traveling?" Her depression deepened.

"Most of the time, no. It's why there are offices in the larger cities."

"How long were you in the military?"

"Two tours, eight years."

"Why did you leave?"

Cody shrugged. "It was time."

When Cody pulled into a parking lot with a large sign over the door of a building that read, "Sparkle and Shine," she was sorry the trip was over. She liked his laid-back attitude and enjoyed being around him. Careful, Riley, she told herself. Need to step back. He's headed to Washington when this is over. Another depressing thought.

Riley hopped out, reaching back to grab the backpack. On the sidewalk, she waited for Cody. He stood by the truck door, gazing at the lot and street.

"Something wrong?"

"Just a twitchy feeling." He turned and walked toward the front door.

"Twitchy feelings? Really! Didn't know men got twitchy

feelings. Seems more like a girlie thing."

He tossed her a wry look. "You're just not going to let me forget that girlie crack, are you?"

She chuckled. "Not anytime soon."

The cleaning service occupied a one-room office with a desk and several chairs. Two women were seated by the front door. A third woman rose from behind the desk. "May I help you?"

"I'm FBI Special Agent Cody Lightfoot. This is Riley Phillips. I called this morning." He pulled out his ID case, opening it for her to see. "I would like to speak to Naomi Meadows."

A worried look settled on her face. "I'm Naomi Meadows. Please have a seat." She motioned toward the chairs in front of her desk.

Riley's gaze swept the two women. Young, in their early twenties, they stared at her with a fearful look. She smiled, hoping to reassure them.

"Agent Lightfoot, this is Emily and Dolores. They cleaned the house you called about. This is highly unusual. We've never had a problem with any homes we've cleaned."

He smiled. "That's not why I'm here. It's not an issue with your cleaning service. I'm investigating a missing person case. I'm interested in the latest rental of the property."

Some of the tension in her body eased. "Well, certainly, we'll help in any way we can."

"Do you know who rented the house?"

"No, I don't. I never know."

"How do you know when the house is rented?"

"At the beginning of the year, Mr. Frisk, the manager, sends me a calendar with the dates of the rentals posted. The house is popular with the college crowd, plus we get a few returning families. If there is an open block of time, and someone rents the house, Mr. Frisk updates the calendar and notifies me. That's what happened this time, a month-long gap the house was available."

"Is that unusual?"

"Not at all. There are a few slack periods, plus sometimes people cancel."

"When did he update the calendar?"

"Hmm … I'd have to check the emails, but I believe it was three or four months ago."

"When do you clean the house?"

"I always schedule it the day after the rental ends."

"I'd like a copy of Mr. Frisk's email and the calendar."

Her brow wrinkled. "I'm not certain I should give you that information. Maybe I should check with Mr. Frisk."

"Ms. Meadows, an Oklahoma City FBI agent is contacting the company. I can assure you there won't be a problem. But if it would make you more comfortable, please call Mr. Frisk."

"All right."

He looked at Riley, cocking an eyebrow to silently ask if she had any questions. She shook her head.

"Ms. Meadows, while you make your call and get the documents, I have just a few questions to ask Emily and Dolores."

He moved his chair to where the two women huddled. With a reassuring smile, he said, "What was the condition of the house when you arrived?" Behind him, he heard Meadows' voice murmuring on the phone.

Emily, the older of the two, said, "It was really clean. There wasn't even any trash in the waste baskets or the outside trash bin. It was like nobody had been there."

"Is that unusual?" Cody asked.

Both women energetically nodded their heads. Again, it was Emily who answered. "Oh, yes, sir. The house is usually a mess, dirty dishes, filthy floors, wine and liquor bottles, beer cans …"

With a smile, Cody interrupted. "I get the picture. I imagine it takes time to clean the house."

"There have been times when we were there all day. Didn't leave until after dark."

"How long did it take you to clean it the last time you were there?"

Emily glanced at Dolores with a questioning look. "A couple of hours?"

Dolores nodded her head.

"Were there any personal possessions left in the house?"

"No, sir."

"Anything unusual, out of place."

"Uh … there was one thing," Emily said. "The shower curtains in both bathrooms were missing. We had to replace them." She nodded to the woman beside her. "Dolores had to go into town and buy new ones."

"What did the ones that were missing look like?"

"Quite pretty. One was blue with swans, the other white with yellow daisies."

Riley's thoughts flashed to the body in the shallow grave wrapped in filthy plastic. Icy tingles raced over her. There was no doubt they had the right house.

The owner walked up with papers in her hand. She said, "I received the email from Mr. Frisk about the rental just over three months ago. I hope this helps."

"It will," Cody said with absolute certainty. "One more question. Do you know the next rental date?"

"Yes. Day after tomorrow."

After thanking the women for their cooperation and leaving their business cards, they walked out. Cody handed the papers to Riley. As his hand reached to start the engine, his phone chimed. He tugged it from a pocket. "It's Scott," he said, tapping the screen.

"Scott. I'm putting this on speakerphone. Riley is with me." He laid the phone on the console.

Riley leaned over with an intense look on her face.

Scott said, "Interesting developments today, but first, fill me in on yours."

For several minutes, Cody talked, giving an abbreviated version of the day's events, starting with the confrontation with the sheriff and ending with what they discovered at the cleaning company.

Scott said, "The shower curtain is a telling piece of evidence. No doubt, the victim and the man living in the rental house are the same person. I wonder what happened to the blue one. Riley, you didn't see it when you found the body?" Scott asked.

"No, just the one with the daisies, though I didn't realize at the time what they were. The EMT at the scene mentioned the daisies on the shower curtain," she said.

"If the man was killed in the house, then I suspect the eye would have been immediately extracted. It could account for what happened to the other shower curtain."

Riley gulped at the sudden image that sparked in her mind.

Chapter 19

Cody said, "Even though the house has been cleaned, I'd like to get a crime scene unit in there, but I don't want to use personnel from the sheriff's department."

"I agree. I'll contact Will Cooper, the SAC over the Austin office. He can get the ball rolling on that one. I'll also contact the Oklahoma City agent, Isaac Franco. He can get the rental company's permission. Do the cleaning people have the key?"

"No, there's a lockbox with the key on the door. I'll need the code."

"Hmm … okay, I'll add it to my call to Isaac. Are you still in Austin?"

"Yes."

"Stay there until I contact Will. He might want to meet you."

"What did you find out from Franco?" Cody asked.

"John Frisk, the general manager, handled the rental. It was rented almost four months ago. Whatever is going down has been planned for some time. Frisk said he received an overnight delivery of a money order. Isaac has already run down the renter's information. It's fictitious. He's trying to trace the delivery and money order.

"Don't they check on who's renting the property?"

"No. The company gets its money upfront, which includes a

very hefty deposit. Any problems, the deposit is forfeited. According to Frisk, the deposit is more effective than any background checks. He had a point."

After Scott disconnected, Cody pocketed the phone.

Riley asked, "What do you think?"

"I think we need to find a place to eat. It may be our only chance. I don't know about you, but I'm starved. You know Austin, where to?"

"Depends on what you've got a hankering for." Buckling her seat belt, she didn't see the spark that flashed in his eyes as he looked at her.

When Cody answered, he was back in control, his voice steady. "How about Tex-Mex?"

"Great, I've got just the one. It's on the way out of town."

Following Riley's directions, he soon pulled into the large parking lot of a hacienda-style building on the west side of Austin.

After walking through huge wood doors with an engraving of a sun-god, they were greeted by a hostess. They opted for a seat inside instead of on the patio.

As they settled into a booth, Cody glanced around the attractive interior with cream-colored walls and multi-colored ceramic bricks as decorative accents.

A waitstaff set a basket of chips and bowls of salsa on the table, then handed them menus tucked under his arm. They ordered iced tea.

Cody asked, "Any recommendations?"

"The place is famous for its homemade tortillas and red-hot fajitas. And I don't mean fire hot," Riley said.

"Just how hot?"

"For someone with twitchy feelings, it may be more than you can handle."

"Ouch," he said. "A direct hit."

She laughed.

Two glasses of iced tea were set on the table. "Are you ready to order?" the young man asked.

With a smug look, Cody said, "Beef fajitas."

"Good choice. And you, ma'am."

"The same."

They nibbled on chips and the spicy salsa as they talked. By some tacit agreement, they stayed away from any mention of the investigation. Instead, they chatted about his family, then hers. Occasionally, Cody glanced around the room or out the window next to their booth that overlooked the parking lot. Riley figured it was a cop thing. Ted was the same way. Go somewhere with him, and his eyes never stopped moving.

Cody exclaimed, "What the …" He jumped up. "Stay here," he said before dashing to the front door.

Riley slid out, the strap of the backpack in her hand.

Their waiter ran up. "What's wrong? Your food is coming."

"Save it," she shouted, chasing after Cody.

Cody burst through the door. From underneath the back of Cody's truck, a man crawled out. Seeing Cody charging toward him, he jumped up, pulling a gun from his waistband.

Even as Cody reached for his weapon, instinctively he hit the ground, rolling as the man fired. Up against a car, Cody peered over the hood. The man was headed toward the street.

Cody took off, zigzagging to keep a low profile. The man darted around parked cars, shooting behind him as he ran. As Cody raced past a car, glass flew when a bullet hit the windshield. The man dashed across the street. With cars passing by, Cody couldn't risk a shot. He ran along the sidewalk, keeping the man in view on the other side. He was gaining ground. Dodging cars, Cody raced across the street. When he reached the sidewalk, Cody picked up the pace. His long strides closed the distance. The man fired wildly over his shoulder. Cody still couldn't risk a shot. Ahead, the man darted into an alley.

Cody came to an abrupt halt at the corner of the building. Going low, he looked around the edge. A dark shape was running toward the other end. Cody took off. "Stop, FBI." The man leaped to the side of the building, turning to shoot. Cody fired. The man staggered into the center of the alley and collapsed. Cody dashed toward the body lying face down. When he spotted the man's gun a few feet from the body, Cody holstered his weapon.

He rolled the man over. The way blood spurted from the chest, Cody knew it was a killing shot. He'd hit an artery. The man was about to bleed out.

In the distance, he heard the sounds of sirens. Cody dropped to one knee. "Who hired you?"

The man stared up at him. His lips moved, then his eyes dulled, the light of life gone. Even before Cody checked for a pulse in the neck, he knew the man was dead.

He stood, walking back to the street. Police cars blocked the entrance to the restaurant. Cody pulled out his phone.

When Riley answered, she cried, "Are you all right? Where are you?"

"Send the cops to the alley down the street. I'll be waiting."

He leaned against the side of the building, pulling in deep breaths to slow his heart. Two officers, guns out, raced toward him. He kept his hands in view. He didn't need a trigger-happy cop thinking he was the bad guy.

"FBI Special Agent Cody Lightfoot. My ID is in my front pocket. My gun is in my holster."

Once the two officers confirmed his identity, they relaxed,

holstering their guns. One got on the radio, informing his supervisor there was a shooting and a dead victim.

Riley came running up. Her eyes anxiously scanned him. "What happened? Who were you chasing?"

More officers had arrived, heading into the alley. One officer was keeping an eye on him.

Cody said, "A man crawled out from underneath my truck. When I tried to stop him, he ran. He was shooting, and I shot back. He's dead." He raised his voice to get the officer's attention. "I'm going back to my truck. I want to find out what he was doing."

The officer nodded, though he followed as Cody grabbed Riley's arm, tugging her toward the street.

"Oh, my god. What happens now?" Riley asked.

"We go to the police station."

Several more police officers were in the parking lot. When one tried to stop them from entering, the officer following them stepped up. "He's the FBI agent."

It cleared the way for him to reach the truck, where he grabbed the flashlight from the console. Kneeling, he spotted a zippered bag near the back tire. Since it was evidence, he didn't touch it. Instead, he flashed the light across the undercarriage. Icy fear rippled over him at the sight of a small IED, an improvised explosive device, with a cellphone attached to a brace near the gas tank. A terrifying thought ratcheted the fear. Who planned to call the phone to trigger the explosion? The dead man or someone else. The blast would kill anyone inside the truck or near it. He'd seen far too many explosions during his military career not to know the horrific damage from one of these bombs.

Even as he slid out from under the truck, his mind raced with options. Moving the truck wasn't one of them. The bomb had to be defused and fast. He trotted to the nearest officer. "Who's in charge?"

The officer pointed to a man standing by a squad car with a phone in his hand. "Lieutenant Curtis Thomas."

Cody headed toward him. When Thomas spotted him, he ended the call.

"Lieutenant, I'm Agent Cody Lightfoot. Do you need my ID?"

"No, one of my officers has already vouched for you."

"There's an IED attached to the undercarriage of my truck, set to be triggered by a phone call."

Stunned, Thomas stared at him for several seconds before saying, "I'll call the bomb squad."

Waiting for the bomb squad wasn't another option. "We don't have time to wait. I don't know who's on the other end of that phone. It might not be the man I shot. I can defuse it. It's part of what I did in the military."

"Are you sure?"

"I wouldn't say so if I wasn't. I don't have a death wish."

Thomas shouted to his men. "Get these people back. I want the area cleared now. Move it." He pointed to a nearby sergeant. "Call the bomb squad."

Cody headed back to the truck, dropping onto his back.

Thomas knelt next to him. "What do you need?"

"Not sure yet."

Riley, standing nearby, had listened to the exchange. She stripped off the backpack. From inside, she pulled out the camera and slung the strap around her neck. With her heart in her throat, she raised the camera.

Chapter 20

On his back, Cody scooted under the truck. The lieutenant crawled alongside him. Cody aimed the beam of light at the bomb. For a few seconds, he studied it, then shifted to get a better look at the other side. The cellphone was taped to a block of C4 with the wires tucked between the two. The bomb was then taped to a metal brace. He couldn't get to the wires without removing the entire device.

"Going to be a bit more of a problem than I thought."

Thomas muttered, "Define a bit more."

Cody handed the flashlight to Thomas, then reached for the knife clipped inside his pants pocket. "Can't get to the wires. Hit this side with the light."

With a quick flick of his fingers, he opened the knife, then gently sliced through the tape. "Now the other side."

While he held the IED in place with one hand, he shifted to get a better position before cutting the tape. Cody let the knife fall to the ground, using both hands to pull it away from the brace. "Let's go."

On his back, Cody waited for Thomas to get clear of the truck. When the light from the flashlight in Thomas' hand flashed across the rear bumper, Cody muttered an oath.

"Everything okay?" Thomas asked, a nervous edge to his voice.

Not wanting to waste time on what caught his attention, Cody said, "Yeah."

Once Thomas was out of the way, Cody eased out from under the truck with the bomb securely cradled in his hands.

As Cody cleared the truck, Thomas asked, "Do you want me to take it?"

With a negative shake of his head, Cody rose, moving a short distance away. He crouched and carefully laid the bomb on the concrete. On his knees, he crept around the device, studying it from every angle. Even though the parking lot had lights, he said, "I need more light."

Thomas hollered, "Get me more flashlights." Then he turned back to Cody, handing him the knife he'd picked up. "What else?"

"See if the bomber left any wire cutters in the bag. Be easier than using my knife."

An officer raced up with three flashlights. While Cody told the officer where to put them, Thomas grabbed the bag and upended it, dumping the contents. He picked up a set of wire cutters.

Cody carefully slit the tape on one side of the IED. Still on his knees, he crawled to the other side. Once the tape had been cut, he eased the phone away from the C4, exposing the wires. He laid the phone next to the block of C4. With two fingers, he pushed the wires apart.

Thomas handed him the wire cutters.

One by one, Cody clipped the wires until the bomb was a pile of inert components with no threat to anyone. Taking a deep breath, he rocked back on his heels, swiping his hand across his brow where sweat beaded. As he stared at the pieces of the deadly device, a jolt of fear wiped out his relief. The screen on the cellphone had just lit up.

Thomas muttered, "Holy mother …" He cleared his throat.

"Someone just called it." He looked at Cody. "I'd say that puts new meaning into the phrase, cutting it too close."

The officers had cleared the parking lot, pushing the onlookers and patrons from the restaurant to the far end of the street. Cody stood, his gaze scanning the people bunched together. Was the caller hidden inside the crowd?

As he watched, a commotion arose. The bomb squad had arrived. Officers cleared the way to let the van pull into the parking lot.

Thomas headed toward it. Once it rolled to a stop, three men climbed out. Two headed to the back of the van. The other greeted Thomas. A short conversation ensued before they headed toward Cody.

"This is FBI Special Agent Cody Lightfoot." Thomas waved a hand at the burly officer next to him. "Sergeant Tony Haslett."

The sergeant nodded, then squatted to eye what lay on the ground. "Who took it apart?"

"I did," Cody answered.

The sergeant looked up at him. "Military?"

"Yeah."

"Figured. Good job." He stood and hollered. "Let's move it. I want to get rid of this."

Thomas said, "Someone just called the phone. Have it checked, though I expect the call came from a burner phone."

Haslett looked down. "God-a-mighty. That was too close for comfort."

Cody stepped out of the way, looking for Riley. She stood beside the truck, her camera raised. He strolled toward her.

"Have you been doing that all along?"

"Yes." She downplayed the horrific terror that raced over her at seeing the screen glowing from an incoming call. "Scary stuff. What happens now?"

As they watched the officers place the C4 in the container, Cody said, "We'll have to give the police a statement. We'll be late getting back." He also figured they'd confiscate his weapon. Routine under the circumstances. He was thankful he had another pistol in the locked container in the truck.

"I'd better call Susan and let her know what's going on. I'm going to file a news story. Anything I can't talk about?"

Cody thought, then said, "Just the bomb and shooting. Don't mention a connection to our unknown victim."

She walked to the edge of the parking lot, out of hearing of any of the officers milling around.

Susan answered on the second ring. "Where are you?"

"Still in Austin. I've got another news flash. Get ready to record."

"Cripes! Wait a minute." There was a pause before Susan said, "Okay, go."

Riley took a moment to organize her thoughts, then began to dictate. "Headline—Terror on an Austin City Street. For this Texas reporter, more than a fine meal was served up during a casual dining experience. When an FBI Special Agent dining at the same restaurant observed a man tampering with a vehicle in the eatery's parking lot, the agent attempted to detain the individual. The suspect fired several shots at the agent. A foot chase ensued, ending in an alley where the suspect was killed. His identity is unknown at this time. Upon investigation, the agent discovered the suspect had attached an explosive device to the undercarriage of the vehicle. Local police and their bomb squad responded to the scene. However, the agent was able to successfully defuse the bomb. Additional details will be published as soon as they are available."

Riley had heard Susan gasp when she reached the part about the bomb.

After Riley finished, Susan said, "This is unbelievable.

Something serious is in the wind. It has to be connected to our mystery man, but you didn't mention it."

"Cody asked me not to. There is more, but I'll tell you about it later. I do have pictures. I'll send them as soon as I can. I don't know when we'll be headed back to Fredericksburg. Any calls about our victim's picture?"

"No."

"How is Milo?"

"He's been restless, pacing, even a couple of howls, but I finally got him settled. Don't worry about picking him up tonight. I'm going to get this on the wire. I'll do a follow-up when I get the pictures."

She pocketed the phone and walked to where Cody stood talking to the lieutenant.

Cody introduced Riley, then asked, "Have you identified the man?"

"Not yet. There was no identification on the body. I will need your weapon, Agent Lightfoot."

"I think we've graduated to first names. I expected it. How long will you need it?" He unholstered, unloaded the weapon, then handed it to the lieutenant.

"I'll have it back to you before you leave town. All I need is a comparison bullet. An officer will take your weapon to our range. If you're ready to go, one of my officers will escort you to my office.

Cody said, "Before I can leave, I have some unfinished business."

"Just let me know." He turned to Riley. "I'd appreciate a copy of the pictures."

Riley figured he could demand a copy but liked that he asked. "I'll have to download them to a computer."

Cody spoke up. "You can use my laptop once we get to the PD."

Thomas nodded and walked away.

Riley looked at Cody. "The restaurant?"

"We did leave rather abruptly. But no, there's something else."

He glanced around. A couple of officers were still on the sidewalk, and with the excitement over, the crowd had dispersed. Most went back inside the restaurant. This was as good a time as any.

Slightly unsettled by his intense stare, Riley asked, "Everything okay?"

"Do you have a flashlight in that pack?" His light was back in the truck.

"Uh … yeah. Why?"

"I need it."

Digging inside, she came up with the small light and handed it to him. "Care to elaborate?"

Ignoring her, he dropped to the ground, rolling under the truck. With a quick twist of his fingers, he dislodged the tracking device. Thoroughly disgusted that he hadn't thought about the possibility, he crawled out.

Puzzled by his behavior, Riley said, "What was that all about?"

He opened his hand. "A tracking device. I suspect there's one on your truck."

Stunned, she stared at his hand. "That's how he knew we were here."

He dropped it, stomping it with the heel of his boot. Then he pulled out his phone and tapped the speed dial.

When Scott answered, Cody said, not pulling any punches, "I shot a man tonight."

"Killed?" Scott asked.

"Yes. He planted an IED on my truck. I caught him in the act. It ended up in a foot chase and shooting."

"Were you injured?"

"No."

"What about the bomb?"

"After I defused it, the pieces were hauled away by the bomb squad."

"Where are you now?"

"Still at the scene, a restaurant parking lot. From here, I'm headed to the police department. My weapon has already been confiscated."

"Any problems with Austin PD?"

"Not so far."

"Just to be sure, I'll call Will Cooper and let him know. He's waiting for the combination code to the lockbox before his team heads to the house. I've got it and a signed release from the rental company with permission to enter. As soon as you can break free from the PD, head to Fredericksburg. When can you get me a full report?"

"Once I get to the PD, I can type it on my computer. I suspect Lieutenant Curtis Thomas is going to want answers. One of which is why an FBI agent assigned to the Tracker unit is in town. How much do I tell him?"

"Use your best judgment. Has the man been identified?"

"I don't know."

"I need that report." He disconnected.

"Let's go pay our bill."

Inside, Cody asked the hostess for their bill.

Flustered, she glanced around. "Please, just a moment." She rushed toward the back of the restaurant and disappeared into a hallway.

Cody looked at Riley. With raised eyebrows, she shrugged.

When the woman reappeared, an older man was with her. Stopping in front of them, the man extended his hand. "Agent Lightfoot, I am Esteban Mata, the owner. One of the police officers told me your name and what you did. Had you not intervened, I shudder to think of the horrific consequences." He spoke with a quiet dignity. "Please accept my profound appreciation. While it is a small gratuity compared to the service you rendered, you are my honored guest whenever you visit my establishment." He turned and sharply clicked his fingers.

Two waiters walked up. One carried two large sacks, the other a drink container.

"With my compliments, this is what you ordered."

Somewhat overwhelmed, Cody's first instinct was to refute the owner's words. Then he realized it would be an insult. Instead, he said, "Mr. Mata, I appreciate the courtesy you have extended."

Riley took the container of drinks and Cody the large sacks with boxes inside. Her mouth watered from the spicy aroma emanating from the contents. It had been a long time since breakfast.

As they strode toward the truck, Cody said, "We may have to fight off a horde of officers when we walk in with these."

Seeing them leave the restaurant, Thomas walked up. "You might be right," he said. "It smells good. If you're ready to go, I've got a squad car waiting."

With the police car leading the way, it didn't take long to reach police headquarters.

Washington D.C.

Her level of irritability had reached a new high. Nicki was pissed. She tapped in another code. While she waited for the program to run, Nicki glumly stared at the wall-mounted monitor where a goblin danced across the screen instead of a spinning circle. One of the many innovations she'd made to her software.

She couldn't remember the last time or that she had ever been so totally flummoxed by a simple search. Nicki still didn't have a name. It was like this guy never had a picture taken. Two yearbooks and nothing. She had just finished loading another yearbook but wasn't holding out any hope. She'd broadened the search pattern, reaching deep into the internet, news articles, social media, anywhere a picture was posted.

The only problem was time. Even with the speed of her computers, it was a massive search. One that could take days, not hours. Time was something they didn't have.

Rising, she stretched, working the kinks out of her shoulders and back. She'd been at it non-stop for hours. She reached for the coffee cup near the keyboard. Empty, the remaining dregs had dried.

"I wondered when you were going to emerge from your lair."

Nicki glanced over her shoulder. Scott stood in the doorway.

"I'm going to start calling our victim the ghost. It's like he doesn't exist."

"You'll find him. Come on, I'll buy you another cup. Just made a pot. There are fresh sandwiches in the fridge."

In the breakroom, Nicki rinsed out the cup and refilled it. Before opting for the large, easy chair, she grabbed a foil-wrapped sandwich from the fridge. With her legs curled underneath her, Nicki peeled back the foil, taking a large bite of the crusted roll filled with tuna fish, a favorite. She washed it down with a gulp of the rich, dark brew, sighing with pleasure. She had to admit that Scott had the touch when it came to coffee.

"I got the initial rundown on Mickey Bennett. The sheriff hired him about six months ago." Mumbling around another bite, she said, "Born and raised in Phoenix, Arizona. Here's what's odd. Bennett moves around a lot. Worked for a couple of police departments in Arizona and New Mexico, then moved to Texas. Before hiring on with the sheriff's department, he'd worked for a police department and another sheriff's department in West Texas. The longest stint was a year or so."

Leaning against the counter, Scott asked, "What reason did he give for quitting?"

"I don't know. The official records state resigned, with no reason given. Nothing ties him to our investigation. Do you want me to go deeper into his background? I'll need to contact the agencies."

Scott hesitated, staring into the cup in his hand. His mind hummed. An odd fact, seemingly without ties to their murder victim. Yet, an inner sense tingled, one he learned to rely on. "Yes. Make the calls. What about the sheriff?"

She crumpled the foil, tossed it into a nearby trash can, and then handed Scott the cup. He refilled it. "So far, he's clean other than an oddity during his run for election last year. From the articles I read, his opponent was leading until he was injured in a hit and run and had to pull out of the race."

"How convenient for Rutherford," Scott mused.

She sipped. "I thought so. What's the status on the house?"

"Isaac Franco sent me the combination code to the lockbox and a copy of a signed waiver by the general manager of the rental company allowing us to go into the house. Before I could call Will, I got a call from Cody. He was involved in a shootout in Austin." He lifted the cup to take a sip.

Nicki, acutely attuned to Scott's moods, didn't miss the grim look that flashed across his face.

"What happened?"

"I'm waiting for his report. He and Riley are on the way to the police department. What I do know is Cody caught someone tampering with his truck. The man planted an IED. A shootout ensued, and Cody killed the man."

A cold chill raced over her. "What happened to the bomb?"

"Cody defused it." He straightened. "I'll be in my office. I still need to call Will. I've already had to explain why one of my agents is on his turf. His response was that most SACs would hang me in effigy for such a jurisdictional violation. Now, it's a shooting and a suspect killed."

"What was his take on the whole deal?"

"Same as mine. Whatever is going down is in Texas. He's compiling a list of companies, including a couple of military installations that use eye scans."

Before heading to his office, he topped off his cup. The evening had all the makings of another long night. Back at his desk, Scott checked his emails. Nothing yet. He tapped Will's number on the phone.

Will answered, "I've got my forensics team ready to head to Fredericksburg. Did you get the combination to the lockbox?"

"Yes, though that's not why I'm calling. Cody was involved in a shooting in Austin." He covered the significant details.

On the other end, muffled curses erupted. "I'll meet Lightfoot at the PD. I want the bomber's name, pronto. Scott, I've put my entire staff on alert. I don't like what my gut is telling me."

"You're not the only one. As soon as we have the name, I'll get it to Nicki."

"That's an amazing reconstruction she did of the victim. I'm surprised Nicki hasn't come up with a name."

"Right now, she'd likely chew your arm off if you asked. She's gone through two Aggie yearbooks and is on number three. Her frustration level is about to redline."

After disconnecting, he forwarded the email from Franco to Will, then propped his feet on the corner of the desk. Scott leaned back and stared at the ceiling. A sense of foreboding crept into his thoughts. He was running out of time.

Chapter 21

Texas

When they strode into the lobby of the Austin police headquarters carrying containers of food, an officer escorted Riley and Cody to a breakroom on the main floor. Cody was told Lieutenant Thomas was on his way. An officer carrying a recorder entered the room. The sacks were set aside while their statements were recorded. Once the officer left, Cody opened his laptop.

"Let's get your pictures downloaded so I can send a few to Scott."

Riley pulled her camera from the backpack. Once the download was complete, she handed him a thumb drive she always carried.

"If you'll copy the pictures to the thumb drive, I can give it to the lieutenant."

Before he transferred the file, he flipped through the pictures. "These are incredible."

A flare of heat brushed her cheeks. Not wanting Cody to see how his compliment had affected her, she quickly turned her head, fiddling with the camera. By the time he'd transferred the file and removed the thumb drive, her emotions were under control.

While he typed, she unpacked the sacks. Once Cody had sent his report, they took advantage of the lull to eat. Not knowing how long they had, they didn't waste time on conversation.

Riley speared the last piece of beef, popping it into her mouth. With a sigh of contentment, she pushed the empty container aside. "Wow, that was good." She sucked on the straw, swallowing the last of the iced tea. "How long will we be here?"

"I'm not sure." Cody shoved the empty containers into the plastic bags, then rose to dump them into a nearby trash can.

Seeing Riley's look of surprise, he grinned. "My mother believed in equality when it came to household chores."

An older man in his late forties with a marine-style buzz haircut and attired in jeans, an open-collared shirt and tennis shoes strolled in. "I bet you're Cody Lightfoot and Riley Phillips."

He stopped in front of Cody, extending his hand. "Will Cooper, Special Agent in Charge for the Austin office. Pleased to meet you."

Astounded the head man showed up, Cody shook his hand. "Same here."

Then Will turned to greet Riley. "I understand you're a reporter for the *Fredericksburg Register*."

"Yes, sir, I am."

"It's Will." He walked to the counter. Eyeing the coffee pot, he said, "Good lord. How long has this been sitting here?" After dumping the muddy contents in the sink, he rinsed the glass container and started a fresh pot.

At the odd look on Cody's face, Will said in a wry tone, "I've been here more times than I care to remember."

Curtis Thomas walked in. The lieutenant eyed Will with a jaundiced look. "I wondered how long it would take you to get here. I'm surprised you weren't at the crime scene."

Will leaned against the counter. "I didn't know about it until I got a call from Cody's boss in Washington, D.C."

Curtis' eyebrows shot up as his gaze shifted to Cody. "You don't work for Will? I figured you were a new agent. Who's your boss?"

"Scott Fleming," Cody said.

"A Tracker. Why the heck didn't you say so? Your boss is well known around here." The lieutenant laughed. "It might have improved my outlook while you played with that IED."

"Wait a minute. What are you talking about, Curtis?" Will asked.

"Cody defused the bomb."

With a new level of respect in his eyes, Will said, "Scott told me about the bomb but didn't mention you defused it."

Curtis said, "We identified the man you shot. Eddie Burgess. Local talent, drugs, guns, assaults. Didn't know he was into bombs."

Cody said, "He probably wasn't. The way it was put together, someone else could have assembled it. All Burgess had to do was tape it to my truck."

Curtis said, "Let's go to my office."

Will grabbed a cup of coffee and followed them.

Once everyone was seated in the lieutenant's office, Curtis handed a box to Cody. "Your weapon. Why is a Tracker in town?"

As he reached for the box, Cody said, "I'm actually in Fredericksburg on an unofficial basis."

"Fredericksburg! I heard a body had been found. Is that why you're there?"

"Yes. Riley and her dog found it."

Curtis looked at Riley with a surprised expression.

"Riley's brother is head of the fusion center for the Dallas Police Department. He's worked with the Tracker unit on other cases and contacted the unit for help. I recently transferred to the unit and was still in Las Vegas. I stopped on my way to Washington."

Curtis frowned. "Why do I sense there's more than you're telling me? Is this one of those, 'I can't talk about the details,' type of case?"

Since Scott left it up to him, Cody hadn't been sure how to

handle the lieutenant. He decided he didn't like stonewalling him. Any officer who crawled under a truck to help defuse a bomb deserved Cody's trust.

"No, it's not." Once he finished explaining the events leading up to their visit to Austin, Curtis's expression was decidedly grim.

Will said, "I have a team ready to head to Fredericksburg. Scott obtained permission from the owner of the house."

"I'd like a picture of the victim."

Riley said, "I have one." She pulled her file folder from her backpack, removing one of the copies she'd made. She handed it to Curtis.

"I'll get this circulated in the department. Has it gone public?"

Riley answered, "Yes, my editor sent it out."

"I also need those pictures you took."

Riley handed him the thumb drive.

Curtis plugged it into his computer. Once he'd transferred the file, he handed the drive back to Riley. After quickly scanning them, he said, "Do you think I could entice you to come work for Austin PD? These are incredible."

Uncertain what to say as the men eyed her, she smiled, though she felt the heat on her face.

Cody said, "There's something else you need to know. The man's eye was extracted. Another agent in the Tracker unit used a picture Riley had taken at the crime scene for reconstruction. That's when the missing eye was discovered. We believe it's why someone has attempted to derail the investigation. To keep us from discovering the man's identity."

Curtis said, "Someone plans to use the eye to hack into a system."

"Or a high-security facility," Cody added.

Will stood. "We need to get going. Anything else, Curtis?"

"No, but I want to be kept in the loop."

Cody reassured him. "I suspect we will need all the help we can get before this is over."

Once they were on the road, reaching the house didn't take long. A convoy of vehicles, led by Cody, pulled into the driveway. Lights flashed across the pitch-black front yard, reflecting off the windows of the house as they parked. Officers pulled out equipment from the crime scene van using the headlights for illumination.

Will strode toward the front porch, followed by Cody and Riley. Cody held a flashlight while Will entered the combination code to open the lockbox. Retrieving the key, he unlocked the front door and pushed it open. Stale air, tainted with bleach, wafted through the open doorway.

An officer rushed up carrying a box with gloves and paper booties to cover their shoes.

While they donned the protective gear, Will said, "This may be a futile effort since the house has been cleaned."

Inside, Cody flashed his beam across the walls. Spotting switches, he flipped them. Lights lit up the entryway and living room, and floodlights illuminated the front yard.

Riley followed Will into the house. "Not a homey place by any means," she observed. Her gaze scanned the cheap living room furniture and stained, scratched linoleum flooring extending into the kitchen.

"Considering its use, I can understand why," Cody said. "I wonder how often the owner has to replace the furniture?"

Sliding glass doors at the back of the living room led to a porch. Bedrooms along the hallway had furniture similar to the quality of what was in the living room.

Riley shuddered. "I'm not sure I'd want to sleep on one of those beds."

Will said, "Let's wait outside; give my people room to work."

As they stood by one of the vehicles, Will began questioning Riley about Milo. While they talked, a black and white SUV pulled across the entrance to the driveway, blocking anyone from leaving.

Cody groaned. "We couldn't have been so lucky as to get in and out without the sheriff knowing we're here."

A man stepped out of the vehicle, looking at the cars parked in front of the house. He lifted his handheld radio, talked for a few seconds, then headed toward them.

"What's going on here?" the deputy sheriff asked, looking suspiciously at the three people.

Will stepped away from the car. He glanced at the man's name tag. "Deputy Jenkins, I'm Will Cooper, the FBI Special Agent in Charge of this district. This is an official FBI investigation."

"Then how come my dispatcher knows nothing about it?"

"There was no reason to contact your department. We should be finished in another hour or so."

From the look on the deputy's face, he didn't like the answer, but he was outranked and knew it. He shot another look at Riley and Cody, then walked away. Leaning against his car, he watched with a phone to his ear.

Cody said, "I fully expect the sheriff will be along shortly."

As time passed, Cody began to hope his prediction was wrong. Then, in the distance, the wail of a siren echoed. Will said, "I'd say you're right. This is your show. How do you want to play this with the sheriff?"

"The less he knows, the better. I'm convinced there is a mole in his department, maybe even the sheriff."

A sardonic grin crossed Will's face. "I'm damn good at stonewalling."

The wail abruptly stopped as another car screeched to a stop behind the deputy's vehicle. Two people erupted, stomping toward them. One was Rutherford, and the other was Bennett.

In a harsh tone, Rutherford said, "Who's in charge here?" His gaze swept over Will and settled on Cody. A vengeful grin lit up his face. "Lightfoot, your ass is grass, and I'm the lawnmower. You've got no right to search a house in my jurisdiction. I'm arresting you on charges of breaking and entering."

Cody, leaning against the car with his arms crossed over his chest, said, "That would be another bad … very bad mistake."

While his tone was low, Will's voice was unyielding as he said, "Sheriff Rutherford, you are not arresting anyone."

Rutherford's angry eyes darted to Will's face. "And just who the hell are you to tell me what I can do and can't do?"

Will pulled out his badge case and flipped it open. "Will Cooper, FBI Special Agent in Charge of the Austin Bureau. As I told your deputy, this is an FBI investigation, and quite frankly, you have no business being here. I suggest you leave."

Dumbfounded, Rutherford gaped at Will. "Uh … uh, you can't do that. I'm the sheriff of this county," he sputtered.

"Yes, I can, and I just did."

Rutherford's hands fisted, and one white-knuckled fist rested on the butt of the gun in a holster dangling from his belt.

Will's eyes flashed to the hand on the gun. "If necessary, my agents will escort you off the property."

Before turning, Rutherford shot a nasty look at Cody and then Riley, standing behind him. "This isn't over, especially for you, Riley."

Anger flashed through Cody like a hot knife through butter. He stepped closer to the man. "Is that a threat, Rutherford? Let me remind you what I told you this morning. If anything happens to Riley, you're going to the head of the list as a suspect. And I've got the clout to make it happen."

Rutherford's lips tightened to a thin line. Hatred flared in his eyes as he turned away, marching back to his vehicle. Bennett shot a hard look at Cody, then at Will, before following his boss. The two sheriff cars peeled away with a squeal of tires.

"You made a bad enemy there," Will said.

With a grim chuckle, Cody said, "I think you're in the same boat."

"Won't be the first or last time," Will observed.

An agent stepped out of the house, slipped off the booties, and trotted across the yard. "Will, we found something."

He handed his boss a sealed clear plastic evidence bag with a piece of paper inside. "This had slid down behind the desk in the living room. It was stuck in the baseboard. It's a list of chemistry textbooks and a formula."

Will glanced at it before passing it to Cody.

Cody studied it before he pulled out his phone and took a picture. "This place is popular with the college kids. Could be one of them left it, though it seems doubtful. I'll send it to Scott."

Will asked, "How's it going in there?"

"So far, this is it. We've found a few fingerprints, which I expect will be the cleaning crew. We're almost finished."

Cody asked, "Any signs of blood?"

"No." The agent turned and headed back to the house, donning another set of booties before walking inside.

Once the agents finished and had loaded their gear, Will secured the house. As they pulled out, the Austin agents went one way and Cody and Riley the other.

In the dark, the hum of the engine was almost mesmerizing. Exhausted, Riley leaned her head against the seat.

Cody glanced at her. "How about I drop you off? Easier than

driving into town to get your car. I'll pick you up in the morning."

She wasn't about to disagree. "I appreciate it." Though she wondered if she'd ever get to sleep. Ever since Riley heard Cody tell the lieutenant there was a bomb attached to his truck, she'd held the terror at bay. Now, it seemed to ripple inside her. A deep sigh erupted.

"You okay?" Cody asked.

"I guess so. I was thinking about what happened."

His hand reached for hers where it lay on the console. "The what-ifs always seem the worst in the wee hours of the morning. I know. Been there, done that."

The gentle tone of his voice and warmth of his hand set off a tingling anticipation. But for what? As chaotic as her emotions were at the moment, this wasn't a path she wanted to go down. Still, she didn't move her hand.

When they reached the house, Cody walked in with her. Before leaving, he checked the rooms, ensuring the windows and doors were locked. He stood on the front porch until he heard the lock click.

As he trotted down the steps to his truck, his thoughts tumbled—his what-if nightmares. Cody had to force himself not to think about what would have happened if he hadn't looked out the window when he did. He knew what a bomb did to a vehicle. They were images he would carry for the rest of his life. This time, it was worse. The killer went after Riley. She'd become more than an assignment, though he wasn't sure he wanted to know why. He just knew he'd do whatever it took to keep her safe.

Chapter 22

Washington, D.C.

Blurry-eyed, Nicki slid off the sofa in the breakroom. She'd spent most of the night altering the search algorithms on her computer, trying to find a match with their victim's face. She'd finally crashed on the couch.

She started the coffee pot, then headed through the office. As she walked by Scott's office, a snore rumbled. When she peeked in, Scott, leaned back in his chair and feet propped on the desk, was sound asleep.

With a grin, Nicki headed out of the office. Bypassing the elevator, she skipped down the stairs to the bottom floor. The gym wouldn't open for another hour, but she had the code to open the door. After a quick shower and fresh clothing, she felt halfway human.

Back upstairs, the office was quiet when she walked in. No sign of Scott. He wasn't in his office, and the breakroom was empty. Figuring he'd done the same as her, headed to the gym to get cleaned up, Nicki poured a cup of coffee. At the sound of the office door closing, she poured a second one.

His hair still damp, Scott stood at his office window, looking down.

"Hey, boss man." She stopped alongside him, handing him a cup.

He gave her a sideways glance as his fingers curled around the handle. "I'd say good morning, but not sure if it is yet." Scott took a deep swig, his gaze returning to the scene below. The morning sun had peeked over the horizon. Cars, bumper to bumper, crawled along the highway.

"It always reminds me of a string of ants," he mused. "When the workday is over, the string reverses itself, crawling back to where they came from. And what have they gained?"

Puzzled, she turned her head to stare at him. Scott was introspective, always keeping his thoughts close to his chest. This wasn't like him at all. She sipped coffee before saying, "An odd thought for this early in the day."

"Probably so, but the image seems so appropriate." He shrugged, shaking off the mood that gripped him. "Cody sent a picture of something they found in the house." Scott stretched his neck. "Dang chair. Not the best place to fall asleep." He sat, tapping the keyboard, bringing up the image.

Nicki leaned over his shoulder to look. "Hmm … chemistry textbooks. College students do rent the place. I wonder what the formula is for."

A thoughtful expression crossed his face. "It's odd. I'd think college kids renting a house would be more interested in other activities than textbooks."

"You're right. They want to party. Send it to me."

In her office, Nicki dropped into the chair, setting her cup aside. When the picture popped up on her computer, she copied the formula, plugged it into the search engine she'd built, and hit enter. Then she settled back, sipping the coffee. Over the rim of the cup, she watched the goblin dancing across the wall-mounted monitor. The goblin vanished, replaced by a leprechaun doing a jig while waving a four-leaf clover over his head. The signal the system had found a match. She hit enter. Mystified, she stared at what appeared on her screen.

Texas

The incessant ring of her phone brought her out of a deep sleep. Groaning, Riley cast a look at the clock. Who the heck was calling this early? The ringing stopped. Grateful, she sank back onto the pillow. Then it started again.

With another groan, she reached for the phone. Ted! Cripes, he must have seen her article.

"I'm here," she mumbled. "I pity any woman you marry. Who wants to get up before the birds are even awake?"

Ted didn't bother to say hello. "I saw your article. What's going on? And don't hold anything back."

"Lord, I wouldn't dream of it since you asked so nicely."

"Riley, if I don't get some straight answers from you, I'm headed to Fredericksburg."

Knowing he'd follow through on the threat, she said, "There's nothing you can do. You've already got the FBI here. Matter of fact, I'm getting quite chummy with the FBI and Austin police."

Wishing she had a cup of coffee before getting into all the details, she gave him the rundown. It wasn't until she finished that he asked, "Do you know the name of the man Cody shot?"

"Eddie Burgess."

"Still no identification on your missing victim, then?"

"Not yet."

"I need to talk to Cody."

"He's picking me up this morning. I left my truck at the newspaper office. I'll tell him. Do you want him to call you?"

"No, I'll call him. I don't want to wait." The line went dead.

She fell back against the pillow. Getting back to sleep was a lost cause. She might as well get dressed.

After a quick shower, she felt somewhat rejuvenated. Dressed in jeans, t-shirt, and vest, she ambled into the kitchen. Without Milo, the house was quiet, too quiet. Riley didn't realize how much she would miss him until he wasn't there.

She started the coffee machine. From the fridge, she grabbed a container of yogurt. Seated at the table, she interspersed spoonfuls with sips of coffee while watching sunlight spread across the backyard. The terror she felt when Cody found the bomb still lingered. So did her attraction for the sexy agent. Pretty dumb when she thought about it. Once this was over, she'd probably never see him again. Not liking the path of her thoughts, Riley gave herself a mental shake.

A quick look at the clock had her pushing back her chair with more force than she intended. "Cripes," she muttered, picking it up. While she'd sat mooning at the table, the time had gotten away from her.

After cleaning up the kitchen, she rushed to her bedroom. She had just tied her boots when she heard a horn honk. Looking out the window brought a warm glow, which she resolutely ignored. The rush to grab the backpack and race out the door was just because she didn't want to keep him waiting.

With a grin, she hopped inside. As she buckled her seatbelt, she said, "You're right on time."

"Did you think I wouldn't be?"

"I absolutely expected you would." She chuckled.

He tossed her an odd look but didn't comment as he pulled onto the highway.

"Have you heard anything from your boss about the note found in the house?"

"No, he hasn't called. I did get an early morning call from your brother."

"I got one too." She gave him a wary look. "And?"

Cody shrugged. "He's worried, and rightfully so."

She groaned.

"Hey, he's a big brother. He's allowed to worry."

"I know, but sometimes, it gets excessive."

"He was ready to leave Dallas, but I convinced him otherwise."

"Thank you for that. I keep telling him there's nothing he can do here."

"Kind of what I told him, as tactfully as I could."

"With Ted, sometimes tact doesn't work. He's hard-headed."

"Hmm … like his sister." Cody laughed.

She sniffed, ignoring the comment. "What's on our agenda other than stopping by the newspaper office?"

"I need to go back to the hotel. Then, I want to research Burgess. Figured I could do it at your office. I'd also like to take a closer look at your pictures from yesterday."

As soon as they parked in front of the newspaper office and Cody turned off the engine, she heard Milo.

Cody opened his door. "I swear that dog operates on another level. There is no way he could know you are out here."

"He does seem to have a sixth sense." She gathered up her bag and hopped out of the truck.

Cody immediately headed to her vehicle, parked a few spaces away. The terror that had laid in her gut like lead blossomed. She knew what he was looking for. With bated breath, she watched as he dropped to the ground, sliding underneath her truck.

The door to the office opened. Susan stood in the doorway, blocking Milo from charging outside. Interspersing yips with sharp barks, the dog strained to push past Susan. "A few minutes ago, he jumped up, barking as he headed to the door. How he knew, I don't have a clue. What's going on?" she asked. "Where's Cody?"

Not taking her eyes off her truck, Riley said, "Milo, sit." The dog sat, though his body quivered with tension. Riley motioned to her truck.

Susan's gaze shifted. Her face tightened in fear. "Oh, my gosh. You don't think …" She stopped as Cody crawled out and stood.

With a grim look, he opened his hand. On the palm was a small object. "No bomb, but another tracking device." He dropped it, stomping on it with his boot.

Bewildered, Susan said, "Another? What do you mean?"

Riley said, "Let's go inside. I'll explain." Milo woofed and twirled as she stepped through the doorway, his tail flying high. She hunkered down to hug him. "Yes, I know you are happy." She laughed, rubbing his head. "Oh, you are such a good, good dog." His nose nuzzled her neck. "Yes, I love you too." She stood.

Behind her, Cody's laughter rumbled. "I hate to say it, but any man in your life may have to take a back seat to a dog."

Milo darted toward him. He sat.

"Feeling bad about forgetting me, are you?" Cody said.

Milo woofed, lifting a paw. Chuckling, Cody gave it a shake.

Susan said, "Good to see both of you. You had quite a trip to Austin."

Riley dropped her bag on a desk. "We did. I still haven't recovered. Dang, that coffee smells good." She poured a cup and took a deep swig. "Hmm … good. Cody, you want a cup?"

Still occupied with Milo, he said, "Not yet. I need to get back to the hotel and check out."

Her eyes narrowed as she stared at him. Though she had a sneaky suspicion about his answer, Riley asked, "And where do you plan to stay?"

With a grin, he said, "Your house."

Riley grumbled, "Is staying at my house how you convinced Ted?"

"He thought it was a good idea."

Riley glared at him.

Susan beamed. "You didn't ask my opinion, but I'm offering it anyway. That's a really dang good idea. Riley, you listen to him."

Riley groaned. "Not you, too."

"You don't need to be staying out there by yourself." With a grim look, she added, "Riley, someone broke into your house. Someone tried to kill you. And don't forget that same someone probably tried to poison Milo. You need all the protection you can get."

Still grumbling, she muttered, "I just hate depending on someone."

"Get over it. Now, let's get to work. I want to send out an update about what happened in Austin."

With a twinkle in his eye, Cody said, "Uh … can I take Milo?"

At the sound of his name, Milo's ears perked up. He woofed, stood, and pranced over to Cody, where he sat, staring up at him with an adoring look.

Riley muttered, "Traitor. Yes, you can go."

Milo's tail thumped the floor. Cody grabbed the leash, and the two headed out the door.

"He's not what I expected for an FBI agent," Susan mused. "Is he married?"

"Cripes, Susan. Don't go matchmaking on me."

"Just asking. Inquiring minds want to know." Her hand swirled in the air. "Well, is he?"

"No, he isn't. Not that it makes any difference."

Susan's lips twitched in a sly smile, though all she said was, "I'd like to see the pictures from yesterday."

"I've got them on a thumb drive." Riley reached into her bag, unzipping the inner pocket where she had stashed the device. She handed it to Susan, who headed to her office.

Riley refilled her cup before settling into the chair in front of Susan's desk.

"I still haven't heard all the details," Susan said. She inserted the drive and transferred the file. While Riley talked, Susan slowly looked at the pictures. The only moment that lightened the grim expression on her face was when Riley reached the part about Rutherford showing up.

"I'd like to have seen that. Rutherford doesn't like to have his ears pinned back."

Susan turned her attention back to the photos. "Over the years, I've seen many pictures of the damage one of these things can cause. Never had the possibility of one coming this close to home. This is so senseless. So, why?" On her screen was a close-up of Cody holding the device as he crawled out from under the truck.

Chapter 23

Once Milo was settled in the backseat, Cody called his boss. When Scott answered, Cody said, "Our bomber has been active. I found a tracking device on Riley's truck."

"I had a feeling this was more bad news. I don't like how this is escalating. Someone is determined to take the two of you out of the picture. It would certainly slow down the investigation. Since time seems to be the motivation, you are both still in danger."

"A point her brother and I discussed. I'm moving into her house."

Scott grunted. "Wise move. Some interesting details on Bennett popped up. Seems he's moved around, going from agency to agency. He hired on with the sheriff's department about six months ago."

"Any reason why he's shifting agencies?"

"Nothing official. Nicki is going to contact the agencies to find out why he left. She's added what you found in the house to her research."

"Chemistry books and a formula did seem out of place in a party house for college students, though I guess it's possible."

By the time the call was finished, Cody had arrived at his hotel. What few items he'd left in his room were quickly gathered up and stowed in his truck. Before leaving, he took Milo to the small grassy section reserved for dogs. After sniffing and marking a few spots, Milo happily pranced to the truck.

Cody's phone rang as he slid behind the wheel. "Lightfoot," he answered.

"Ted Phillips. I've got some information for you. Eddie Burgess is from Dallas. It looks like he moved to Austin about six months ago. He's been in and out of jail since he was a juvie. Mostly drugs and assaults. He was a suspect in a drive-by gang shooting, which didn't stick."

"What happened?"

"Witness disappeared."

"Convenient."

"The driver of the car was Pablo Hernandez, an enforcer for the Camargo drug cartel. Burgess was riding shotgun."

Cody's instincts kicked into high gear. "That puts a whole new spin on whatever is going down."

"I thought the same. I contacted a couple of detectives in the narcotics division. Word is Burgess was moving up in the cartel. I sent what I found to your unit, though I imagine Nicki has already found most of it."

"Check out another name for me. Mickey Bennett. I'd be interested if your department had any contact with him. He works for the sheriff's department. The man's got an attitude. I'm wondering why. Nicki ran him, found out he's moved from agency to agency. Bennett hired on here about six months ago."

"Six months."

"Yeah. About the same time Burgess moved to Austin."

Ted said, "I don't like coincidences. I'll get back to you."

The line disconnected.

On the way back to the newspaper office, Cody didn't like the direction of his thoughts. While he'd never had any dealings with the cartel, he knew their reputation. Planting a bomb was one of their more humane ways of killing people.

After parking in front of the newspaper office, he opened the back door to let Milo hop out. The dog raced to the front door, where he plunked down, patiently sitting until Cody caught up with him.

Inside, Milo woofed as he trotted to where Riley was seated at one of the desks. She reached down to give his head a good rub. "Did you have a good time?" Milo barked.

Cody laid his laptop on the other desk and walked to the coffee pot. "How are you coming with the article?" He filled a cup.

"Susan just sent it."

Susan spoke up. "Since it seems we have some downtime, is anyone interested in lunch? There is a deli close by that delivers."

Seated in front of his computer, he sipped before saying, "Sounds good. I'm not particular." He typed his report to Scott, adding the cartel connection from his conversation with Ted. Once it was gone, he turned his attention to the folder with Riley's pictures of the bomb.

Sipping the coffee, he slowly studied each picture. Many were of the device, but interspersed were pictures of the crowd and police, from a distance and close up. Riley had done an amazing job of capturing the emotion on their faces. It was these that garnered his attention. He scrutinized each one, magnifying the image before moving to the next.

Peering over his shoulder, Riley asked, "What are you looking for?"

"I'm interested in who was in the crowd."

"Finding anyone you recognize?" she asked.

"Not so far."

Susan asked, "Who are you looking for?"

"Whoever called that phone after I had detached it from the explosive."

A look of horror crossed Susan's face. "You never said …"

The door opened. A teenager carrying a sack labeled *Artful Deli* walked in. After a short discussion on who would pay, Cody finally conceded the battle to Susan.

For the rest of the afternoon, Cody and Riley studied the pictures she took at the restaurant. They finally had to admit that if the caller was in the crowd, they couldn't identify him. While Riley worked on another article, Cody turned his attention to researching Burgess. Ted's information about the cartel was unexpected and extremely disturbing. He hadn't wanted to mention it to Riley or Susan. When he called his old office, he stepped outside on the pretext of taking Milo for a walk. What he learned added to his anxiety.

Washington, D.C.

Scott stood at the window, staring at the faint illumination from street lights as the sun slowly disappeared on the horizon. His thoughts circled over the emails and reports he'd received. The latest intel from Ted about the connection to one of the deadliest drug cartels was a kick to the gut. Every instinct said time was running out.

"Bingo!" Nicki's victorious shout echoed in the office. He hustled into Nicki's office.

She flipped him a high five as he stopped alongside her chair. "I found him."

On the large monitor on her wall was a picture of a group of people. Using her laser pointer, she aimed it at the head of a person standing at the back. "Meet our victim, Gary Jamison, a chemist at the R&B Lab near Austin." She magnified the picture.

Nicki's reconstruction was almost on the money for accuracy, Scott realized as he studied the face.

"This may be the only picture of the guy. Talk about being camera-shy and no social media presence. This picture was taken at a conference on drug trends six months ago."

"How the devil did you find him?"

"From the note Cody sent you. It was a snippet of a formula for a drug to treat nerve diseases. I added nerve drugs to the parameters in my search program and found him."

"I need everything you can get on R&B Lab and Jamison."

Nicki smirked. "Already on it, boss man. Check your computer. About Bennett, I contacted the agencies where he'd worked before. At all of them, he just up and quit. No reason given."

Scott rushed back to his office. On his computer, he accessed Nicki's data. He settled back and began to read. R&B Lab, a small, privately owned company, was located about halfway between Austin and Fredericksburg. The company had already been recognized for its work in plant-based drugs for neurological diseases, with a new patent pending.

Scott steadily worked through article after article, absorbing the company's details. In none of them could he find a reason for Jamison's death, let alone the removal of an eye.

At the drug conference, Jamison had been part of a team from the company presenting a paper on their new drug. The article praised the drug for its lack of side effects, an ongoing problem with most drugs.

Nicki's voice rang out. "Just sent you a list of employees and a schematic of the building."

After perusing the list, he sent Cody an email, then hit the speed dial on his phone.

When Cody answered, Scott said, "Our mystery man is no longer a mystery. Nicki found a picture of him at a drug conference. His name is Gary Jamison. He was a chemist working at a drug company, R&B Lab. The company is headquartered about thirty miles east of Fredericksburg."

Cody said, "Another link to drugs. How did she find him?"

"The paper Will's agent found in the house was a part of a drug formula. She added nerve drugs to her search. I'm sending you what I've got so far. Get someone to shut down access to their security system."

"I'll handle it. Scott, after I talked to Ted, I called an agent I worked with in Las Vegas. He recognized Burgess' name. He said he runs with a couple of cartel enforcers, Stan Delbert and El Sombra, the shadow man. No one knows his name or even what he looks like, but he's their top assassin. I'll be in touch once I've contacted someone at the lab." Cody disconnected.

Scott's next call was to Will. When the man answered, he said, "We've got an identification." After explaining, Scott asked, "Know anything about R&B Lab?"

"Never heard of them. I'll start on my end, see what I can dig up. I'll get back to you," Will told him.

Scott turned back to his computer. It was going to be another long night.

Chapter 24

Cody pocketed the phone. Wide-eyed, Susan and Riley, seated in nearby chairs, had avidly listened to his end of the conversation.

"We've got an identification, Gary Jamison. He worked for a drug company." He quickly filled them in on the details. "I've got to locate someone who can open the building and shut down their security access for Jamison."

"Dang, that company isn't that far away. Why hasn't someone come forward to identify him?" Riley said.

Susan exclaimed, "I want to know more about this cartel connection, and the two men, Delbert and El Sombra, but I'll wait."

Cody booted his laptop, accessing the email from Scott. He studied the blueprint of the building before perusing the employee list. "Thank god for small favors. There are telephone numbers. Zachery Warner is the CEO." Cody tapped a number on his phone.

"Will Cooper."

"Will, Cody Lightfoot. Have you read Scott's latest email with the list of employees?"

"Yes."

"I've got to get someone who can access the security system to meet me. I may need you to verify my identity. I'm starting with Warner, the CEO. I'm headed to the lab. And I need a search warrant for Jamison's apartment. Scott included the address."

"I'm already working on the warrant." The line went dead.

Before shutting down the computer, Cody pulled up a satellite image of the location. R&B was set back a considerable distance from the highway. The parking lot spanned the length of the single-story, U-shaped structure. Heavy woods encircled the sides and back of the building. From the schematic Scott sent, Cody knew the center of the building and one wing housed the offices, while the other wing was the laboratory. With the image locked into his memory, he shut down the computer. Rising, he picked it up. "I'll call as soon as I know something."

"I'm going with you." Riley grabbed the backpack, slinging it over her shoulder.

His tone was firm as Cody said, "No. It's best if you stay here. After what happened in Austin, it's too risky."

With a pugnacious expression, her fisted hands on her hips, she said, "You've got two choices. Either I go with you, or I follow in my truck."

Susan spoke up. "You can leave Milo with me. I'll stay here until I hear from you."

Faced with two resolute women, a prudent man didn't argue. With a shrug of resignation, he said, "Let's go."

Outside, Riley ran toward her truck. Over her shoulder, she shouted, "I need to get something." Clicking open the door lock, she opened the passenger door and leaned across the seat. From inside the console, she pulled out a pistol in a holster and a belt. Brushing back the vest, she threaded the belt through the loops on the waistband of her jeans, then clipped the holster to the belt, tugging to be sure it was tight against her hip. She grabbed the extra magazine from the console and stuck it into a back pocket.

She trotted back to Cody's truck and slid inside.

He eyed her with a wary look. "Did I just see you grab a gun?"

She shot him a smug look. "Dang straight you did. And don't think I don't know how to use it. My dad, then Ted made sure of that. One of these days, I'll take you out to the range. See who's the better shot."

"Dare I ask if you've got a license to carry it?"

"Of course I do."

Suppressing a groan, Cody started the engine. While Riley buckled her seatbelt, he programmed the GPS with the address for the lab before connecting his phone to the truck's computer. As he pulled out of the parking lot, he called the number for Warner. After several rings, the call rolled to voice mail.

"Mr. Warner. This is FBI Special Agent Cody Lightfoot. It is imperative I speak to you. To confirm my identity, please call the FBI Special Agent in Charge of the Austin Bureau, Will Cooper." Cody rattled off Will's number, then added his own.

Next, he called Norton Johnston, the vice president. It rolled to voice mail. Cody left the same message, then called Brewster Cavanaugh, the head chemist and two other personnel. It wasn't until he reached an executive assistant that a woman answered.

"Ms. Davis. This is FBI Special Agent Cody Lightfoot. It is imperative I contact someone in your company who can access the security system."

"What is this? Some kind of joke?"

"No, ma'am. I am deadly serious. I have a number for you to call to verify my identity. It is Will Cooper, Special Agent in Charge of the Austin FBI Bureau. Please write this number down and then contact someone to meet me at the lab. This is extremely urgent. I will be there within thirty minutes or so."

When he didn't hear anything, he asked, "Ms. Davis, did you get the information?"

"Yes. Though this is probably nothing but some type of scam." She disconnected.

Riley said, "How did you remember all those phone numbers Scott sent you? You didn't even write them down."

"I'm good at remembering details."

Keeping an eye on the rearview mirror, Cody weaved around the evening traffic, heading out of town. He'd just passed the city limits sign when his phone rang.

"Agent Lightfoot, this is Zachery Warner. I just spoke with Agent Cooper. He said you would explain."

"Mr. Warner, do you use iris scans at your facility?"

"Yes, we do. What's going on?"

"How soon can you get someone to your building? I'm leaving Fredericksburg and will be there in about twenty minutes. I need access to your security system. I don't want to explain over the phone."

"It will take me thirty or so minutes to get there." The line went dead.

While listening to Cody's calls, Riley pondered what they'd learned. Their victim was a chemist. She couldn't see a connection unless it was a grand scheme to steal drugs, which didn't make a lot of sense.

Once Cody finished, she voiced her thoughts. "We're missing a piece of the puzzle. This still doesn't make sense. Why such an elaborate scheme?"

"Let's hope we can find the missing piece when we get there."

Once they cleared the city limits, he sped up until he turned onto the road leading to the lab. The truck's headlights were two solitary pools of light in the pitch-black night. As the satellite image of a parking lot with several light poles flashed in his mind, a faint stirring of alarm trickled over him. The GPS showed the driveway just ahead. His gaze shifted over the terrain. The trickle surged at the sight of pinpoints of lights flicking on and off.

Cody kept driving while curses rolled in his thoughts. It wasn't likely it was Warner or one of his personnel. His gut told him he had just landed in the middle of whatever was going down. He should have tied Riley to a chair and taken her truck keys.

Riley had also seen the lights. "It looks like Mr. Warner is already here. Hey, you just missed the driveway."

"I know. We've got a problem. I don't think it is Warner or one of his employees."

The grim tone in his voice set her pulse racing. Riley turned her head to look over her shoulder at the building as they passed.

"Uh … what do we do now?"

"I'm going to find a place to park and go back on foot."

Ahead was an intersection. Cody turned, stopping on the shoulder. "Stay in the truck."

Riley snorted. "Forget that. You need backup, and I'm all you've got."

After a muffled curse, Cody said, "If I tell you to do something, you do it. No questions. Make sure your phone is off. Don't slam the door shut." He pulled his phone from his pocket, tapped it, then reached to turn off the overhead light.

"Understood." She quickly turned the phone off. Before opening the door, she dug inside her backpack. "I've got a flashlight."

"Keep it in your left hand, and don't use it unless I tell you."

She hopped out, easing the door back, though she didn't shut it.

"Stay behind me," Cody whispered. He climbed over the bar ditch, heading into the woods.

The moon rising on the horizon barely provided enough light to see the dark shape in front of her. While she stumbled behind Cody, she wondered how the devil the man could see where he was going.

He never made a misstep. She couldn't even hear his footsteps while hers crunched dried leaves.

Cody abruptly stopped. She slithered alongside him. Ahead, Riley could see the outline of the building and a van parked in front. An occasional light flashed inside.

He leaned over to whisper in her ear. "I'm going to disable the vehicle. Stay here." He glided into the darkness.

A cold chill settled between her shoulders. Her heart thudded from a fear unlike anything Riley had ever felt.

With his gun tightly clasped, Cody moved with a stealth honed from his military days. He eased across the parking lot, but his luck ran out when two men exited the building. One headed toward the van, and the other, holding a flashlight and a box tucked under his arm, fiddled with the door.

Stuck in the middle of the parking lot, Cody shouted, "FBI. Put your hands up."

The first man spun, firing wildly. Cody shot back. Even as the man fell to the ground, Cody was already twisting toward the second man. Too late, he didn't have a shot. The man disappeared on the other side of the van. Cody raced toward it. The engine roared, wheels spun, spitting gravel as the driver backed up, then skidded out of the parking lot. Cody repeatedly fired, though the van kept going.

Behind him, Riley shouted, "Cody."

"I'm okay." Cursing, he ran to the man on the ground. He pulled a flashlight from the side pocket of his pants. Face down, the man lay in a pool of blood, his gun a few feet away. Cody holstered his gun, then knelt, feeling for a pulse.

Riley slid to a stop beside him. "Is he dead?"

"Yes." He rose, moving to the front door. The key was still in the lock, and the door was unlocked. Stepping inside, he flashed his light around, spotting the bank of switches near the door. He flipped them. Lights lit up a small reception area and the parking lot.

Before walking out, he called Will. When the man answered, Cody said, "Two men broke into the lab. One is dead. It's not a good idea to call the sheriff."

"I agree," Will told him. "What happened to the second man?"

"Got away in a van."

"Did you get the number on the license plate?"

"No, it was too dark to see."

"I'll get a team headed your way." He disconnected.

Cody headed out the door to where Riley still stared at the man.

"Will is sending a team of agents. Nothing we can do except wait. Can you find your way back to the truck and bring it around?'

When she didn't answer, he put his hand on her shoulder. "Riley, are you okay?"

He finally broke through the shock. Wide-eyed, she looked at him. "Uh … sure."

"Don't call Susan with the story. I want to keep a lid on this until we figure out what's going on." He handed her the keys.

The adrenaline still pumping in her system propelled her toward the truck, making the trip back seem a lot shorter.

While he waited, Cody knelt on one knee alongside the body, careful to avoid the blood staining the cement. Unshaven, with stringy hair and arms covered with tattoos, the dead man looked like a typical street thug. The gloved hands told him it was a waste of time to check for fingerprints inside the building.

Cody patted the man's pockets. Feeling a bulge in one, he eased out a wallet. He flipped it open and read the name on the driver's license. His sense of trepidation deepened. He recognized the name. The man lying at his feet wasn't a typical street thug. It was Stan Delbert, an enforcer for the Camargo cartel.

****

In the woods bordering the parking lot, a figure slithered around trees. A dark shadow living up to his name, El Sombra. He'd doubled back after leaving the van hidden behind an old barn. As he silently slipped through the woods, acid burned his gut. There was only one reason for tonight's fiasco, one that cost him another man. Jamison had been identified. At least they'd accomplished what they had to do inside the lab. No one would ever know unless Stan talked. To make sure, he had to find out if he was alive. While he didn't believe Stan would tell the cops anything, he couldn't risk it. If his partner was still alive, he had to kill him.

By the time he was close enough to see, lights lit up the parking lot. Judging by the actions of the agent bent over the body, Stan was dead. El Sombra felt no relief at not having to kill him. After all, it was business, not personal. The agent straightened. Light reflected off a face that triggered another surge of rage. Lightfoot!

The agent should be dead, killed by the bomb on his truck. Instead, he killed two of his men. His hand curled around the butt of the gun stuck in his waistband. Lightfoot was personal. The agent had been a thorn in his side since he hit town.

He braced his arm against the tree to steady the gun. Before he could fire, a vehicle raced up the driveway, forcing him to duck back to avoid the flash of headlights. The driver angled the truck along the side of the parking lot, blocking his shot.

Cursing the bad luck that continued to plague him, he started to turn away, then caught a glimpse of the driver. Exhilaration mixed with the rage eating away at him. The night wouldn't be a total loss after all. If it hadn't been for the woman and her damn dog, Jamison's body would never have been found. When Phillips stepped out of the truck, he couldn't miss.

His irritation built as he impatiently waited. The damn woman was on the phone. From his position, he didn't have a clear shot at her inside the truck. In the distance, he heard sirens. Still, he waited. His hand trembled from the urge to pull the trigger. As the sounds grew louder, he couldn't risk waiting. He had to leave. It was more important to get rid of the container with the eye and ditch the van he'd stolen.

He ran, darting around the trees. Another failure pushed the acid into his throat. The woman and the dog, like Lightfoot, were personal. Next time, he wouldn't miss. No one defied El Sombra and got away with it.

Chapter 25

Parked on the far side of the lot where the truck wouldn't be in the way, Riley had checked her phone. She'd missed two calls from Susan and an urgent voicemail to call.

When Susan answered, her voice quivered with anxiety. "Riley, is everything all right? I got worried when you didn't answer. Milo is going crazy, howling and jumping at the door. I don't know what's wrong with him."

In the background, Riley could hear Milo howling. "I had the phone turned off."

"What should I do? I've tried everything, even bribing him with his favorite biscuit. Nothing is working."

"I don't know. I've never known him to act like this."

"Are you sure there isn't anything wrong? Something you're not telling me?"

"I'm fine. Explanations will have to wait. Put me on speakerphone. Maybe I can calm him."

"I'm willing to try anything. I'm really worried about him. I've been afraid he'd hurt himself. Talk to him."

"Milo, sit." The dog howled, a spine-chilling sound. Abruptly, it stopped.

"Dang," Susan said. "He sat. He's panting, looking at me like nothing was wrong. This is weird, way too weird."

Riley heard sirens. The agents were about to arrive. "Are you sure you want to keep him tonight? It will be late, but I can stop by your house."

Susan said, "Of course, he can stay with me. But you really have my curiosity going."

Riley had to grin. Susan was like a bulldog when she scented a story. She wouldn't let go. "I'll see you in the morning." She disconnected before Susan could interrogate her further. However, she did have to wonder what got into Milo. *Surely, he hadn't been able to sense …,* the thought was cut off as a car raced up the driveway, screeching to a stop, followed by several vehicles, including a van and ambulance. She hopped out of the truck.

The driver erupted from the first car, running toward Cody. He shouted, "Are you Agent Lightfoot?"

Before Cody could respond, the man spotted the body. "Good god. Is he dead? What happened?" Then he looked at the front doors. "Why are the inside lights on?"

Will Cooper walked up.

"You made good time," Cody told him.

"When needs drive or some such nonsense," Will said.

Cody turned to the man, who stared down at the body with a look of disbelief.

"Are you Zachery Warner?"

The man looked up as he nodded.

"I'm Cody Lightfoot. This is Agent Will Cooper."

"I hope one of you can tell me why I have a dead man in my parking lot. Who is he?"

Cody said, "He's one of two men who broke into the lab."

"Good lord! I've got to check the inside." He started toward the front door.

Cody stopped him. "You can't go inside. It's a crime scene."

"Why would someone break in?" Baffled, the man thrust a hand through his hair. "I don't understand any of this."

Will knelt, examining the man's face. "Never seen him before."

Cody handed him the wallet. "His ID is inside."

Will flipped it open. After a quick glance, he grimaced, looking at Cody, who only nodded.

Warner said, "Well, who is he? Why would he break into my building?"

Cody said, "At this point, we don't know. We need you to wait here until we can check the inside."

As Will turned to walk toward the door, an eyebrow cocked when he spotted Riley standing beside Cody's truck. "I didn't know you were here."

As she walked up, Will said, "This time, no camera."

Warner exclaimed, "What did he mean by camera? Who are you?"

"Riley Phillips, a reporter with the *Fredericksburg Register*."

"For cripes sake, can this get any worse? Now, I've got a dang reporter here."

Before opening the door, Will spotted the key. "Interesting."

"Yeah. The second man didn't get a chance to lock the door. I turned on the lights."

Will signaled to one of his agents, pointing to the key.

Once inside, Will asked, "What do you know about Delbert?"

"His name cropped up in a number of homicides in Vegas, but there was never any evidence to connect him to the killings. Have you crossed paths with him?"

His hands in his pockets, Will rocked back on his feet. "By name only. Rumor has it he's one of the cartel's top hit men, second only to El Sombra."

"The shadow man. As deadly of a killer as ever came out of a cartel. His name came up a few times, too. No one knows what he looks like, and we never had a witness who lived to identify him." Cody looked out the door to see an agent snapping pictures of the body. "Why do I have this nasty feeling El Sombra was the other man?"

"Probably because it's true. The two ran together."

"Earlier today, I called an agent I worked with in Vegas. I ran Burgess' name by him and found out Burgess was also running with Delbert and El Sombra. Which confirms what Ted Phillips told me. He'd heard Burgess was moving up the chain in the cartel."

A worried look settled on Will's face. "Two dead men, both enforcers for the cartel. Why would the cartel be interested in a small drug company?" He squared his shoulders. "Let's see if we can find out. I'll get Warner in here."

An agent walked in and handed Will an evidence bag containing a key. "It's clean. What about prints in here?"

Will glanced at it and handed the bag to Cody, who did the same before giving it to the agent.

After introducing the agent, Phil Ketloff, Will said, "Probably a waste of time since the dead man was gloved, but tell Hardy, when he's done with the body, I want pictures of the inside of the building. Warner and Riley can come inside."

Riley walked in, followed by Warner and another man in his middle forties with a troubled expression. Riley settled in a chair behind the receptionist's desk. It was the best place to not be in the way.

Warner said, "This is Vice President Norton Johnston."

After the introductions, Cody asked, "Mr. Warner, do you leave the parking lot lights on?"

"Yes, we do. It's for the safety of the employees. It's not unusual for someone to work late in the lab. The lights are on a timer, though the system can be overridden by the switch on the wall."

"What type of security other than the iris scan do you have? Any cameras?" Cody asked.

Warner shot a disgruntled look at Johnston. "No, we don't. I didn't think we needed anything else."

Will asked, "Do you see anything disturbed in here?"

Warner looked around. "No."

Cody, remembering the layout of the building, said, "Let's check the rest of the building starting with this side." Warner, followed by Johnson, led the way. Two agents trailed behind Cody and Will as the group quickly checked offices.

Unable to find anything out of place, Warner said, "There really isn't any point in checking the lab. Whoever broke in couldn't get inside. Access is restricted to a few personnel."

Not wanting to get into the details to correct him, Cody said, "We need to make sure." When they reached the lab, they waited while one of Will's agents dusted the scanning device and door for prints. When the agent finished, he said, "About what I expected. Nothing but smudges."

Johnston stepped up to the iris scanner, pressing his face against it. A few seconds later, the door clicked.

Cody opened it to step inside a spacious room about half the size of the entire building. Microscopes and medical equipment covered multiple counters in the center of the room. Several small offices lined one wall. Bookshelves, overflowing with books, covered another wall. At the back were two large metal doors.

"Whose offices are these?" Cody asked.

"The chemists."

"Is one Gary Jamison?"

"Yes. Why do you want to know?"

"Once we finish in here, I'll explain. Which office is his?"

Warner pointed. Cody walked inside, followed by Warner. A desk with a computer faced the window that overlooked the parking lot. On each side were bookcases and file cabinets. "Would you know if anything is missing?" he asked, eyeing the bookcases.

"I wouldn't," Warner said.

"Who would?"

"Maybe one of the other chemists or Brewster Cavanaugh. He's the head of the lab."

Making a mental note to follow up, Cody walked out. "What are those large doors at the back of the room?"

Johnston said, "A storage unit. It's where we keep chemicals and sample drugs."

Will and Cody wandered along the aisles separating the counters, scrutinizing what was on top of them as they headed toward the back of the room.

"Does anything look out of place?" Cody asked.

Johnston and Warner looked around.

Warner answered, "Not that I can see, but then I'm not in here daily to know."

"I was in here today," Johnston said. "I don't see anything has been disturbed."

"Let's look at the storage unit," Will told them.

Johnston opened one of the large doors. Inside, he flipped a switch, and bright overhead lights lit up the room. Rows of shelving ran along the walls and in the center of the room. Most were filled with varying sizes of plastic containers, boxes, and glass jars. On one shelf, four containers held glass vials inserted into individual compartments.

Cody stepped over to look at them. "What are these?"

Warner said, "Doses for a group of volunteers for the test phase of a new drug we have developed. Tomorrow morning, the vials will be transported to a clinic in Austin for the start of the FDA, Food and Drug Administration's trial."

Cody's eyes roamed over the vials, slowly studying each container. "How many?"

"There are eighty-seven in the test group, but we've prepared ninety doses. The extra vials are for the FDA."

"Could someone have tampered with them?"

"Impossible." Warner reached for one of the vials, holding it up. "Each label has a distinct number and is sealed with a uniquely designed cap. Any attempt to open the vial will break the seal. The vial is never opened. A needle is inserted through the cap to withdraw the liquid. Any needle marks would be clearly visible."

Cody took another lingering look at the vials.

Will said, "Let's go to the conference room."

Chapter 26

A frown crossed Warner's face when Riley entered the conference room. "I object to the presence of a reporter."

Cody said, "Nothing will be printed without the permission of the FBI."

Warner flashed a razor-sharp look at Riley. "Is that correct, Ms. Phillips?" he snapped.

Her shoulders squared as Riley faced Warner. While a spurt of anger flicked through her, she understood his concern. "I can assure you the FBI has my and my newspaper's full cooperation."

In a calm, controlled tone, Cody said, "What we haven't had a chance to tell you is that Riley is the reason we are here."

His face flushed with ire and frustration, Warner exclaimed, "What do you mean, she's the reason?" His voice rose. "I have a dead man in my parking lot, my building broken into, FBI agents crawling all over the place, and now you tell me *she's* the reason. Someone had better have a good explanation."

Cody said, "If everyone will take a seat, I'll explain."

As Cody talked, astonishment, then disbelief, settled on the faces of the two men.

Warner wiped his brow. "Why would someone kill Jamison and steal his eye?" A look of horror flashed across his face. "Don't tell me you think someone used his eye to access the lab."

"That is exactly what we believe. Does your system maintain a log of entries?"

"Yes. I need my laptop." With a quick shove of his chair, Johnston rushed out the door. When he returned, he opened the laptop he carried, tapping the keyboard. A few seconds later, his eyes widened. The color leached from his face. "My god, he's right. A dead man was in the lab tonight."

Warner shook his head as if he still couldn't assimilate what he'd heard. "How is that possible? How could a dead man's eye be used?"

"A cadaver eye, if properly stored, can be used for up to three weeks after death." Cody's eyes flicked toward Riley. "We don't understand why no one came forward when his picture was published in Riley's newspaper and online. The major news stations picked up Riley's article."

Warner said, "I never saw it, and I guess none of my staff did either. We had no reason to believe he was missing. Gary has …" he cleared his throat, "was on vacation. Since he wasn't involved in the testing phase, Gary asked if he could use the vacation time he had accrued, which was six weeks."

"When was the last time either of you saw Jamison?"

Warner spoke up. "It was on a Sunday afternoon. I stopped by the office, and Gary was coming out the front door. I was surprised to see him since he'd left on vacation on Friday. Gary said he forgot some of his personal items and stopped by to pick them up. He had a satchel over his shoulder. It appeared to be full."

"Did he say anything about his plans?"

"No. Gary didn't talk much about his personal life."

Cody looked at Johnston.

He said, "I stopped by his office the last day he worked. I asked if he had anything special planned for his vacation. He told me no. He was just going to hang out."

"When did he ask for vacation time?"

Warner pursed his lips as he thought. "About two months ago. It was the same day we received final confirmation of our trial date from the FDA. I remember Gary commented that he wouldn't be needed, now that we had a date."

"How many times was Jamison in the lab after he left?"

Johnston tapped the keyboard, studying the screen before he pulled a notepad from a stack in the center of the table toward him and wrote.

He tore off the paper and slid it across the desk to Cody. "Four times. Those are the dates and times. The first date is the Sunday Zachery saw him."

Cody quickly scanned them before passing the paper to Will. "Since he was on vacation, did you ever question why he was in the lab?"

Johnston said, "I didn't know it. We've never had a problem, so there was never a reason to check the logs."

"There's something else you should know," Warner said. "He didn't have a key." With a look of chagrin, he said, "That Sunday, I asked for his key. I stuck it in my desk drawer and forgot about it."

His face troubled, Johnston said, "Then how did Gary or the men who broke in tonight get into the building?"

Cody said, "They had a key. Mr. Warner, was there a reason you asked for the key?"

The man hesitated before saying, "I'm not sure. It might have been because he would be gone for six weeks. There wasn't any reason for him to have access."

"Was his demeanor normal?" Cody asked.

"Come to think of it, it wasn't. He was somewhat nervous, hurrying to explain why he was in the building on a Sunday. Looking back on the encounter, I don't think he expected to see me."

"Who else has keys to the building?"

Johnston said, "Most of the staff. The keys are numbered and assigned to specific personnel. I printed the list." He rose and left the room.

Cody said, "May I see your key, Mr. Warner?"

Warner pulled a set of keys from his pants pocket, selecting one to hand to Cody.

After looking at it, Cody passed it to Will. "The one used tonight didn't have a number. It was a copy."

Johnston walked in and handed a piece of paper to Cody.

Warner's face tightened. "If the key was a copy, one of our personnel must be involved. How else could the men get a key?"

Cody said, "Something we need to find out. Who has access to your computer system?"

Warner said, "We have a dual system. One is for the company's administration. The other has all the records for the development and production of RB2. Like the lab, it's restricted to a few personnel."

Cody's brow wrinkled as he thought. "Can the lab system be accessed by a computer outside of the lab?"

Warner shook his head. "No."

"If someone accessed the drug program, what damage could they do?"

Warner said, "If the formula was altered and we didn't know it, it would be disastrous. Throughout the FDA process, the drug is independently analyzed, and the results are compared to the documentation submitted by the drug company. Not only would the paperwork not match, but the next round of production would be different. Such a disaster would stop the FDA process and put my company out of business."

Will leaned forward. "Can you tell if someone accessed your

computer system?"

Johnston answered, "No. Limiting access to the room seemed to be sufficient security."

"Obviously, we need to reexamine our security system. It looks like we've got holes." Warner's hand flashed up before Johnston could say anything. "I know. You don't need to tell me I told you so." His gaze flicked from Will to Cody. "For the last year, Norton has tried to convince me we needed to beef up our security."

Cody said, "Run a thorough check of your computer system. Since we still don't know why two men hacked into the lab, the answer could be in the software program for the drug. I'll be back tomorrow morning to speak with each of the personnel assigned to the lab and anyone else who has a key."

Cody and Will left business cards with the two men before they and Riley walked out.

Once they stepped outside, Cody took a deep breath of the cool night air. "We don't know much more than we did before we got here."

"Maybe we'll find some answers in Jamison's apartment. I've got the warrant."

"Let's go," Cody said. "I'll follow you."

Will headed to his car, and the agents got into the van. Cody followed them out of the driveway.

As soon as he cleared the driveway, he activated a call on the truck's computer. When Scott answered again on the first ring, Cody had to wonder if his new boss ever went home or slept.

"What happened?"

"We walked into the middle of something, though I'm not sure what yet."

"We?"

"Riley is with me. Two men broke into the lab." Cody went on to describe the shooting and identity of the dead man. "Will and a team of agents processed the crime scene. Here's what we know." He went over the results of the meeting, adding, "I'll be back at the lab in the morning. Jamison got a copy of the key from someone."

Scott said, "It's an inside job. Do you know who had keys?"

"I've got the names. Do you want them now or in an email? It will be a while as we're headed to Jamison's apartment."

"Go ahead and give them to me."

Cody rattled them off while Riley stared at him in amazement. She knew he had only glanced at the list.

"I'll get Nicki started on them. How about the man you shot?"

Cody said, "Stan Delbert. With two of their enforcers dead, there's no doubt the cartel is running the show."

Scott said, "Watch your back. If the rumors are true, El Sombra was giving them their marching orders."

"I'll let you know if we find anything at the apartment. By the way, are both of you still at the office?"

"Welcome to the Trackers. Right now, it looks like we'll be here most of the night. Hopefully, we will have found some answers on this end. Send me a report as soon as you can." He disconnected.

Riley said, "This is the second time I've heard you mention a drug cartel. At the newspaper office, you mentioned two men, Delbert and El Sombra. Who is El Sombra?"

"Translated, El Sombra is the shadow. He's the cartel's top hitman. No one knows who he is or what he looks like. The man deals in death."

Chapter 27

A chill crept down her back. "Why would a cartel be involved? What could they possibly want from a company like R&B?"

Cody said, "Whatever it is, it's dang important."

"Okay, what's with the memory bit? This is more than I'm good with details type of thing. I know you only glanced at that list of names."

Even in a truck lit by just the dashboard lights, she couldn't miss the look of chagrin on his face.

"I don't like to talk about it since it makes people uncomfortable, especially for someone who worked in Las Vegas. It's one reason why I never gamble. I have a photographic memory. It only takes one glance."

"Wow, I've heard about it but never met anyone who had it. I don't know why it would make people uncomfortable. It would seem to be a definite asset in your line of work."

"From that standpoint, yes. But over the years, I've won a lot of bets based on what I can remember. It tends to irritate people."

Ahead, Will's car pulled into a brightly lit apartment complex parking lot, stopping in an empty spot near the office.

As Cody parked, Riley asked, "Do I need to stay here?"

"No. I doubt we're going to find anything. I expect the place has been sanitized just like the rental house."

Will and two of his agents waited on the sidewalk. One hoisted a large case.

"The complex had an emergency contact number. I was able to talk to the manager. He's on the way with the key," Will said.

Cody cast an eye over the parking lot filled with cars. "Jamison was driving a blue car. Maybe the manager has his vehicle information. It will save running the license plate on every blue vehicle. I've wondered several times what happened to his car."

A bright red car zipped into the parking lot and screeched to a stop. The driver hopped out. With an eager look of anticipation, the nerdy-looking young man bolted toward the sidewalk. "Are you the FBI? I'm Jeff Dalton, the manager."

Will swapped looks with Cody before pulling out his badge case. Flipping it open, Will handed it to Dalton. "I'm Agent Will Cooper."

Dalton reached for it. He breathed, "A real … honest to god … FBI badge." He held it as if it was the Holy Grail. "Oh, man, this is awesome, dude. Oh, sorry, I mean Agent Cooper."

Will held out his hand. Dalton gave it one more wistful look before slowly handing it back.

"Do you have the key to the apartment?" Will asked.

"Oh, yes." He fumbled in his pocket before extracting a key, proudly holding it high. "I can't believe this. Wait until I tell Gloria—she's my girlfriend—I helped the FBI. She thinks my job is so totally boring."

"This is the search warrant. You might want to look at it."

A gleam of excitement flashed in Dalton's eyes as he shoved the key into a pocket. "Oh my gosh, yes, I want to see it. Not because I don't believe you, because I do. A search warrant, an actual search warrant." One finger pushed the glasses further up the bridge of his nose as he closely scrutinized the document. "Can I take a picture of it with my cellphone? That will prove it to Gloria. And can I get a picture of all of you, maybe with your badge cases held open?"

"No pictures," Will said with a firm tone. He held out his hand. "The key."

"Oh, gosh, sorry about that." He retrieved the key from his pocket, dropping it onto Will's palm along with the warrant. "What did this dude do to get his apartment searched?"

Cody said, "Gary Jamison was murdered."

A ghoulish look crossed Dalton's face. "Really? I mean, that's awful. How'd it happen?"

Cody ignored his question. "Did you know him?"

"Not really. He'd come in each month and leave a check for the rent. That's about the only time I ever spoke to him. He never had much to say. Holy smokes, what do I do now about his apartment? He didn't list anyone as an emergency contact. I'd better call my boss and let her know."

"What about his vehicle?" Cody asked.

Dalton looked around before pointing. "It's over there, the blue Mazda."

Will looked at one of his agents. "Hardy, stay here and get a tow truck out here. Mr. Dalton, where is Jamison's apartment?"

"Oh, yeah, yeah, okay. This way." He loped along the sidewalk, turned the corner, stopping in front of a door.

Will said, "Why don't you wait in your office until we're done."

Dalton's face fell. "I don't get to watch. Well, dang," he muttered, turning to walk away.

Will waited until Dalton disappeared before opening the door.

Once inside, Cody quickly found the light switch. It was a small one-bedroom apartment. On one side was the kitchen with a table and a doorway leading to a bedroom. A TV screen was mounted on the other side. The furniture was bare bones, a recliner, coffee table, desk, bookcase, and wall-mounted TV.

Cody observed, "Guess he didn't do much entertaining. No place to sit."

In the doorway, Riley said, "I'll wait out here."

Cody nodded. "This isn't going to take long." He pulled on a pair of gloves Will handed him, then headed to the desk while Will and the other agents checked the rest of the apartment.

Within minutes, it was obvious they weren't going to find anything. "Whoever killed him cleaned out the place," Will said. "Even the clothes are gone."

"Same here. There's a surge protector, so he had a computer." Cody closed the last desk drawer. "All empty. Not even a checkbook." He eyed the empty bookcase. "It seems a bit over the top to completely strip the place. I wonder why."

Standing by the door, waiting for the other agent and Cody to leave, Will said, "I'll stop by the office and give Dalton the key,"

Cody and Riley headed toward his truck.

Riley asked, "Does that happen often?"

"What?"

"A dry well."

Cody grimaced. "More often than not."

"Okay, where do we go from here?"

"Back to Fredericksburg. Once we get to your house, I'll send Scott a report. Then, I want to know more about R&B Lab."

Washington, D.C.

Scott settled in one of his favorite positions, feet propped on the corner of the desk, elbows resting on the arms of the chair, and his fingers steepled under his chin. Unsettled by Cody's phone call, the details swirled in his mind. Dots and more dots. Some he could connect, but not enough that he could get a clear picture.

Nicki wandered in, plopping into a chair, her feet mirroring her boss's on the other corner of the desk. "Was that Cody?"

"Yeah." He brought her up to speed on the call. He pushed a piece of paper towards her. "More names. Maybe one of them might break the logjam."

Nicki knew her boss only too well. The tight-jawed look, a portent of his thoughts, meant his sharp intellect was probing every detail.

Used to being a sounding board, she asked, "Okay, what are you thinking?"

He leaned back to stare at the ceiling, dropping his hands onto his belly. "The body count is rising. Another one tonight with links to a Mexican drug cartel. A murdered chemist, his eye extracted, his body stolen, the attempts to eradicate Riley's pictures and prevent an identification, a bomb. And in the middle of this swirling vortex is a small independent drug company. In the scheme of things, not even a significant player in the hierarchy of drug companies. What does this small drug lab have that would justify such an elaborate scheme? Serious money is in play. Why?"

He dropped his feet. "Set up a new search. This time, I want everything you can find on related drug companies, any controversies, lawsuits, or takeovers. Dig deeper into the financials for R&B and this new drug. I'd like to know when they went public with it."

"You got it."

In one of his swift about-faces, he asked, "Is it too late for a pizza?"

"Dang, boss man. It sounds good. Better order two. I'm hungry. Though I guess this means we're working through the night."

"I still have this itchy feeling a clock is ticking down, and people will die if we can't figure out the why. I hope you didn't have any plans or a hot date." He reached for the phone and tapped the speed dial for the pizza parlor in the next block.

As Nicki wandered back to her office with the list of names in hand, an unwelcome thought crossed her mind. If only he knew. She hadn't had a serious hot date since she started working for Scott. Any other man paled in comparison.

Frustrated by her thoughts, she banged away on the keyboard, setting up the parameters for a new search on drug companies. Then she turned loose her new search engine, Warlock, to mine the internet for answers.

Next on the list were the employee names. Dealing with each one took time. She was still typing when the wafting aroma of pepperoni, garlic, and onions invaded her space. Voices echoed in the outer office. Her nose twitched. With a few quick taps, she entered the last name before hopping out of the chair. In the breakroom, steam rose from two open boxes on the counter. She grabbed a piece, flipping the hot trailing cheese back on top.

"Coffee or soda?" Scott asked.

Nicki mumbled around a large bite. "Soda. Whatever is in the fridge is okay." She moaned with pleasure. "This is so … so good."

Scott eyed her. "You might want to sit down before it drips down your shirt. Though I doubt you'd notice it in all those bilious colors." The t-shirt boasted a multitude of discordant colors around the gaping mouth of T-Rex.

"Hey, don't knock it. T-Rex was badass. It fits my mood." She grabbed another piece, though she did drop onto a chair at the table.

Scott shook his head, giving her an indulgent look as he slid a plate under her hand.

"Did I tell you I have a name for my new search engine?"

With her penchant for computer games, Nicki's labels became a constant source of amusement. The unit had been waiting for her to come up with a name. Bets had been placed on when it would happen. He noted the time since he was the keeper of the bets.

"What?"

"Warlock. I don't know why it took so long. It's a perfect fit for dungeon sweeps and goblins. I even created a new icon."

He grinned. "Of course you did."

Conversation lagged as they consumed the large pies. With one piece of pizza left, Nicki shot Scott a sly look. "Flip you for it."

Since he had lost more than he won by flipping coins with her, he laughed, saying, "I'm tired of being the patsy. You take it."

While she polished off the last piece, he stuffed the boxes into the trash can. With a full cup of coffee in hand, he wandered back to his office. The respite over, his thoughts shifted back to Texas. How much time did they have left?

Chapter 28

Feeling the aftermath of the long night, Scott stepped out of the elevator. Even the hot shower in the gym on the first floor had done little to alleviate stiff muscles.

Most of the night had been spent in research. Nicki's program was still running down the background on R&B's employees. He had weeded through news articles and online research papers from the search on drug companies.

With a wide yawn, he opened the door to hear Nicki's hard rock music rolling through the office. Her music selections were often an indicator of her progress. The clashing, metallic sounds of guitars and drums were a good sign.

He paused in the doorway to her office. Nicki's eyes were fixed on the monitor while her fingers tapped the keyboard in sync with the music. She was in what she called the zone, oblivious to anyone or anything around her.

With a smile, he stepped away. In the breakroom, he started a fresh pot of coffee, then looked in the fridge for breakfast. A couple of old deli sandwiches weren't inspiring. He pulled out his phone and tapped a number on the speed dial. It seemed his life was run by speed dials to fast food eateries.

When the call was answered, he ordered two ham and cheese omelets with hashbrowns, toast, and two containers of orange juice. Unknowingly, when he had selected a location for the Tracker office, it was in a suburb riddled with restaurants and retail shops.

By the time he finished, the coffee was ready. He poured a cup, inhaling the rich aroma before taking a deep swig. He refilled it, poured a second cup, and headed to Nicki's office.

Numbers flashed across the wall monitor. Probably someone's bank account. He set the cup alongside her, then tapped her shoulder. She jerked, twisting her head up. A quick tap on the keyboard and the music died.

"Morning," she said with a cheerful tone.

Grumpily, he wondered how someone could be that perky so early in the day. "I ordered breakfast. Find anything?"

Her lips twisted with a smug smile. "Maybe the inside man, or should I say, woman."

With a quick flick on the keyboard, a picture came up. "I found this. It was taken at the company's annual meeting." Her laser pointer moved to a woman standing in the front row. "Francis Snyder, another chemist. Over the last two weeks, she's made numerous deposits totaling five thousand dollars, all in cash. So far, this is the only red flag for the employees. I'm still running the background on the guy Cody shot last night."

She drum-rolled her fingers. "Wait for it … wait for it."

Knowing this was Nicki's alert for significant developments, Scott held his breath.

"There may be trouble brewing with another drug company. I found a short news article about Goldmark, Inc., filing a complaint with the FDA over R&B Lab's new drug. The article didn't give any specifics. I sent it to you. As soon as their offices open, I plan to call the FDA to find out why."

"When was the complaint filed?"

"I wondered how long it would take you to ask. I'm not sure about the complaint, but the article appeared three weeks after the drug conference, where I found Jamison's picture. Goldmark is headquartered in Austin."

Scott's spider sense tingled, vanquishing the hangover from sleeping in his chair. Rising, he said, "Get me everything you can on Goldmark." He hurried to his office and dropped into his chair. He took a sip, then set the cup aside. He avidly stared at the screen, perusing the article. Despite the reporter's generalization and lack of details, dots started to connect, prompting another thought to rear its ugly head. The lab had been broken into the night before the FDA's trial of R&B's new drug was to begin. Every instinct said the two events were connected.

Texas

Riley awoke to the aroma of fresh coffee. Disoriented, her first thought was Ted. When did he get here? Then her memory kicked into gear. It wasn't Ted, but Cody. When they got back to the house, she was too exhausted to do more than show him the spare bedroom. She left him unpacking his gear. After a quick shower, she collapsed in bed.

Feeling somewhat rejuvenated after another shower, attired in jeans and a t-shirt, Riley padded barefoot to the kitchen.

Seated at the table, his laptop in front of him, Cody looked up when she walked in. "Good morning. I hope you don't mind. I brewed a pot of coffee."

"Not at all. It's a pleasant surprise. Help yourself to anything in the kitchen."

From the cupboard, she pulled out a cup and filled it. She glanced at his cup. "Refill?"

Cody pushed the cup closer to her. "Please," then went back to typing.

As she settled in a chair across from him, Riley sipped her coffee while she watched his concentration, the slight frown on his brow. A warm glow spread through her. She liked seeing him at the table. Maybe a little too much. Wanting to divert her thoughts, Riley asked, "Finding anything useful?"

"So far, all I've turned up is probably useless trivia. Compared to other drug companies that develop and manufacture drugs, R&B Lab isn't even in the same league, small payroll and personnel. The company's focus is plant-based drugs. Evidently, it's a controversial concept, even though aspirin is the most commonly known drug. R&B has developed a new drug for the treatment of neurological disorders. Still, it could take years before they get it to market, and that's assuming they get FDA approval. I can't find any reason why the company would be a target, and for what?" Frustrated, his hand scrubbed his face.

"Why would anyone go to such lengths to break into the place? And I don't like that it happened the night before a trial of the drug is about to begin." Unknowingly, his thoughts echoed those of his boss. His face troubled, he said. "There was no visual evidence of why the two men were even in the lab. What were they doing?"

"Are you certain about the vials?"

"Yes. If someone tampered with them, it would be obvious." Cody shut down the laptop and closed the lid. "There's something I'm missing, but for the life of me, I can't figure out what. It has to be in their computer system." He finished the coffee and rose, walking to the sink where he washed the cup.

"I can fix breakfast, or we can stop somewhere on our way to the newspaper office." Riley wanted to check on Milo before leaving town.

"Let's stop."

"Do you like taquitos? There is a Mexican restaurant on the way. We could grab a bagful."

"Sounds like a game plan to me."

When they arrived at the newspaper office, Milo's barking greeted them as Riley opened the door. Behind her, his arms full of takeout bags, Cody followed her inside.

Milo rushed toward them with quick, sharp barks of joy. He danced around Riley, his nose nuzzling her hand.

After tossing her backpack on a desk, she dropped to one knee, giving his neck a big hug. "Have you been a good boy for Susan?" Milo barked. His tongue scraped the side of her face. "Yes, I'm glad to see you too."

Susan stepped out of her office to greet them. "He's been dancing around for the last several minutes, so I knew you'd be walking through the door. What is that wonderful smell?"

"We stopped at the El Americano and picked up breakfast, sausage, egg, and cheese taquitos. I also got an order of cinnamon sticks."

"Oh, that sounds good. All I had this morning was a container of yogurt."

As he set the bags on a desk, Cody's grimace had Susan chuckling. "I take it you aren't a fan of yogurt."

"He probably thinks it's girlie," Riley said. When Cody groaned, Riley shot him an impish grin.

"Obviously, I'm missing something," Susan said, prompting a chuckle from Riley.

After Riley stacked the paper-wrapped taquitos, cinnamon sticks, and packets of salsa in the center of the desk, they settled in chairs.

Behind them, Milo circled while Riley laughed at his antics. "Having trouble trying to decide who your best target is?" Milo woofed before sitting next to Cody. "He's got *you* pegged for a sucker."

Cody patted Milo's head. "Hey, he's got good sense, and he

knows who his buddy is. Don't you, Milo?" His tongue hanging out, Milo gazed at Cody with an adoring look.

"Boy, does he have you conned," Susan observed.

Another laugh erupted from Riley. "This from the woman who has a whole drawer full of dog treats."

Once the laughter faded, Susan's tone turned somber. "Tell me what happened. I'm about to bust a gut from not knowing."

"I'll let Cody explain. We can't print anything yet." She bit into a taquito.

In between bites, Cody talked.

As she listened, Susan's expression turned grim, though she didn't comment until Cody finished. "That's why Milo went crazy last night. I bet he somehow sensed you were in danger."

Still chewing, Cody shot her a questioning look.

"Riley didn't tell you?"

Cody swallowed. "No, she didn't." After listening to Susan's explanation, mystified, he stared down at Milo, still sitting beside him. He plucked a chunk of sausage from the taquito. "Guess you deserve another bite."

Once they finished, Cody crumpled the paper wrappers, stuffing them into one of the bags. "We need to leave. I want to stop by Will's office before we head to R&B."

Pleased she didn't have to argue with him, Riley started to pick up her mess.

Susan said, "Leave it. I'll clean it up. Are you taking Milo?"

Riley looked at Cody.

"Probably best if he stays here."

Milo let out a whine. His head drooped. All three looked at him.

At his woebegone look, Riley dropped to one knee. Her arms wrapped around his neck. "Susan has a treat." Even the word "treat" didn't spark a reaction. Sighing, Riley stood.

Susan chuckled. "He's got you trained. How often does he change your mind with his guilt trip?"

Milo tilted his head to look up at Susan. His tongue lolled out.

Laughing, Riley grabbed the backpack. "I'll call later."

Despite the traffic, Cody made good time, parking near the front of the FBI building. Inside, a receptionist behind a desk looked up.

Cody pulled out his ID case. "I'm Special Agent Cody Lightfoot. Will Cooper is expecting me."

She picked up the phone, tapping a number, informing someone that Agent Lightfoot was here to see Agent Cooper.

"Please have a seat. Someone will be here in a moment."

The someone who walked up was Will. After greeting them, he said, "Come on back to my office."

Will escorted them along a hallway to a large corner office, motioning toward chairs inside the room. "Would you like something to drink?"

Riley declined, and Cody did the same.

Will dropped onto the chair behind his desk. "I didn't come up with much we don't already know about Delbert. The man had been arrested several times, mainly for assaults and homicides. No convictions. Witnesses had a way of disappearing. Several were in Arizona. I called our office there to confirm our intel. Delbert was one of the cartel's top men."

"So, the question is," Cody said, "who hired Burgess and Delbert, and why is the cartel interested in R&B Lab?"

Cody's phone rang. He pulled it from his pocket. "It's Scott."

When he answered, Scott asked, "Are you where you can talk?"

"I'm in Will's office."

"Good. Saves me a second call. Put me on the speakerphone." His voice echoed in the room. "I've found some interesting details."

Will grinned. "Does this mean you've solved the case?" He was all too familiar with how Scott worked.

"Not yet, but it's coming together. Nicki may have found the inside person at the lab. Another chemist, Francis Snyder, has made several cash deposits over the last couple of weeks. They add up to five thousand bucks."

Cody said, "My next stop is the lab. I'll start with her."

Scott said, "That's not all. There may be another player involved. We're looking into Goldmark, another pharmaceutical company. Nicki found an article that appeared about three weeks after a drug conference Jamison attended. It's where she found his picture. Goldmark filed a complaint with the FDA over R&B's new drug. The article didn't give a reason. Nicki is going to contact the FDA. Cody, ask Warner about it. I'd be interested in his reaction. I'd also like to know when they went public with the drug. We're working that angle, but Cody, you can find out faster than we might. I don't like that the lab was broken into the night before the trial."

Cody said, "I had the same thought, but the way the vials are sealed, any attempt to tamper with them would be quite obvious. It might not be the vials but the formula itself. The only access to the drug's computer program is from the computers in the lab. I told Warner to examine the program."

"Will, Goldmark is headquartered in Austin. Know anything about them?" Scott asked.

"I've heard of the company. That's about it. I'll check some of my local sources, though."

After Scott disconnected, Cody said, "Unless you've got something else, we're headed to R&B."

The lab was closer to Austin than Fredericksburg, so it was a short drive once Cody cleared the downtown traffic.

When Cody turned into the driveway, a muffled curse echoed. Square in front of the door were two squad cars.

Chapter 29

Riley said, "What is the sheriff doing here?"

"Good question. If it's about last night's shooting, I'd like to know how he found out," Cody said in a grim tone.

He braked to a stop. Snatching the keys out of the ignition, he jumped out. Riley was close on his heels.

When Cody flung open the door, Sheriff Rutherford, his hands fisted on his hips and his jaw thrust forward, faced Warner and Johnston. Billy Thatcher stood alongside him. A woman with a wild-eyed look sat behind the reception desk. Bennett, his arms crossed, leaned against it.

Rutherford's voice roared. "I don't give a damn what the FBI said or did. A man was killed in the county, and you should have immediately notified my office. As far as I'm concerned, that's obstructing a criminal investigation, and I can haul you in on charges."

Cody's voice, though mild, carried. "No, you won't."

Rutherford whipped around. "Son-of-a-bitch. You've interfered for the last time. Get the hell out of here, or I'll have my deputies lock you up. This is county business, and you have no jurisdiction."

From the corner of his eye, Cody saw Bennett straighten, his hand slipping to the gun on his hip.

Cody shot him a quick look. "You do, and I can guarantee you'll spend the rest of your life locked in a federal prison."

Despite the sneer on Bennett's face, his hand shifted away from the gun.

"Were you working last night?" Cody asked him.

Rutherford's head snapped toward the deputy. "Mickey, you don't have to answer that. Lightfoot, you get a warrant if you want to question my deputies."

Bennett leaned back against the desk. His lips twisted with a smug smile.

Cody turned his attention back to the two men. "Mr. Warner. I suggest you and Mr. Johnston return to your offices and take the young lady with you. I'll handle this."

With a quick swipe at the sweat beading on his forehead, Warner said, "Gladly." He had the final word before he walked away. "Sheriff Rutherford, I plan to call my attorney. If there's any legal action I can take concerning your threats, I will do so. And that's not a threat but a promise."

Warner motioned to the woman.

Once they were gone, Cody said, "Rutherford, you overstepped your authority this time. This is a federal investigation. You have no authority here. Leave, or I'll be the one to file charges. It won't look good come election time. You've bungled this case from the beginning, and now you have a prominent company in the community threatening legal action."

As the words sunk in, overriding his hot rage, Rutherford's eyes gleamed with loathing. "Boy-o, this isn't over."

He huffed his way out the door, followed by the two deputies. While Thatcher had an apologetic expression, Bennett stared at him with a menacing look.

"Riley, wait here." Cody followed them out. Once they drove away, he retrieved his briefcase from the truck.

Warner, Johnston, and the receptionist had returned when he walked in. He figured they'd waited in the hallway out of sight.

Cody said, "I'm sorry you were caught in the middle of a jurisdictional battle. Unfortunately, it happens. If you have any more problems, let me or Will know."

Warner said, "We have the conference room set up."

They followed the two to the same room they'd been in the night before. From a coffee machine on a table against one wall, an enticing aroma wafted in the air. Next to the coffee pot was a large box of donuts.

"Please, have a seat wherever you like. Help yourself to the coffee and donuts," Warner said.

Riley poured two cups of coffee. She set one next to Cody. Busy opening his briefcase, Cody nodded his thanks.

Johnston laid the laptop he carried on the table.

Cody said, "This will be very informal. It's more about my understanding your business. Once we finish, I'd like to speak with each of the personnel who work in the lab. I'd also like a list of all your employees."

Johnston tapped the keyboard. "I'll get the printout."

After he left, Warner asked, "Do you have any information on the man you shot?"

"We're still digging into his background."

Johnston walked back in, handing Cody a set of papers. "It's a complete list with home addresses."

Cody quickly scanned it before laying it aside. "What is the status of the review of your computer system?"

Warner said, "I don't know yet. I had the IT personnel start on it first thing this morning. They are still cross-checking the data. Quite frankly, the break-in has us mystified."

"As soon as you have an answer, let me know." He reached into his briefcase, pulling out a recorder. At the wary look on Warner's face, Cody gave him a reassuring smile. "It's easier than taking notes. Tell me more about what you do here and what's happening with the FDA."

In anticipation of writing a news article, Riley pulled out a notepad from the backpack she'd set next to her feet. As Warner talked, she scribbled. The CEO was articulate, even passionate at times. His hands gesticulated as he discussed the basis for the new drug and its impact on neurological diseases.

"RB2, our designation for the plant-based drug, uses the sap of the mesquite tree. Native Americans have long used mesquite trees for medicinal purposes. We use a derivative of the sap to target the body's neurological system and boost the immune system."

"I understand there is a problem with another company, Goldmark, and even a complaint with the FDA."

Warner stiffened. A flush of anger stained his cheeks. "Is Goldmark behind this?"

"We haven't found any evidence to believe they are involved. It's a connection we need to eliminate. Why would Goldmark file a complaint?"

Warner's voice pulsated with hostility. "It was nothing more than an underhanded stunt to slow us down. We should have started testing months ago."

Cody asked, "How did Goldmark benefit?"

"Goldmark is marketing a similar drug. The cost of developing and getting a new drug approved can run into millions of dollars. If our drug reaches the market first, it will represent a heavy financial loss for Goldmark. Plus, if the tests prove out, our drug will be superior to Goldmark's due to the lack of side effects, which has been an ongoing problem in the development of drugs. It's why a commercial has about ten seconds of what a drug will do and fifty seconds listing all the side effects it can cause. Too many times, drugs fix one problem only to create others. The reason for phase one testing is to identify side effects."

Cody asked, "What was the basis of their complaint?"

A derisive snort erupted from Warner. "Some of the top brass at Goldmark made accusations that were totally unfounded. Goldmark claimed RB2 would escalate the progress of the disease, causing death."

"Did Goldmark provide any evidence?"

"Some outdated research. Nothing concrete. Like I said, just a delaying tactic. One that worked. Of course, the FDA had to investigate. It took several weeks before they finally ruled Goldmark's claims were unsupported by any factual evidence, and we got a new date for the trial. Because of the delay, though, Goldmark is ahead of us. They are already into phase two. Still, we are hopeful the results from the testing that starts today will prove RB2 is the better choice."

"You mentioned the test was supposed to have already started. When was that?"

"Almost six months ago," Warner said.

A tingle of nerves raised the hackles on his neck, though he kept his tone casual. "When did you first announce the drug?"

"At the Southwestern Regional Drug Conference in Dallas. It was just before we were to start phase one. We presented a paper on RB2 at the conference. Why? Is there a connection?"

Not wanting to raise Warner's suspicions, he said, "Not necessarily. It's more about a timeline of events. When did the FDA rule on the complaint?"

"I'd have to check the FDA documentation, but I believe it was about two months after the conference. Do you need the exact date?"

Cody said, "No. An approximation is fine for now." Though

mentally, another link snapped into place, the house rental. "What's happening with the vials?"

Warner said, "We double-checked each one this morning before we shipped them to the clinic. None of the seals were broken. Do you need anything else from me?"

"Not at the moment."

"Then I need to get to the clinic for the start of the testing."

After Warner left, Cody said, "Mr. Johnston, I'd like to talk to each of the personnel with access to the lab, starting with the head chemist, Brewster Cavanaugh. I would appreciate speaking to them without your presence."

A frown crossed Johnston's face, but he didn't make a complaint as he rose to leave the room.

Cody rose, refilling his cup. He wandered to the window overlooking the back of the property. Somewhere in the building was the answer. He just had to find it.

Behind him, footsteps sounded. Cody turned to see an older man with thick white hair and a round face, oddly reminiscent of Santa Claus, walk in.

Cody stepped toward him to shake hands. "FBI Special Agent Cody Lightfoot." He motioned toward Riley. "This is Riley Phillips."

The man nodded at Riley. "Brewster Cavanaugh. We've all heard about what you and your dog did. Unbelievable. Learning Gary was killed and his eye used to access the lab has been a nightmarish blow for all of us."

Cody stepped around him to close the door.

As the man took a seat, he eyed the tape recorder Cody had on the table.

Cody sat across from him, wondering at the nervous tension in the man's body. "I'm going to record this. Easier than taking notes." He smiled reassuringly, hoping to ease the man's discomfiture as he pushed the button to record. "Mr. Cavanaugh, I have a few questions about the employees and lab procedures. Gary Jamison worked for you, is that correct?"

"Yes."

"What was your opinion of him?"

"Bright, intelligent, very competent chemist, though he was somewhat of a loner. He kept to himself, never attended any of the employee events."

"Do you know anything about his family?"

"Only from sporadic comments. His parents are dead. Gary graduated from Texas A&M University. He worked for a hospital in Houston before Mr. Warner hired him."

"What did Jamison do?"

"He was part of the research and development team that created the new drug, RB2. It's the second version. We changed the initial formula about a year into the process."

"According to the security logs, Jamison was in the lab after he left on vacation, even before he was killed. Did you know?"

"Norton Johnston asked me the same question. I didn't."

"Can you think of a reason Jamison would need to return to the lab?"

"No. He wasn't involved in the next phase."

"After he left, what were you doing with the drug?"

"Finalizing the production of ninety doses. Every step of the process, inventory of the formula's components to the final step of sealing the vial, must be documented according to FDA requirements. The paper trail is unbelievably complicated."

"Mr. Warner said the vials were checked before they were shipped out."

"Considering the break-in, we double-checked each one to ensure no one had tampered with them."

"Mr. Johnston said the computer system examination was still ongoing."

"It's a slow process. So far, we haven't found anything suspicious."

Cody's jaw tightened with frustration as he turned off the recorder. "I may need to talk to you again. Are you going to Austin?"

The man rose. "No. I'll be here. Who do you want to talk to next?"

"Ms. Snyder."

After the chemist left, Cody looked at Riley. His fingers drummed the table. "I feel like the answer is staring me in the face, but I just can't see it."

Chapter 30

A knock sounded on the door. A woman in her middle forties, frumpish and overweight, walked in. "Mr. Cavanaugh said you wanted to talk to me."

"Yes, please have a seat. I'm FBI Special Agent Cody Lightfoot. This is Riley Phillips."

The woman, her back straight, perched on the edge of the chair with her tightly clasped hands resting on the table. Her eyes nervously flicked between Cody and Riley. "It's just awful about Gary, but I can't tell you anything about his murder."

Cody said, "I'm interested in the procedures in the lab and will be talking to all the personnel."

"Oh, it's not just me, then."

"No." He motioned toward the recorder, providing her with the same explanation as he had the others. "How long have you worked here?"

"A little over three years."

"What are your duties?"

"I am part of the team that developed the formula for the new drug."

"Are you involved in the testing phase?"

"Um … yes."

"In what way?"

"I was responsible for the FDA documents."

The innocuous questions had put her at ease. Her hands and body had relaxed. Cody felt he could step up the questions. "How well did you know Gary Jamison?"

"We worked together, that's about it. Gary wasn't much for making friends."

"Mr. Cavanaugh mentioned Jamison didn't attend any of the company events. Did you ever see him outside of work?"

"No, never," she declared in an indignant voice.

"I just wondered if you knew any of his friends."

"Oh. No, I didn't."

"Did Gary say anything about his plans for his vacation?"

"No. None of us in the lab knew he was going to be gone until he didn't show up one day."

His eyes focused on her face, Cody said, "So … you didn't see him after he left."

Her body tensed. "No, I didn't."

She's lying, Cody thought. "The intruders had a key. Do you have any idea how they got a key?"

A nervous titter erupted. "How could I possibly know? Most everyone who works here has a key."

Cody leaned forward. "Since Gary left on vacation, you've made several deposits totaling five thousand dollars to your bank account. Where did you get the money?"

She couldn't control the gasp. "You had no right to check my bank account."

"Yes, I do. An employee has been murdered, his eye extracted and used to gain entry to a secure area of this building. Ms. Snyder, the break-in last night involved someone inside this company. It's the only way they got a key. Jamison didn't have one. He'd given his key to Mr. Warner."

Her face blanched. "That's not what he told ...." She stopped and gulped.

"Told you what?"

With a fearful look, she said, "Gary called a few days after he left on vacation. He said he lost his key and wanted to make a copy of mine. At first, I said no. Gary begged me. He was afraid he'd be fired if Mr. Johnston found out he'd lost his key. He was almost hysterical on the phone, going on and on about losing his job. Gary said he'd pay me for helping him out."

Her eyes flicked between Cody and Riley. "I ... uh, I met him after work at a hardware store in Austin. He got a copy made, then handed me an envelope with the money. I didn't know until I counted it just how much was in the envelope. I figured it would be a hundred bucks or so, not five thousand dollars."

"Didn't it strike you as strange he'd pay you five thousand dollars for a copy of your key?"

Her eyes flicked away, though she couldn't hide the guilt on her face. "I just didn't think about it. I was just trying to help him out."

Yeah, you did, but you couldn't pass up the lure of money, Cody thought.

She stretched her hands toward Cody. "I didn't think I was doing anything illegal. After all, Gary worked here. Am I going to go to jail? I'll lose my job." She covered her face as deep sobs shook her body.

Cody said, "Riley, find Mr. Johnston for me."

She nodded and hurried out of the room.

Cody rose and followed Riley. Standing in the hallway where he could keep an eye on the distraught woman, he tapped the speed dial on his phone.

When Will answered, Cody said, "I found out how the intruders had a key." He explained what he learned, then added, "I bet

Jamison was in a panic. No key. He couldn't get into the building. I wonder if his handlers knew it."

"Good question. It could have derailed the whole plot. I'll send out an agent to get a notarized statement. Anything else?"

"Another confrontation with Rutherford. When we got here, he and two of his deputies had already arrived." After explaining, he said, "I'd sure like to know how he found out."

He disconnected as Johnston rushed up.

"What's wrong with Francis?"

Cody told him.

"Oh, my. Have you arrested her?"

"No. At this time, it looks like she was an unwitting dupe. An agent is on the way to take her statement."

A grim look crossed his face. "I may have to fire her. Can I talk to her?"

"Not until after the agent gets her statement."

"Do you mind, then, if everyone takes their lunch break?"

"Go ahead."

Riley had retrieved a box of tissues from somewhere and walked inside, setting them on the table in front of the woman.

Cody followed her back into the room, closing the door.

After grabbing a wad of tissues and wiping her face, Snyder asked, "What happens now?"

"An agent from the FBI office in Austin will be here shortly to get a written statement," Cody told her.

His brow furrowed, Cody wandered to the window, staring at the rough terrain behind the building. Bits and pieces of conversation floated in his mind, along with the desperation of a murdered man to have access to the building. Something hovered on the edge of his thoughts. Something he couldn't grab.

While Riley watched him, she stirred uneasily in her chair. A multitude of questions, none of which she could ask in front of the woman, tumbled in her mind.

Cody abruptly turned. "Mr. Cavanaugh said each step in preparing the doses had to be documented. I am assuming all this documentation is in the computer."

"Yes."

"What did that entail?"

"The actual production of the serum, then filling the vials and attaching a label. Each label has a unique number that has to be recorded."

"When were the doses prepared? Before or after Jamison left?"

"It was the first week after he left. The same week, he called me about the key."

"Is that when the vials were filled."

"Yes. I attached each label, then recorded the number on the FDA form."

"When did you print the labels?"

"The same day we started to fill the vials."

"Where are the components of the formula kept?"

She swiped her swollen, tear-streaked face with another wad of tissues. "Most are kept in the lab's storage unit. Though the stems and leaves used to extract the sap are in another storage room."

"Could Jamison have recreated the formula outside the lab?"

"I suppose so. Everything he needed was in the lab."

"How long does it take."

"Depending on how many doses, at least a couple of weeks."

"What about the vials and labels?"

"In the lab."

In his mind's eye, the dates of when Jamison had been in the lab came up. Then, another image flashed. In an instant, he knew.

"Riley, let's go." He stuffed the recorder into the briefcase. "Ms.

Snyder, do not leave the building before the agent gets here. If you do, a warrant will be issued for your arrest." He headed out the door.

Mystified, Riley grabbed her backpack, running behind him.

The receptionist looked up when Cody burst into the room.

"Where is Johnston?"

"He just left for lunch."

"I need Warner's cellphone number."

"I … uh."

"Now!"

Startled, she hastily told him.

Cody tapped it into his phone, but the call rolled to voice mail. "This is Agent Lightfoot. Stop the trial. I repeat, stop the trial. I'm on my way to the clinic." He disconnected.

"I need the address."

Wide-eyed, she wrote it down and handed it to him. Cody tapped the number for Will.

He muttered a curse when the call rolled to Will's voicemail. Cody said, "Send agents to the Walker Medical Building at 4101 Cambray Street. Stop the trial. I repeat, stop the trial."

His next call was to Lieutenant Thomas at Austin PD.

"Lieutenant Thomas."

"Curtis, it's Cody Lightfoot. Send officers to the Walker Medical Center. Eighty-seven people are about to participate in testing a new drug. Stop it. I'm on my way." He ended the call.

He turned, looking for Riley. "Let's go."

By the time he slid behind the wheel, Riley was buckling her seatbelt.

Cody peeled out of the parking lot. As soon as he turned onto the highway, he punched it. He said, "Type this address into the GPS. I need to know where I'm going."

Once the map came up, she said, "I know this area of town. I can help get us there. What did you figure out?"

"If I'm right, several of the vials were swapped out. It means some of the volunteers aren't getting the real drug. No telling what's in the vial."

"Oh, my god. How did you figure it out?"

"The labels. The printing on several was slightly different."

In amazement, she stared at him. "How come no one else spotted it?"

"I guess they just didn't look close enough."

"No, I think it's that thing you do with your mind, the photographic bit."

His cellphone rang. He answered using the link to the truck's computer.

"Lightfoot." In the background, he could hear sirens.

"It's Curtis. Explain why I am running hot across Austin to get to a clinic."

Once Cody explained, Curtis said, "What time was it supposed to start?"

"I'm not sure. I've left a message for Will, so agents may be on the way."

"Did you, by chance, call the National Guard? Would just like to know if I should expect them too."

"If this wasn't so serious, I'd have a witty comeback."

"Save it. I'm sure you'll get another chance to use it. We're about ten minutes out." He hung up.

After parking behind a line of squad cars and FBI vehicles blocking the driveway, Cody jumped out, racing toward the large glass front doors. Riley was hot on his heels.

Inside, pandemonium reigned. Visitors milled around, visibly upset by the commotion. In loud voices, cops and the medical staff argued. He spotted Curtis and Will talking to Warner. He loped toward them. Riley dropped onto a chair, figuring the best thing she could do was to stay out of everybody's way.

Warner, his face troubled, said, "What's this all about, Agent Lightfoot? Agent Cooper and Lieutenant Thomas said you ordered the trial stopped. Something about the doses. I told you they had not been tampered with."

"Has anyone received a shot?"

"Yes, four volunteers. Then the police rushed in, followed by the FBI. I've got a lot of unhappy people, including representatives from the FDA. All demanding to know what's going on."

Cody's heart was in his throat. All he could do was hope the four didn't get one of the substituted vials.

"I need to see those containers."

A man in a white coat walked up. "I'm Doctor Edwards. This is a clinic. There are sick people here." He waved his hand at the lobby. "Someone needs to stop this."

Curtis stepped away, taking charge to clear the room.

Doctor Edwards said, "Now, who is going to tell me why my clinic has been invaded by the police and FBI?"

Cody introduced himself, then added, "Before I can, I have to see the vials."

Doctor Edwards escorted Cody, followed by Warner and Will, to a room at the back of the clinic filled with a large group of people of varying ages. Edwards walked into a small treatment room. Inside, he motioned toward boxes on a long counter.

Cody stepped past him. A chill rippled through him at the sight of four empty holes. "Where are the empty vials?"

"In that box." Edwards waved toward one on the end of the counter. "We need to keep them in the event there is a problem."

Cody reached inside the box, picking up one of the empty vials. Slowly turning it, he studied the label before laying it aside. He picked up another. It wasn't until he'd looked at the fourth vial that he heaved a sigh of relief. Then he turned to the container with the remaining vials, studying each one. Some he set aside; the others went back into the container. By the time he finished, he had ten vials lined up on the counter. He turned to look at Warner and the doctor.

Fear shimmered in his eyes as Warner stared at Cody.

Cody said, "These need to be analyzed. What's in them isn't the real drug."

Warner's face lost what little color was left. "How do you know? We examined all the vials. No one had tampered with them."

"That's correct. It wasn't tampering. It was a substitution. These vials were substituted for the real ones."

Warner exclaimed, "My god, what about the four people who got a shot?"

"That's the only good news. All four got the right dose. If you want to be certain, test the residue in the vials."

Will said, "You still haven't told us how you knew."

Cody pointed to the label on one of the tainted vials. "The print is out of alignment compared to the real labels. These ten were printed on a different printer. According to one of the chemists, Francis Snyder, the labels were all printed at the same time in the lab. There shouldn't be a difference."

Warner picked up a good vial, comparing it to one lying on the counter. "My god, you're right. There is a slight difference. It isn't obvious if you don't know to look for it. Was vials and labels what Jamison came back to get?" Warner asked.

"Probably. I also think one of Jamison's trips back to the lab was to get a copy of the FDA documentation with the numbers on the vials. He had to have the number to print new labels. Snyder told me Jamison could have recreated the drug outside the lab. Cavanaugh mentioned an inventory. What is inventoried?"

Warner had collapsed onto a chair. "Everything. Drugs, medical supplies, even the vials and labels."

"Do an inventory. Find out what is missing."

Will said, "I have to take all of this into custody. Doctor Edwards, send everyone home except the four individuals who received the shot. I suggest you keep them under observation."

Cody said, "Will, how fast can you analyze the contents of the vials?"

Doctor Edwards spoke up. "I can help. The tests can be done in my lab. I need to know what to look for."

Warner said, "Could the chemist in charge of my lab, Brewster Cavanaugh, help?"

"Absolutely. In fact, it would shortcut the process."

"Before I call him, are there any documents he should bring?"

"Yes, a copy of the formula and list of components."

Warner pulled out his phone. After glancing at the screen, he said, "I missed your call, Agent Lightfoot. I had turned off the phone." After a short conversation, he disconnected. "He should be here in thirty minutes or so. As you heard, I told him to have the lab inventoried and at least two people verifying the results."

Dr. Edwards said, "I need to get the lab personnel alerted. We can have everything ready. Other than the four who received a dose, I'll tell the other volunteers they can go home."

Will said, "While we wait, I can get pictures and document the evidence." He followed Edwards out the door.

Cody looked at Warner. "Let's wait in the other room. It should be more comfortable."

Warner rose, looking as if he had aged ten years. He walked into the waiting room where most everyone was leaving, though another group still sat nearby. One person rose.

"Zachery, please tell us what happened."

"Harold, this is FBI Special Agent Cody Lightfoot. Harold Gibson is head of the team from the FDA."

Cody shook hands with the man.

Warner added, "Let's have a seat."

Cody said, "While the two of you talk, I need to make a call." He walked back to the front of the clinic.

Most everyone in the lobby had left. Only Riley and another person were seated in chairs. Riley stared at him with an anxious look in her eyes.

He sat down next to her, taking a deep breath. "God, Riley, it was close. Too damn close." His hand scrubbed his face.

"Then none of the four got the wrong dose?" Riley asked.

"No. But the order in which the vials were selected, number five, would have received a tainted dose. Ten vials were switched. The lab here is going to analyze the contents. I need to call Scott and bring him up to date." He pulled out his phone.

Riley said, "I could use a cold drink. How about you?"

"Sounds good." While Riley wandered off to find the breakroom, Cody tapped his phone.

When Scott answered, Cody said, "I've got news." Scott occasionally interrupted him with a question but, for the most part, listened until Cody finished.

"What's your gut take on who is behind this?" Scott asked.

If the man wanted to know, he'd tell him and hope he wasn't making a fool of himself.

"Goldmark. They have motive and resources."

"I agree. I had planned on calling you. We received a copy of the complaint Goldmark filed with the FDA. They claimed the drug would escalate the disease and, instead of healing, kill the patient."

Cody said, "That's what Warner told me. The question is whether the tainted dose would kill or just make the volunteer sick."

"We're digging into the company. By the time Nicki gets done, there won't be a rock that hasn't been overturned. There has to be a link somewhere to the cartel. If we can find it, I want to hit the company with a search warrant and a full team of agents before they have time to react. First, Riley, and then you have been kicking sand in their faces from their sandbox. Now, their plan to sabotage the FDA trial just got flushed down the toilet by you. Revenge is how they operate. Until we find out why, the two of you are probably in their crosshairs."

Cody felt a fear unlike any he'd ever felt. It centered around Riley. He had to keep her safe, but was it possible?

Chapter 31

Riley strolled up, carrying two cans of soda. "Will is looking for you. He's grabbing a cold drink."

Will walked up. He popped the top on a can, took a deep swig, then said, "Curtis got another call and had to leave. I told him one of us would contact him as soon as we knew something. The doc said once they started, it would take a couple of hours to get the results." He sat next to Cody, stretching out his long legs.

After taking a drink, Cody said, "I think this has been in the works for the last several months."

"How did you come to that conclusion?" Will asked.

"Goldmark has a similar drug. The difference is the side effects, which, according to Warner, is a big deal. Goldmark could lose a ton of money if R&B gets their drug on the market before Goldmark does, and even more, if R&B's drug is the better drug." Cody swallowed a gulp of cold drink.

"Six months ago, Jamison was at a drug conference where RB2 was introduced. I'd be willing to bet someone from Goldmark was also there. Not long after the conference, Goldmark filed its complaint with the FDA. Scott finally got a copy. Goldmark claimed R&B's drug would escalate the disease, killing the patient. Warner said they didn't have any solid proof to back up the claim, just old research. From his comments, I gathered the FDA blew off

Goldmark's complaint, though it did delay the start of phase one."

He waved the can toward Will. "If, however, today's stunt had gone off without a hitch, Goldmark would have their proof. R&B would be dead in the water. I'd also bet Jamison was a dead man as soon as he agreed to their plan. They couldn't afford to let him live. Once he recreated the formula, they got rid of him. They just needed to make sure no one knew he was dead. When he didn't show back up for work, he'd have been listed as missing."

He took the last swallow, crushing the can with his hand. "Until Riley and Milo found the body, it was smooth sailing. Then it started to unravel. That's when someone began to get nervous."

Will said, "That's dang good reasoning. If Goldmark is behind this, then what is their connection to the cartel? We've seen an uptick in drugs hitting the streets. I have something working in that area."

In cop-speak, that could mean Will had an informant. "Scott's digging into Goldmark."

This brought a laugh from Will. "I'm sure both he and Nicki are. If there is anything to be found, those two will come up with it. I know you're new to the Tracker unit, but what they have accomplished in other cases has been phenomenal."

"I've heard rumors. Scott wants to hit Goldmark with a team of agents if he finds anything."

"I'm one step ahead of him, which doesn't happen often. I've already canceled all leave. Anyone on vacation is headed back to the office. All the agents have been notified an immediate call-out is in effect. Once I have the results of what happened here, I plan to meet with the District Attorney and get him on board."

Cody's phone rang. He pulled it from his pocket and glanced at the screen. "This is Warner."

"Lightfoot."

"Zachery Warner. I received a call from my office regarding the inventory. Eleven vials and labels are missing. Are you still in the clinic?"

"I'm at the front with Agent Cooper. Do you have any word yet on the analysis?"

"No. Doctor Edwards is still waiting for Brewster to arrive."

Cody spotted the man walking through the doorway carrying a large briefcase.

"He's on his way in." He disconnected.

Cavanaugh, his face creased with a worried expression, hesitated, looking around.

After tossing the can in a nearby trash container, Cody walked over to him. "Follow me."

They headed to the back of the clinic.

****

The wait had been long and tedious. Cody rose, stretching his neck and shoulders. "These chairs aren't made for long sessions of sitting."

In the hallway, Will paced, a phone to his ear as he handled some issue with a warrant. In a corner, Warner slumped in a chair. His face reflected the catastrophe that had hit his company.

Riley said, "It's already been over four hours."

Even as she spoke, Edwards appeared in the doorway with Brewster Cavanaugh behind him. Edwards said, "I have the results."

Warner and the FDA representatives shoved back their chairs. Will hurriedly disconnected from the call, following the two men into the room.

His expression was grim as Dr. Edwards said, "First, the good news. The shots the volunteers received were not tainted."

It was as if the room itself relaxed as those gathered around the doctor heaved a sigh of relief. Despite his conviction the doses were safe, Cody even took a deep breath.

"Now the bad news. The vials Agent Lightfoot identified contained thallium. It was originally used in rat poisons and ant killers. It's highly toxic, and in the mid-1970s, the U.S. banned its general use, though some thallium compounds have limited applications in optics and nuclear medicine."

His voice deepened with anger. "It's odorless, tasteless, water-soluble, and nearly undetectable during an autopsy unless the medical examiner specifically targets thallium or one of its derivatives."

His voice as harsh as the doctor's, Cody said, "Ten people would have died."

"Very likely. The patients would have exhibited gastrointestinal symptoms, abdominal pain, nausea, vomiting and neurological symptoms, muscle weakness, headaches, seizures, and eventually coma."

"Dear god," Warner whispered. In a louder tone, he said, "RB2 was designed to target the neurological system."

"Precisely," Edwards said. "The thallium would have piggybacked on the molecules in RB2. An autopsy would have identified RB2 as the culprit, not the thallium."

Will asked, "How long would it have taken?"

"Since RB2 is injected instead of ingested, it would have sped up the onset of symptoms. Problems in the gastrointestinal tract would have appeared within a few hours. The neurological symptoms within twelve to eighteen hours. A coma, then death in maybe forty-eight hours or so. Emergency rooms wouldn't have known how to treat this because they wouldn't have been looking for thallium."

Cody turned to Cavanaugh. "Did Jamison ever talk about thallium?"

Cavanaugh shook his head. "No. He didn't."

"How would someone acquire it?" Will asked.

Dr. Edwards said, "It can be ordered from chemical companies since it has medical and manufacturing applications. It's still available in other countries."

"As in Mexico?" Cody said.

"Probably."

"Zachery, I am postponing further trials until we get this sorted out. Doctor Edwards, please forward a full report on your findings to my office." Gibson handed him a business card.

Then Gibson turned to Will, giving him a card. "Since you are head of the Austin FBI office, I would appreciate it if you could keep me in the loop on the results of your investigation." A grimace crossed his face. "Or at least as much as you can share." He shook hands with everyone, then walked out, followed by his team.

"Doctor, please send me a copy," Warner said. Then Warner looked at the two agents. "Do you need anything else from us?"

Will looked at Cody, who gave a negative shake of his head. "Not at the moment," Will answered.

Warner and Cavanaugh walked out.

Will said, "How fast can I get a report?"

"I can give you a copy of the preliminary report, then follow up with the final one."

"I'll take it. In fact, I'd appreciate two copies. One for me and one for Agent Lightfoot. His boss will want a copy."

"He doesn't work for you?"

"No, Cody is assigned to a specialized unit in Washington, D.C."

Once they had copies of the analysis, Will asked, "Are you headed back to Fredericksburg?"

Cody nodded. "I have to file a report with Scott. I'll be in touch."

Outside, Riley sucked in a deep breath of the evening air before sliding into the truck. As she buckled her seat belt, she said, "Can I file a news story about any of this?"

"Not yet." He shot her a grin. "Don't worry, you'll have an exclusive."

She chuckled. "I won't. I already figured out I had an in."

Using the truck's connection, Cody set up a call to Scott.

His boss answered, "Did you get the test results?"

"Thallium had been added. Doctor Edwards said it would have killed the volunteers."

"Never heard of it."

"I hadn't either." Cody explained what he'd learned.

"What about the volunteers who received a dose?"

"No traces of thallium. We got lucky."

Scott grunted. "That's one way to put it. Did R&B use it?"

"No, which leads to the next question. How did Jamison get it? I think it came from Goldmark. The poison, mixed with RB2, would have been undetectable during an autopsy unless the medical examiner was looking for it, making RB2 seem like the cause of death. I can't see the cartel coming up with this scenario or supplying the poison. They're the muscle, not the brains. Plus, there was a risk for Goldmark. Whatever is sold in another country may not be the same as what was needed for the tainted formula."

"Companies that sell the stuff just went to the top of the research list," Scott said.

"I've got a preliminary copy of Edwards' findings. Once I get it loaded onto my computer, I'll send it to you."

After Cody disconnected, Riley asked, "What's our next step?"

He grimly said, "Take a closer look at Goldmark. Tomorrow, I plan on dropping by for a surprise visit. Some face-to-face time with the head man."

"What good will a meeting do? We still don't know if they are responsible."

"People could have died. I want to see his reaction when I tell him."

Chapter 32

Washington, D.C.

Nicki had sent Scott several documents, including financial details for Goldmark. Engrossed in reading an article on his screen, when his phone rang, Scott slowly reached for it. "Fleming."

"Scott, it's Ted Phillips. I've got some info for you."

At the intensity in the man's voice, a sharp sense of alertness shifted his attention.

"Cody asked me to look into Mickey Bennett's background. He told me what Nicki had found. How this guy moves around. Cody was interested in any local connections to Burgess. I didn't find a connection to Burgess, but I found something else. Everywhere Bennett worked, there's been an increase in drugs hitting the street. It didn't happen until he appeared on the scene. He could be the setup man. Once the distribution network is in place, he moves to the next town."

Scott said, "It makes sense. As a cop, he'd know when and where the cops would react. He could probably even steer an investigation in the wrong direction. It does raise a question about the sheriff's investigation."

"I had the same thought," Ted said.

"I'll let Nicki know what you've found. It may dovetail with her research. Today, we found out what they had planned." He went on to explain.

After Scott finished, Ted's voice was harsh. "No wonder there was such an elaborate scheme to hide Jamison's identity. Someone is paying the freight, but who, Goldmark or the cartel? Any idea what the cartel is getting out of this?"

"Not yet."

"What is disturbing is how close they came to getting away with it. I'll be in touch."

Scott laid the phone on the desk. From the doorway, Nicki said, "Well, boss man, what did Ted have to say?"

"Listening, were you?"

Unrepentant, she said, "I always do." She plopped in the chair, tossing her tennis shoe-clad feet on the corner of his desk.

With a slight shake of his head, he told her what Ted had found out.

"Now, isn't that interesting," she mused, leaning back to stare at the ceiling. "I came across a report from a DEA agent in New Mexico. The agent reported a rash of drugs hitting the streets in several small communities. She said it seemed to move from town to town. While the agent suspected it was the Camargo cartel, she had no evidence."

"I need to talk to her."

Nicki bounded out of the chair, racing out the door.

Scott wondered where she got the energy. At times, the decade difference in their ages seemed a lot older. His computer beeped. She'd just sent him the report. A welcome distraction to his gloomy thoughts.

As he read, she bounced back into his office. He glanced at the time on his computer. Considering the time difference, he might get lucky and get the agent on the phone.

A voice answered, "DEA, how may I direct your call?" He tapped the speakerphone so Nicki could hear.

"This is FBI Special Agent in Charge Scott Fleming. I'm calling from Washington, D.C. I would like to speak to Agent Maria Gutierrez."

"Please hold. I'm not sure if she is in the office."

A few seconds later, a woman said, "This is Agent Gutierrez."

"This is Scott Fleming with the FBI in Washington, D.C. I'm looking at a report you wrote about eighteen months ago regarding the increased drug distribution in your state."

"I remember that report."

"My office is involved in a case similar to what you reported. A surge of drugs hitting small towns. Were you ever able to identify the supplier?"

"No, and it's still an ongoing problem. We don't even know how the drugs are being shipped."

"You mentioned the Camargo cartel."

"The general consensus is the cartel is running the drugs. We make an arrest, and either a witness disappears, or our suspect is murdered. No one wants to talk, though we have picked up some intel from tapped phones. One name keeps surfacing, El Sombra. Like his name, he's a shadow. No one knows what he looks like, or if they do, they won't admit it. We do know he is an enforcer for the cartel."

Scott thought for a moment. "Something we've come across might be of interest."

Gutierrez said, "I'm open to any suggestion."

"Check the employment records for local law enforcement agencies. See if someone hired on, stayed a while, and then moved to another agency in another town."

A whistle echoed. "A setup man?"

"It's a lead we're following up on in a case in Texas."

"Wait a minute. I thought you said you were in Washington, D.C. How did you get connected to a case in Texas?"

"I'm in charge of a special unit, the Trackers. We cross over division boundaries."

"Dang, I've heard of you. You've got quite a reputation beyond just the FBI. Let me do some digging. How can I reach you?"

Scott relayed the phone number and his email address.

"If I find anything useful, I'll be in touch." She disconnected.

Scott stared at the computer screen as he processed what he'd learned.

"Another series of dots connecting?" Nicki said. Not long after she'd gone to work for Scott, he talked to her about his theory of connecting dots in an investigation in one of his rare moments of openness. For Scott, it was more than a theory. It was how his brain was wired.

"There's a pattern. Did Bennett ever live in New Mexico?"

"No, he didn't, just Arizona and Texas."

He picked up his pen, tapping the desk as he thought. "The cartel. Goldmark. What links them?" Tap, tap, tap. "Did you run a background on the top management of the company?"

"Underway. So far, I've got Lewis Braxton, CEO, and James Montgomery, his second in command. I haven't found anything raising a red flag, though each is quite wealthy."

"Send me what you have. What about the structure of the company?"

"Several separate divisions, development, manufacturing, and wholesale distribution."

"Financials?"

"This is where it gets even more interesting. On paper, Goldmark appears to have a healthy portfolio, though I picked up on a few idle comments indicating there could be some problems. I called Savi. If there is any scuttlebutt, she'd find out."

"How's Savi doing?" A few months earlier, Scott brought

Savannah Roth on board to deal with a threat to the Federal Reserve Chairman. Her financial background and expertise had proven to be invaluable. She was currently assigned to an investigation of a Ponzi-style retirement scheme involving several companies in Atlanta.

"Great, though she's up to her eyebrows in financial reports. I told her what was going on in Texas and asked her to take a look at Goldmark. I got a call from her, which is why I was headed to your office when you were talking to Ted."

If Scott had been a dog, he would have just gone on point. His instincts flared.

"Rumors are floating that Goldmark is in trouble," Nicki said. "The company has invested heavily in the development of its new drug. There have been costly setbacks, even to the extent the drug might not be as good as the company has touted. So far, investors haven't panicked, but if Goldmark's new drug doesn't pan out, it spells disaster for the company."

"Cody said Warner mentioned RB2 could mean a heavy financial loss for Goldmark." He looked across the desk at Nicki, who calmly waited. "Who was at the conference Jamison attended?"

"Good question. I'll contact the company sponsoring the event in the morning and get a full list of attendees."

For a moment, Scott stared toward the window, his brow furrowed with a worried look. "Why would Goldmark's financial difficulties involve the cartel? What am I missing? How soon before you complete the financial research?"

"Another couple of hours. With three divisions, the search is complicated."

With razor-sharp clarity, it hit, stiffening his spine—what he'd been missing. "Wholesale distribution. What's involved?"

Nicki's lightning-quick mind grasped the connection. "Goldmark is a wholesale distributor for several drug companies, in addition to the drugs they manufacture. Goldmark ships drugs to pharmacies, doctor's offices, and hospitals all across the country. Is this what it's all about? Is the cartel piggybacking on the shipments? If Goldmark goes under, they could lose their shipping network. I sent you the company's portfolio."

Scott tapped his keyboard, searching the documents Nicki had sent. When he found it, he quickly scanned the details. "We need the locations of their shipping centers."

She jumped up. "I'm on it."

Scott grabbed his phone, tapping the number for Will.

When Will answered, Scott could hear muted voices and music in the background. "This had better be important. I'm about to cut into a mouth-watering, perfectly cooked rib eye steak at one of Austin's finest restaurants."

"Tell the waiter to put it in a takeout box."

Will groaned.

"Then get to a secure location where you can't be overheard," Scott told him.

"Hold on, I'm moving."

"I'm adding Cody to the call."

With a quick couple of taps, Cody answered.

Scott said, "I'm setting up a conference call with Will. Are you where you can talk?"

"In the truck. We just picked up Milo at the newspaper office. Do you mind if I put this on speakerphone so Riley can hear?"

"Go ahead."

Will's voice came over the phone. "I'm outside."

"Cody is on the line. Goldmark has a wholesale division that sells and ships legitimate drugs to pharmacies, drugstores, doctor's offices, and hospitals. Ted Phillips called. He discovered that everywhere Bennett has worked in Texas, there is an increase in illegal drugs hitting the streets. Nicki came up with a similar report put out by a DEA agent in New Mexico. They have the same problem. A proliferation of drugs moving across small towns. No one has been able to figure out how. This could be our connection. The cartel is using Goldmark's trucks to move their drugs."

Will whistled. "Who would suspect a legitimate truck transporting drugs?"

"We need evidence. Nicki is compiling a list of warehouse locations."

Cody asked, "What about the agent in New Mexico? Any help there?"

"I've thought about it, but here's my dilemma. We already know the cartel has infiltrated local law enforcement agencies. How far have they gone? I don't believe we can afford to take a chance. If the cartel discovers we're on to them, they'll shut their shipping network down. I'm betting there is a warehouse, maybe more than one in Texas. If we work it from our end, we can hopefully control any leaks."

Nicki raced in, dropping a paper on Scott's desk.

"Hold on," Scott said. He glanced at the paper. "There are twenty-two across the country. There is one in Burnet, Texas, northwest of Austin. We need to find out where those trucks are headed when they leave the warehouse."

Will said, "It will take a couple of hours to set up the surveillance. It sure would help if we could find a way to get inside to see the shipping invoices. Second best option is to put a tracking device on the trucks."

Cody spoke up. "I'd planned to visit Goldmark's corporate headquarters in the morning. In light of what happened with R&B, Goldmark's FDA complaint gives me a reason to talk to them. Any reason I should hold off?"

Scott said, "No. I'd be interested in their reaction." On that note, Scott ended the call.

He leaned back. "The wheels are in motion. I wonder where they will lead."

Texas

A few seconds after Scott disconnected, Cody's phone rang. He answered, "Will, what do you need from me?"

"I'll let you know once I get my agents in place. You're close to Burnet, and that can be handy. If we can get an idea of where trucks are headed, one option is to set up a roadblock using the highway patrol, checking truckers' logbooks, that type of stop. I'll use a sniffer dog to check the truck. If we are stopping all trucks, it won't be suspicious."

"Good idea, though how can you control any leaks?"

"Pull a typical FBI stunt. Won't tell them why." Will disconnected.

Cody started the truck. "Well, tomorrow is still a go."

Standing with his head hanging over the console, Milo nuzzled Riley's shoulder. His tail thumped the back seat.

Laughing, she slid her arm around his neck, her face against his head. "You think you are going, do you?"

Milo woofed. "Hey, I don't even know if I'm going." Riley looked at Cody over Milo's head. When he didn't answer, with a bit of a huff, she said, "Well!"

He shot her a mischievous grin. "Not sure I could get out of town without you."

"Humph. Dang straight, you couldn't." She slumped back into the seat.

"I think having Milo with us might be a good idea."

"Really! Why?"

"Having you and Milo with me takes away some of the tension

of my walking in and demanding a meeting with the CEO, Lewis Braxton. Another way to test his reaction. I do want to stop at the lab first. I want to find out more about the conference Jamison went to six months ago. Let's plan on an early start."

"Cody, do you think we're still in danger?"

Not wanting to share Scott's concerns, he said, "I'm not sure. If the cartel's gravy train is about to come to a grinding halt, there's no way to anticipate what they might do. No one would blame you if you backed out."

With an adamant shake of her head, she said, "Not going to happen. Milo and I have been in this from the start. I'm not quitting now."

The image of seeing the camera in her hand while he had defused a bomb mere feet from her flashed in his mind. A new and uncomfortable feeling crawled through him. She had already earned his respect and admiration. Now, her spunkiness had snuck under his skin. He liked her, maybe too much. Cody made himself a promise. No matter the cost, he'd protect her and Milo.

Chapter 33

Early the next morning, Cody's phone chimed as he braked to a stop in front of R&B Lab. He looked at the screen. "It's Will."

"Cody, quick update. I've got agents in place at the warehouse. Tracking devices are on the trucks. It turned out to be more of a problem than I anticipated. The parking lot where the trucks are parked is surrounded by an eight-foot-high chain link fence." In a droll tone, he quipped, "Good thing we didn't have any moonlight last night. I've got our command center van set up outside Bertram, about ten miles away. My team will be watching the tracking devices for any movement from there. I'm sending you directions. Are you still planning on going to Goldmark?"

"Yes. I'm at the lab. Once I finish here, we're headed to Austin."

When Cody pocketed the phone, Riley asked, "Are you sure it's okay to take Milo inside?"

"He's not going to be a problem. Let's go."

Cody held the door open for Riley and Milo. Inside, the receptionist turned a wary eye toward the dog before greeting them.

"We'd like to speak with Mr. Warner or Mr. Johnston."

After a brief call, Warner walked into the lobby.

He greeted Cody before turning toward Riley. "Ms. Phillips, is this the dog that found Gary's body?"

"Yes, this is Milo. I hope it's okay to bring him inside."

Warner said, "It's just fine. There's no reason he can't stay with you. Is it all right to pet him?"

"Oh, yes. Milo, greet."

Milo sat, his tail sweeping the floor. Lifting one leg, he extended his paw. Warner chuckled as he shook it, then ran his hand over the dog's head. "It would have been nice to meet you under better circumstances." He straightened. "What can I do for you?"

Cody said, "I have a few more questions. I'd like to speak to you, Mr. Johnston, and Mr. Cavanaugh."

"Come on back to the conference room." He looked at the receptionist. "Call Norton and Brewster. Tell them to meet me there."

Warner led the way. As they stepped inside, he asked, "Would you like coffee or a soft drink?"

Riley said, "Thank you, but I'll pass."

Cody said, "I will, too."

Riley glanced around, deciding to settle Milo in a corner where he would be out of the way. She pulled out a chair next to Cody's. From the backpack, Riley removed a notepad and pen before dropping it at her feet. They'd already agreed that she would take notes of pertinent details instead of using the recorder.

While they waited for the two men to arrive, Cody asked about the fallout from the aborted FDA test.

"I'm still waiting for a copy of the analysis from Doctor Edwards. I did speak with Harold Gibson, the FDA representative, this morning. Between us, we came to an agreement about how to proceed with a second test. A chemist from the FDA will be here to monitor the production of the new doses. Which doesn't bother me one iota. As far as I'm concerned, they can send an entire team. Whatever it takes to ensure the volunteers' safety and the testing's accuracy."

Cody was impressed with his openness and willingness to work under what would likely be difficult scrutiny. Johnston and Cavanaugh walked in. A look of surprise crossed the men's faces at seeing Riley and Cody.

Cody rose to reach across the table to shake their hands. "I had a few more questions."

Cavanaugh spotted Milo in the corner. His head was on his paws, and his eyes intently scrutinized the two men.

Cavanaugh said, "So this is the remarkable animal responsible for saving the lives of ten people."

Warner's gaze shifted toward Milo. "I hadn't considered it from that context. But you're right. If Milo hadn't found Jamison's body, people would have died."

A warm glow started in the pit of her stomach, spreading throughout her body. "Milo, say thank you."

Milo's head snapped up. A sharp bark erupted.

Johnston laughed. "Well, how about that." He pulled out a chair and sat. Cavanagh did the same.

Cody said, "I'd like to know more about the conference Jamison attended in Dallas."

Warner's brow shot upward. "Why would the conference be an issue?"

Not wanting them to know the real reason, he fobbed off Warner's question by saying, "Not sure it is, but it's a connection I need to explore. I'd like to know what other employees were at the conference."

Cavanaugh spoke up. "I was there along with Jamison."

"What was the purpose of the conference?" Cody asked.

He answered, "A forum for drug companies to discuss new drugs on the horizon. I presented a paper on RB2. Since Gary played a key role in its development, he was there to help answer questions."

"Do you have a list of the attendees?"

"Yes, I do. I'll get you a copy before you leave."

"Could anyone attend?"

"No. Invitation only. We had to apply with a synopsis of our presentation. Once we were approved, I had to follow up with the names of the individuals attending."

"What type of activities were there?"

"It was a three-day conference. During the day, different individuals gave presentations and answered questions. On the final night was a banquet. There really wasn't much time to do anything other than go to dinner at night."

"Who did Jamison socialize with?"

Brewster thought, then said, "Other than casual conversation, I don't remember seeing him with anyone. We sat together at a table during the day. During the breaks, we talked to other people. The university hosted the conference lunch, where there was some interaction. Jamison and I had dinner on both nights at the hotel, then the banquet the final night. Afterward, we went to our rooms, or I assume Jamison did."

"Was anyone from Goldmark there?"

Warner shot a quick look at his head chemist.

"Yes, though I'm not sure how many."

"Did they make a presentation?"

"Goldmark was first on the agenda, talking about their new drug. We made our presentation on the second day."

Warner leaned forward over the table. "Agent Lightfoot, this isn't the first time you've raised questions about Goldmark. Why the interest if you don't think they are involved?"

"Goldmark's complaint to the FDA about RB2 is a loose end that we need to clear up. This is just part of our investigation. Who would have known about your drug before the conference?"

Before answering, Warner looked at his two employees as if for confirmation. "I can't say with absolute certainty, but I don't believe anyone did. The conference was the first time we went public with it."

"Mr. Cavanaugh, did Goldmark show any interest in your drug?"

He pursed his lips for a moment as he thought. "No, they didn't. At the time, I didn't think anything about it. Looking back, it does seem odd. After my presentation, many of the attendees from other drug companies approached us, asking questions. I don't mind saying, RB2 is somewhat of a breakthrough in plant-based medicines. Goldmark didn't show any interest."

"How about Jamison? Did you ever see him talking to anyone from Goldmark?"

"No. I didn't."

"One more question. Was there any change in Jamison's demeanor after the conference or any odd incidents?"

Cavanaugh said, "If anything, he seemed more nervous, but that was his personality, high-strung."

After thanking them, Cody rose. Cavanaugh left to get the list of persons at the conference. Riley stashed her notepad and pen back into the backpack, then motioned with her hand. Milo stood, following her outside.

While she waited for Cody, Riley let Milo run to burn off some of his energy. When Cody walked out, she whistled. After loading Milo in the back seat, she slid inside. "What do you think?"

Seated behind the wheel, Cody's gaze quickly scanned the documents Cavanaugh had given him. They included the agenda and list of conference attendees. With a grim look, he tossed the documents on the dashboard. "Five names from Goldmark. I think someone got to Jamison at that conference. I wonder how much money they used for bait." He started the engine. "Let's see what Lewis Braxton has to say."

Cody parked in the lot adjacent to the multi-story building with "Goldmark" embossed over large glass front doors. After they exited, Riley hooked the leash to Milo's collar, ordering him to heel. She slung her backpack over her shoulders. Unable to control the flutter in her chest, she took a deep breath. If they were right, someone with this company was a cold-blooded killer. Someone who didn't dirty his hands but had the power to order the hit.

Cody asked, "Ready?"

Though tension tightened her jaw, she said, "You bet."

Inside, Cody stepped toward a wall-mounted computer screen with a list of offices. "Braxton is on the twenty-first floor."

A security guard shouted from behind a desk across the lobby. "Hey, you can't bring a dog in here. Take it outside." The man rose, rushing toward them.

Cody pulled out his badge case. Flipping it open, he said, "FBI Special Agent Cody Lightfoot, and the dog is with me." After the man had taken a close look at it, Cody slid it back into his pocket.

He pushed the elevator button while he watched the guard scurry to his desk and pick up a phone. As they stepped inside, he said, "It looks like we've been announced."

The surge of apprehension in Riley's gut wasn't from the swift movement of the elevator as it shot upward.

The doors slid open, revealing a luxurious reception area with a pale green, thick piled carpet. Floor-to-ceiling windows overlooked the Austin skyline. In the middle of the room, a dark, highly polished wood desk held a computer monitor and phone. The woman behind the desk was replacing the telephone receiver.

As they stepped out, Riley said, "Milo, heel."

The woman's gimlet-eyed scrutiny sharply raked over Riley and Milo before shifting toward Cody. "I assume you are the FBI agent. I would like to see your identification."

Cody stepped toward the desk, glancing at the name, Marsha Shroeder, engraved on a wooden nameplate. "Ms. Shroeder, I'm FBI Agent Cody Lightfoot." He removed his badge case from a pocket, flipping it open for her to examine. "This is Riley Phillips. We need to speak to Lewis Braxton."

The woman studied it for a moment, then looked at Riley. "Are you an FBI agent?"

"No. I am a reporter with the *Fredericksburg Register*."

Her lips thinned as she picked up the telephone and pushed a button. "An FBI Agent, Cody Lightfoot, is here, asking to meet with you. There is also a reporter, and they have a dog with them. Yes, sir, I'll tell them." She hung up the phone.

"Please have a seat. Mr. Braxton has a very busy schedule and can only give you a few minutes." She motioned toward a grouping of chairs along one wall.

Riley, nervous, elected to walk around, looking at the pictures on the wall. Milo kept pace next to her body.

The woman's strident voice rang out. "Ms. Phillips. Please restrain from letting that dog roam any more than is absolutely necessary."

At Shroeder's disapproving tone, she spun. "I can assure you, Milo is very well-mannered."

Whatever comment Shroeder was about to make was cut off by the ding of the elevator. When the doors slid open, a short, compact man stepped out. Flat, dark eyes scrutinized them as he passed, sending chills racing down Riley's back.

The woman greeted him. "Go on in, Mr. Wetherby. Mr. Braxton is expecting you."

A few minutes later, a light flashed on her telephone. She answered, listened, then hung up. "Mr. Braxton will see you."

Cody opened one of the doors, allowing Milo and Riley to go

ahead of him. Large windows overlooked a view of Austin. Braxton, a broad-shouldered man in a dark grey suit that bespoke money, was seated behind a desk similar to his secretary, only twice the size. Riley knew from her research he was fifty-four, but his face belied his age. She suspected it wasn't natural. The other man, Wetherby, was seated in a nearby chair.

Determined not to be intimidated, she held her head high and strode across the room. Riley slid the backpack off her shoulders, setting it on the floor beside her feet. Still holding the leash, she sat, ordering Milo to do the same.

On his haunches, his ears forward and his body tense, the dog's gaze shifted between the two men. Riley laid a calming hand on his head. Too low to be heard, she felt the deep growl rumble in Milo's chest. Milo didn't like the two men.

Other than a quick flick of irritation at the sight of Milo, Braxton's face showed no emotion. The other man, though relaxed in the chair, gave the impression of a coiled snake, ready to strike. Riley decided it was the eyes. They didn't even appear to blink as he fixed his gaze on her. Milo was right. She didn't like the men either.

Braxton said, "Agent Lightfoot, I hope you have a good reason for this intrusion, though I can't imagine what it could be. I especially don't appreciate the presence of a reporter or a dog."

Unperturbed by the less than cordial greeting, Cody settled into a chair beside Riley. He pulled out his badge case and opened it.

Braxton waved it off. "Whatever you have to say, make it brief. I only have a few minutes to spare."

Cody looked at the second man with a questioning look.

The man said, "Marlin Wetherby, head of security."

With a wolfish smile, Cody turned his attention back to Braxton. "I thought you might be interested in meeting Ms. Phillips. Her dog, Milo, is a search and rescue dog. He found the body of a man murdered and buried on a farm outside of Fredericksburg. You must have read about it. The story has been a major news headline for days."

Braxton's stoic demeanor never changed as he dispassionately studied Cody.

"I'm investigating the murder."

"How could that possibly interest me? Why would you assume I want to meet a reporter and her dog? Obviously, this is a waste of my time."

Cody said, "The murdered victim was Gary Jamison."

"Never heard of him."

"I'm not only investigating the homicide but also Jamison's connection to R&B Lab. I'm sure you must have heard of the company."

"I haven't. If that's all you wanted to know, I have another meeting."

Cody ignored him, saying, "Your company's name came up during my investigation."

Braxton straightened in his chair. "Are you suggesting Goldmark was involved in the murder of this man?"

"I'm not suggesting anything. About six months ago, five Goldmark personnel attended a drug conference in Dallas to make a presentation on your company's new drug." With a taunting twist of his lips, he said, "I have their names if you don't know."

"Personnel from this company attend many events. I fail to see any relevancy to some man murdered and buried at some abandoned farm."

"Gary Jamison was a chemist working for R&B Lab. He was also at the conference for a presentation on R&B Lab's new drug. A drug that competes with your new drug." Cody slid in another taunt. "Are you unaware of that fact?"

Braxton didn't rise to the bait. "Whoever was at the conference beyond my personnel is a moot point."

"Yesterday, R&B Lab planned to start the first trial of their drug. The test was stopped." While Cody's gaze never shifted away from Braxton's face, he could see Wetherby in the corner of his eye. Wetherby's face tightened with anger. "Several of the doses were poisoned. Had the volunteers received the sabotaged dose, it would have killed them."

The first hint of uneasiness flicked in Braxton's eyes before he concealed it by glancing at his watch. "This is all news to me. But then, I'm not interested in R&B Lab or whatever problems they are experiencing. None of this is of any importance to my company."

Cody crossed his legs. He settled deeper into the chair, making it easier to see Wetherby. "Your company filed a complaint with the FDA, claiming R&B's new drug was dangerous. Is this something else you don't know?"

Braxton shifted in his chair. "I'm aware of the complaint."

"I thought you said you had never heard of R&B Lab."

Braxton's nostrils flared. "It was your mention of the complaint that reminded me. As a major pharmaceutical company, we have a responsibility to ensure the safety of the drugs hitting the market. Some of my staff were concerned. The FDA overturned the complaint. That ended Goldmark's involvement."

Cody mused. "Therein lies the problem. It's all a matter of timing. At a drug conference, your personnel learn about another drug the FDA is getting ready to test. If RB2 hits the market, especially before Goldmark's new drug is approved, it would mean heavy financial losses for Goldmark. Several days after the conference, your company filed a complaint informing the FDA that RB2 could be deadly. Had sabotaging the test worked, it would have appeared that R&B's drug caused the death of the volunteers, stopping the production of the drug. It certainly would appear to validate your claim the drug was dangerous."

Rising, Braxton shoved back his chair.

Wetherby also stood. Cody flicked a glance at him. Though his eyes still had that flat stare, the tension in his body was revealing.

Braxton, his face flushed with anger, said, "This is nothing but a blatant fishing expedition because of a legitimate concern my company raised regarding a new drug. We are not connected to whatever problems R&B Lab is experiencing. Any more questions can be directed to my attorney."

Before Cody rose, he said, "I do have one more. How did you know Gary Jamison had been buried at an abandoned farm?"

Blustering, Braxton said, "Uh … you said so."

Cody stood. His tone was low and grim. "No. I didn't." He glanced down at the raised hackles on Milo's back. The dog's lips curled, showing his teeth. "I don't think Milo likes you."

Riley rose and picked up her backpack. With a tug on the leash, she turned toward the door.

Braxton's fist thumped his desk. "I'll have a few words to say to Will Cooper about your reprehensible, defamatory conduct."

Before walking out, Cody said, "Waste of your time and Will's. I don't work for him. I'm assigned to a special unit, the Trackers, in Washington, D.C. My boss, Scott Fleming, would like to speak with you. Agent Fleming can be reached by contacting Special Agent in Charge Will Cooper, who, I'm quite certain, would be interested in speaking to you as well."

As the elevator slid to the bottom floor, Riley remarked, "I don't know who was spookier, Braxton or Wetherby. I can still feel the chill from the way Wetherby looked at me."

Chapter 34

Washington, D.C.

Nicki stood in the doorway. "I hit more than one jackpot."

Scott looked up from his computer screen. "Money or otherwise?"

"In this case, otherwise, though, I wouldn't mind a raise."

He groaned. "You already make more than any other agent."

With one of her cheeky grins, she said, "Yeah, and you know I'm worth it."

Not wanting to pander to her ego, Scott ignored her, but silently, he agreed. Every dime and more. "Okay, tell me what you've got."

"The sponsor of the drug conference had someone taking pictures throughout the event. I got the entire file, and there are several of Jamison. I just sent them to you. I also have a full list of attendees."

Scott turned back to his computer, opening the file. As pictures filled the screen, Nicki scooted around behind him.

"In each picture of Jamison, I've identified the individuals he talked to. There are two with Goldmark personnel. One on the second day, and one on the last day."

As he scrolled through the pictures, Jamison was in the background, usually standing near Brewster Cavanaugh.

"There," Nicki said. "That's the first one with Goldmark personnel. It was taken after Brewster Cavanaugh's presentation."

In the picture, two men and Jamison were seated at a table in what appeared to be a breakroom. On the side of the picture were long tables with coffee and food.

"The two men are James Montgomery, Vice President and R.T. Waters, their head chemist. They made the presentation for Goldmark on the first day."

In the next picture, Jamison and a man were seated at a similar table.

"Here's where it gets interesting. The man's name is Marlin Wetherby, head of security for Goldmark. He's not on the list of attendees. He was only at the conference on the last day and didn't attend the banquet."

Nicki propped her hip on the corner of the desk. Her eyes gleamed with excitement. "I think we just found our link. I'm running him through the dungeon sweep, but I haven't got the results yet. But that's not all. One of the suppliers of thallium is in Boston, Massachusetts. The company shipped an order to Harton Corp in Austin four months ago. Harton's a shell company owned by Goldmark, Inc. It wasn't hard to trace."

A grim look settled on his face. "They weren't concerned. After all, no one would be looking for thallium in the autopsies of the dead volunteers. Plus, I'd bet they have a cover story. It was used for testing in their lab."

His cellphone chimed. "It's Cody." He tapped the screen, then the speakerphone, and said, "How did the meeting with Braxton go?"

"My opinion, he's knee-deep in this, even though he denied everything. I've got another candidate for you, Marlin Wetherby. He's head of security. Before we were allowed into the inner sanctum, Braxton called Wetherby. His presence raised a few red flags. Why did Braxton need Wetherby in the meeting?"

"He's already on our radar. The drug conference sponsor had a photographer there. On the second day, there is a picture with Jamison sitting at a table with two Goldmark employees, a chemist and VP. On the third day, Jamison is talking to Wetherby. He wasn't on the list of attendees."

"That dovetails with what I learned when Riley and I stopped at R&B on our way to Austin. Goldmark made their pitch on the first day. R&B was on the second day. After the conference, Goldmark filed a complaint to stop R&B's production. When that didn't work, they sabotaged the FDA test. Now, we just need the evidence to back it up. I have a list of attendees, but it sounds like you already have it. I'm on my way back to Fredericksburg to drop Riley off. Then I'm headed to Will's location, where he has the command center set up."

"We may have just found part of the evidence." Scott explained about the purchase of the thallium.

Texas

Cody braked to a stop in front of Riley's house. Before Riley could hop out, his phone rang.

When Cody answered, Will, his normally calm demeanor stoked, exclaimed, "We got them. One of the trucks went south on Highway 281. I alerted the highway patrol to set up their checkpoint south of Marble Falls. The trooper's dog alerted on the truck. I'm on my way there now."

Since Cody had automatically hit the speakerphone, Riley said, "Call me when you know something. I'm going to the newspaper office." She quickly hopped out. Once Milo was out of the truck, Cody backed up and tore out of the driveway.

While Riley backed her truck out of the garage, Milo ran around the front yard, chasing a squirrel until it scrambled up a tree. Milo looked up at where the squirrel perched on a limb, calmly twitching its long tail, undisturbed by the dog's sharp barks.

Riley whistled. Milo leaped, spun around, and raced back towards her. She opened the back door and said, "Lost another one, did you?" Milo gave her one of his tongue hanging out of his mouth looks before hopping in the backseat. "I swear that dog can grin," Riley muttered as she climbed behind the wheel. As if in agreement, Milo woofed.

When they arrived at the office, Riley held the door open, and Milo eagerly raced inside, heading toward Susan's office.

"He's looking for a treat," Riley hollered.

"I got one," Susan shouted as she dug into a desk drawer. After handing him a chew bone, Milo happily settled into a corner of her office, gnawing away.

Riley swung by the coffee pot, filling a cup before dropping into a chair in front of Susan's desk.

"Why are you here, and where is Cody?"

Swallowing a swig of the hot brew, Riley filled her in on the latest details, ending with the truck the highway patrol stopped. "Cody was already headed to the command center, which is why he dropped me off at the house. A stakeout wasn't the place for Milo and me."

"Hard to imagine a company like Goldmark would go to such lengths, though I don't know why I should be surprised. When it comes to money, greed and evil have no boundaries. If they do find drugs, what's next?"

"The FBI will go after the company's records. Boy, I'd sure like to know what's going on with that truck."

Susan grinned. "It would be good to have a few pictures to go with the story."

Riley shot her a narrow-eyed look. "It certainly would. Can I leave Milo here?"

"Not a problem. Call me. Let me know what's happening."

Riley grabbed her backpack and headed out the door.

****

Cody passed the barricades set up to stop southbound traffic. He slowed and moved onto the shoulder. Once there was a break in the traffic, he did a U-turn, stopping behind a row of marked and unmarked cars. As Cody passed them on foot, a dog inside one of the patrol cars barked.

Ahead, several people clustered around a large box truck. A man, handcuffed, was seated on the shoulder of the highway.

Will spotted him, waving him over. "This is Agent Cody Lightfoot. He's heading up the investigation." Will introduced the troopers.

"What did you find?" Cody asked. He walked toward the back, where the large truck doors hung open. The interior was stacked with boxes.

A trooper, Dan McDougal, spoke up. "I'm waiting on a tow truck to get here. We're not sure where the drugs are. There could be a false floor in the truck, or they could be in the boxes. I'll wait until the truck is in our maintenance building to search it." He nodded toward Will. "Cooper is sending his forensics team to help."

Cody motioned to the handcuffed man, who angrily glared at them. "He have anything to say?"

McDougal gave the driver a disgusted look. "Says he doesn't know anything and wants a lawyer."

Will walked up, handing Cody a set of papers. "Found these in the cab. A list of locations and what gets dropped."

Cody shuffled the pages, quickly scanning each one. He walked to the nearest squad car, laying the papers on the hood where he could take a picture of each page. Then he set up a text message to Scott, attaching the pictures. Once it was sent off, he picked up the papers, handing them to Will.

As they waited for the tow truck to arrive, Will pulled Cody aside. "What happened with Goldmark?"

Cody hit the highlights of the meeting, then added what Scott had found out about the thallium. Will said, "That's icing on the cake, though I already have search warrants on their way to a judge at the Travis County courthouse. I want to hit both locations simultaneously, Goldmark headquarters and the warehouse."

"Do you think the driver alerted anyone?"

"No. The way this was set up, all the vehicles were stopped. Plus, a phone was inside the truck. No outgoing calls. Here's my concern. Does the driver check in at each town? If that's the case, and there is no phone call, it could blow this wide open."

"How long before you can serve the warrants?"

"Uncertain, though I hope no more than an hour or so. I'm getting spread thin here between the warehouse and headquarters. I've already alerted Curtis Thomas. He's got officers on standby, ready to help with the headquarters warrant."

"Where do you want me?"

"Either one. Take your pick."

"Then put me on the team for the headquarters. I'm going to give Scott a heads-up."

When his boss answered, he said, "Got your pictures. Nicki is feeding the locations into the computer. Never know what might pop up. Where do you stand on the investigation?"

Cody explained about the warrants.

"We got the results of the background check on Wetherby. He's been operating under a very good set of false credentials. He's Felix Lorenzo, with ties to the Camargo cartel. He's wanted for several homicides in California and New Mexico."

Cody's phone buzzed for an incoming call. It was from Susan. He let it roll to voice mail. A few seconds later, a second call came in.

His gut took a lurch. "Scott, incoming call I need to take." He switched calls.

Her voice frantic, Susan said, "Please tell me Riley is there with you." In the background, he could hear Milo howling.

"No. She isn't. Why would you think she was here?"

Her voice rose. "She left, wanting to get pictures of what you were doing. Something is wrong, terribly wrong. Milo is going crazy, running and jumping against the front door. Riley isn't answering her phone."

Chapter 35

Sharp pangs of terror pierced his gut. Cody hit the disconnect button, shoving the phone in his pocket as his head swiveled. Will leaned against the side of the truck, his phone to his ear. Cody ran.

Hearing the footsteps racing toward him, Will looked up. At the grim expression on Cody's face, he straightened, ending the call. "What's wrong?"

"Riley has disappeared. She was on her way here." He explained Susan's call, then added, "I'm going to backtrack her."

"I'll follow you." He hollered at McDougal, who was talking to the tow truck driver who had pulled up.

Cody was already running to his truck. Hopping behind the wheel, he didn't waste time with the seatbelt. Once he was clear of the vehicles and the officer directing traffic around the box truck, Cody stomped the accelerator.

His best-case scenario was an accident. The worst case, the killer had made a final strike. With crystal clarity, he pictured the twists and turns of the roadway he'd just traveled.

When he rounded a curve, he saw Riley's truck parked on the shoulder. Cody's foot hit the brakes. The truck fishtailed, sliding to a stop. With his heart in his throat, he jumped out, racing across the road. He tugged on the door of Riley's truck. It opened.

Behind him, vehicles screeched to a halt. Will shouted, "Is she there?"

"No." Cody took a deep breath, pushing back the emotion that threatened to overwhelm him as he leaned inside, searching for bloodstains.

Will stopped alongside him, peering through the windows. McDougal was right behind him.

Cody climbed behind the wheel to look into the backseat. "Keys are gone, and so is her backpack." He opened the console. "And her gun." Cody stepped out. "Look for tire tracks, evidence of another car."

McDougal shouted, "Here."

Cody and Will rushed toward him.

Several feet behind Riley's truck, the ground was churned up with long scuff marks.

McDougal said, "I'd say she put up a fight, then was dragged."

Despite the churning fear, Cody looked around, his mind building a scene. "She wouldn't have stopped without a reason."

Will said, "A cop?"

"That's what I figure. I need to get Milo, then I'm headed to the sheriff's department."

"I'm going with you," Will said.

"I'll take care of the truck," McDougal told them.

At a dead run, the two men rushed to their vehicles.

Will said, "I'll meet you at the sheriff's department."

In front of the newspaper office, Cody slid to a stop. Not bothering to turn off the engine, he jumped out. From inside the building, he heard Milo howling.

When he opened the door, the dog lunged toward him.

Despite the fear churning in his gut, he spoke to Milo in a calm voice. "Sit, Milo. We're going to find her."

The dog, panting, stared up at him, then sat.

Susan rushed up, her eyes fearful. "What's happened?"

"I need his leash. We found Riley's truck, but she's missing."

Susan ran to her office, grabbing the leash.

As she handed it to Cody, she said, "Can I help?"

"I don't know. I'll call if you can."

Uncertain he could control the dog once they got outside, he clipped the leash to Milo's collar, then wrapped the other end around the palm of his hand.

"Let's go."

While the dog strained against the leash, he seemed to pay attention to Cody's commands.

Outside, Cody opened the back door. He didn't let go of the leash until Milo was safely inside. Jumping behind the wheel, he took off.

Milo, his head hanging over the console, whimpered. His nose nuzzled Cody's shoulder.

"We're going to find her."

Will had already arrived when Cody pulled into the parking lot. As he parked, Will trotted toward him.

Opening the back door, Cody quickly grabbed the leash. The dog hopped out and, for a moment, stood, then threw back his head. A spine-tingling howl erupted as he strained against the leash.

Will said, "He's onto something."

Cody eased his grip on the leash, letting Milo set the pace.

The driveway curved around the building to the back, where the squad cars were parked.

Another howl echoed, prickling the hairs on Cody's neck. Milo lunged toward a patrol car parked at the end of the row. He sharply barked, lifting a paw to scratch at the side of the car.

"Milo, down." Insistent, the dog howled again, butting his head against the metal. Cody dragged him away from the car with a sharp command to sit. The dog's head tilted up. Cody would swear what he saw in Milo's eyes was fear.

Will said, "You stay here. I'll find out about the car." He headed inside the building.

A few minutes later, Will, followed by a deputy, came out.

Cody said, "Is that car assigned to anyone?"

"Thatcher and Bennett drive it," the deputy said.

"Are they here?"

"No. It's their day off."

"I need the keys."

Milo howled.

"What the hell is going on out here? For god's sake, shut that damn dog up, or I'll call the pound and have it removed."

Cody and Will turned to face Rutherford.

"When was the last time that car was driven?" Cody said.

"I don't have to tell you a damn thing. Now get that dog out of here."

Cody stepped forward. Beside him, Milo growled.

"If that dog comes any closer, I'll shoot it," Rutherford said. His hand moved to the butt of his gun.

With a quick side step, he put himself between Milo and Rutherford. "You'll have to shoot me first," Cody told him. "Riley Phillips is missing. One of your deputies is involved. I want to know who last drove that car. I want the keys to look inside."

"I'm in charge here, and you don't get anything unless I say so. If Phillips is missing, it's not my problem."

"I'm about to make it your problem," Cody declared.

Will spoke up. "Sheriff, I'm warning you that your interference in an investigation is grounds for a charge of malfeasance. I will have you removed with one phone call to the attorney general. A woman's life is at stake. If she is killed, I'll take it a step further and have you charged with conspiracy to commit murder."

Rutherford paled. Blustering, he said, "You can't do that. I'm an elected official."

Will pulled out his phone. "I'm not bluffing. We don't have time for these games."

Rutherford's hand flashed up. He growled at the deputy. "Get them the damn keys and the logbook."

When the deputy returned, he handed the logbook to Cody. "No one drove it today."

Cody glanced at the last entries, then stepped to the front of the car, laying a hand on the hood. "Then why is the engine still warm?"

Will had taken the keys. First, he unlocked the trunk, then the car doors.

Milo lunged toward the backseat. Cody handed the leash to Will before he leaned inside. His gaze searched the floor and under the backseat. He slid his hand around the seats. Between the seat and the back cushion, his fingers felt something. He pulled it out. It was a dog biscuit, the kind Riley carried in her backpack for Milo.

Cody backed out of the car. Milo whined. "Good boy. But this time you can't have it. It's evidence."

Will said, "What did you find?"

Cody held it up. "A dog biscuit. Riley's been in this car."

Still fuming over Will's threats, Rutherford said, "That doesn't prove anything. Anyone could have put it in the car."

"I don't give a damn what you believe. I want this car impounded. I know who to call," Cody said.

Rutherford shook a fist in the air. "By god, you can't take one of my cars."

"I can and am." He looked at the deputy still standing beside Rutherford. "Get me the home addresses for Bennett and

Thatcher." The deputy turned tail and ran into the building. Rutherford turned to follow, but not before he shot a look of loathing at Cody and Will.

Cody pulled out his phone and did a quick search for the number. When a voice answered, he said, "I'd like to speak with Sergeant Ingram."

A man's voice came on the line. "Sergeant Ingram."

"This is Cody Lightfoot. Riley is missing. I need your help. I'm in the sheriff's parking lot. How soon can you get here?"

"I'm on my way." The line went dead.

As they waited, Will mused, "It doesn't make sense they'd grab her." He handed the leash to Cody.

"I was on the phone with Scott when I got the call from Riley's boss. Marlin Wetherby, head of Goldmark's security division, is actually Felix Lorenzo. He's wanted and works for the cartel. They had a sweet operation going. Wetherby was in the meeting I had with Braxton. Wetherby has to know this is coming apart. We're onto Goldmark. It all started because of Riley. They could have killed her. They didn't, which tells me they have other plans for her."

"Only one reason comes to mind," Will said. "She's headed to Mexico."

A grim look crossed their faces. They knew, only too well, what it meant.

Will asked, "How much of a lead do you think they have?"

"Can't be much. Whoever grabbed her had to switch to another car, then get the patrol car back here. They may wait until it's dark to move her. Easier to get her across the border."

The deputy ran up, handing Cody a piece of paper with two addresses. Cody waited until he was out of earshot before saying, "It would be near impossible to check every vehicle going into Mexico, and we don't know where they'd try to cross."

Two police cars pulled in. Artie Ingram climbed out of the lead vehicle and headed toward them.

Will said, "I need to make a call." He walked away.

Artie stopped in front of Cody. His voice tense, he asked, "What happened to Riley?"

After Cody explained, Artie said, "Bennett, I can believe, but Thatcher?" He shook his head. "Tell me what you need."

"Impound the car and dust it for prints. I also need to have all the personnel interviewed. Find out if anyone saw Bennett or Thatcher here today. Did anyone see one of them driving the car?" Then he handed the paper with the two addresses to Artie. "Their home addresses. Are you familiar with the locations?"

Artie took a quick look. "Both are apartments. I doubt Riley would be there. If she was conscious, she'd be fighting every step of the way. If she wasn't, then someone would have to carry her. Either way, too risky that a passerby or neighbor might see."

"Can you send someone to find out if Thatcher and Bennett are home?"

"I'll do it myself as soon as I get the car squared away. Do you want me to hold them if I find them?"

"No. If we locate them, I want to set up surveillance."

Artie nodded, then walked off, signaling to the other officers.

Beside him, Milo whined. Cody laid a hand on his head. "Doing everything I can." Milo barked.

Chapter 36

Will walked up. "There is another possibility. A few days ago, a report came across my desk about planes arriving late at night at a small airport about thirty miles from here. It's an unattended airport the locals use, and private pilots bring in tourists and hunters. Seldom does anyone use it at night. Some of the neighbors became suspicious. This could be how the drugs are coming in. From there, they get transported to Goldmark's warehouse."

In Cody's mind, the pieces started to fit. His gut told him Will was on to something.

Will added, "We need a place to work out a plan. I don't want to lose time going back to Austin."

"I've got one. Susan's office. I'll tell Artie to meet us there once he's finished."

When Cody entered, followed by Will, Susan rushed out of her office. Her voice trembled as she asked, "Any news?"

Cody took off Milo's leash, though the dog didn't move from his side. "Not yet." After introducing Will to Susan, he added, "We need to use your office. Artie Ingram will be here shortly."

"Do you want me to leave?"

Will said, "No. In fact, you could probably help."

Nothing could have pleased Susan more than to hear those

words. "I'll get a fresh pot of coffee going."

"I need to call her brother."

When Ted answered, Cody cut to the chase. "Riley's missing."

Curses echoed over the phone line. "What are you doing?" After listening to Cody's explanations, he said, "I'm on my way. Where are you?"

"Right now, the temporary office for the *Register*." The line went dead.

Cody said, "Phillips is on his way."

Susan, listening to Cody's side of the call, said, "It doesn't surprise me you're looking at Bennett, but Billy?"

"Both drive the patrol car, and both are off today," Cody told her.

"Susan, what do you know about Billy's background?" Will asked.

"Not much other than he's always been friendly and cooperative. He's never given me any grief over stories I've filed."

As they settled at the two desks, Will's phone rang. He listened, then said, "Go ahead with the warrants. Wait until Kathy has the one for the warehouse before you execute the one for Goldmark. If you encounter any problems, give me a call. I'm in Fredericksburg." He disconnected. "The judge signed the warrants."

Cody only nodded. He booted his computer.

"Treat, Milo?" Susan said. Milo ignored her, keeping his gaze on Cody's face. Cody rested his hand on the dog's head for a minute. Milo sighed.

Will's phone rang again. He looked at the screen. This time, as he answered, he pushed back his chair and walked outside.

"Now I wonder what that is all about?" Susan said.

A comment Will made about the increase in drugs crossed Cody's mind. Will said he had something working in that area. At the time, Cody figured it was an informant. A small kernel of hope began to build.

Susan shrugged, saying, "Come on, Milo. You'll get a treat whether you want it or not." She grabbed his collar. Though the dog yipped, he didn't resist the tug as Susan pulled him toward her office.

Will walked back in and settled in the chair. After a quick look at Susan, in a soft voice, he said, "I've got an undercover agent in Mexico. He has connections to the cartel. A few days ago, I fed him some names, Bennett, El Sombra, Goldmark, Jamison, and R&B Lab."

He paused, again looking toward Susan. "That was my agent calling. The head of the cartel, Julio Juarez, went on a rampage. Something to do with Goldmark. Then Juarez got a call that had him gloating. A package is on the way, but my man doesn't know what."

"Did he say how?"

A gleam lit Will's eyes. "A plane."

"When? Did he know?"

"He overheard the order to the pilot. The plane will be here in about three hours."

"Damn, that doesn't leave us much time. I don't suppose he knew where."

"Somewhere near a warehouse."

"You keep things close to the vest," Cody remarked. The kernel blossomed.

"Have to, when the life of one of my agents is on the line."

"What do you know about this airport, and how certain are you it's the right one?" Cody asked.

"I'm not certain at all, but it makes sense. It's a small airport, one runway, unmanned, no control tower."

Cody pulled out his phone. When Scott answered, he tapped the speakerphone. "Riley's missing." He explained the details and what he and Will were doing. "I need another background check as fast as

Nicki can run it. Deputy Billy Thatcher."

"She's right here. What else do you need?"

Cody said, "Any other intel you can dig up on Bennett and Thatcher."

Will spoke up. "Scott, this is Will. We are getting ready to hit the warehouse and Goldmark's headquarters with a search warrant."

"Sounds as if you are spread thin on personnel."

"I am, but Austin PD is backing me up at Goldmark."

"What about Fredericksburg?"

The door opened, and Artie Ingram walked in. "Our backup may have just arrived," Will said.

Scott said, "As soon as I've got something, I'll call." He disconnected.

Hearing the last of the conversation, Artie said, "Backup to what?"

After bringing him up to speed, Cody asked, "Are you in?"

"Yes."

"What about your chief? Any problem?"

"No. But I'd appreciate it if I could give him a heads-up. I haven't told him what's going on. Didn't want to create more problems for you."

Respect for the man swelled. By not saying anything, Cody knew Artie was putting his job on the line. "Can you get him to meet us here? I don't want this conversation in his office."

Artie couldn't hide the relief as he punched a number on his phone. Once he finished, he said, "He's on the way."

Cody said, "Did you find out if anyone saw Thatcher or Bennett?"

"Both were at the PD early this morning, though no one saw either one driving the vehicle. I found out they each have a set of keys to the car. I checked their apartments. They aren't there."

Artie stepped to the coffee pot, pouring a cup.

Cody asked, "Artie, what do you know about Thatcher?"

Artie sat in a chair, tilting it on the back legs. "He hired on a year or so ago. Always pleasant, easy to work with. Beyond that, I don't know much. What about the airport? How did you find out about it?"

Will answered. "I got a report about planes landing there. We also know a plane is coming in later this afternoon. It's coming from Mexico."

Artie eyed the two men. "I suspect that's one of the need-to-know pieces of information."

Will said, "We need a printout of the terrain around the airport."

Susan, who had walked out of her office when Artie arrived and leaned against a wall to listen, said, "I'll print it."

The door opened, and a tall, lanky man walked in. The name tag read Harley Perkins. The five stars on each side of his shirt collar proclaimed his rank.

After Artie handled the introductions, Cody didn't waste any time. He quickly explained about Riley's abduction and their plans. When he finished, Perkins said, "You've got the full support of my department. Artie, get whatever you need, just keep me in the loop."

Artie said, "I could use Tucker."

"Consider it done. Good luck." He walked out.

Will's phone beeped, signaling a text message. Will read it, then looked up. "Wetherby's in the wind. Cleaned out his office."

Cody said, "I bet he split before we left the parking lot."

"According to the agent in charge of the search, Braxton was unaware Wetherby had hightailed it. It means we have to add him to the mix. Two of my agents are on the way. One is a sniper."

Susan walked up, laying a map in front of Cody. The others gathered around him to study it.

"Okay, with the three of us and the three on their way, that's six. It's all we need. I don't want to turn this into a full-fledged SWAT takedown. In this case, finesse is better than brawn. Here's what I suggest."

He gestured to a place on a ridge bordering the runway. "A sniper here could cover the entire airport." His finger shifted to the small structure. "This is probably an office. We can put one or two of us in there. Or one inside and another sniper on the roof if there is a way to hide. The pilot is sure to be looking for anything out of the ordinary."

He turned to his computer. On the screen was a smaller map showing the connecting roads.

Will, using the tip of his pen, pointed. "Put one of us here. No matter which way they come, they have to turn here to reach the airport. It will give us a heads-up."

Artie asked, "What about gear and communications?"

Will said, "My agents are bringing what we need."

Cody said, "I have my gear and weapons in my truck."

Will's phone chimed. For a few seconds, he listened before exclaiming, "Bingo. We got them. No wiggle room on this one."

Once he was off the phone, he said, "They found the drugs in the truck. Boxes labeled as prescription drugs were filled with cocaine. No one would give them a second look in a truck full of legitimate drugs."

Cody exclaimed, "Son of a gun. Here's what I bet we'll find. Goldmark sent fake boxes to the cartel, where they were filled with cocaine. Fly them back in the country and deliver them to the warehouse, where they're added to a shipment of drugs to different towns. No wonder no one could figure out how the drugs were coming in. Heck of a slick operation."

Will's next call confirmed his team had found boxes filled with cocaine in the warehouse. All personnel were under arrest.

Cody said, "Susan, get busy writing. With all the activity with the warehouse and Goldmark, some local reporter will get wind of it. Go ahead and break the story. Just say that at this time, significant quantities of cocaine have been discovered. Stay tuned for details type of thing."

A spark of excitement lit Susan's face for the first time since they arrived. "I'll write and even let you read it before I put it out."

While she typed, Cody sent a quick email with the update on the warrants and their plans to Scott. He'd just hit the send button when the door opened. Two men and a woman walked in. Two were attired in tactical gear with FBI on their back. The third, in similar attire, had a patch for Fredericksburg PD.

After the introductions, the two agents, Janet Hancock and Grady Addick, and Tucker Monroe, the police officer, grabbed chairs while Cody briefed them.

Artie asked, "What about vehicles?"

Will said, "We can use my SUV. Four will fit in it."

Cody added, "I've got my truck. The problem is there isn't anywhere to hide a vehicle at the airport." He studied the map on the computer before indicating a small cluster of buildings about a half mile from the intersection. "We can park the vehicles here. They shouldn't be suspicious."

He looked at the two agents. "Who is the sniper?" Janet lifted her hand. "I want you on the ridge." He pointed to the map. "As soon as you have a clear shot at the tires, disable the plane, stop it from taking off. Will, you and Grady are with me on the ground. Artie, take up a position here," pointing to a cluster of trees near the intersection. "Tucker, after we get dropped off at the airport, you'll be with the vehicles. Once the suspect's vehicle reaches the airport, you and Artie block the road. Don't let them leave."

While the officers checked their gear, Cody leaned back in his chair. What-ifs rolled in his head, pushing at the fear bubbling inside him. Even his logic and training couldn't stop them. Despite what Will had discovered, what if they were wrong? What if Riley was already on her way to Mexico? What if she was already dead?

He felt a cold nose nuzzle his hand. Milo stared up at him, then whined. All afternoon, Milo had paced. He'd sit next to Cody for a few minutes, then, restless, he'd get up. Susan had taken him for a walk twice. He even rebuffed the food and Susan's treats. At least the dog had stopped that god-awful howling. Cody suddenly realized the dog hadn't howled since leaving the sheriff's department. Cody slowly straightened. Was it possible? The dog seemed to sense when Riley was in danger. Though restless, as if he knew something was wrong, there had been none of the bizarre behavior Milo had exhibited on other occasions. Did it mean, for the moment, Riley was okay? If she was dead, something told Cody that Milo would know. Hope flared. *My god, was he actually putting his faith in a dog?*

Susan asked, "What about Milo?"

Hearing his name, Milo's ears twitched forward, his gaze still locked on Cody's face.

"I can't see a reason for him to go with us," Cody said. "I'm not sure I can control him, or that when it comes to Riley, he'll listen to my commands."

Artie said, "I know Riley. Whatever has happened, it might help to have him there. He could stay back with us in your truck."

Cody thought. Though his combat experience said to leave Milo with Susan, another deeper, elemental instinct said to take him.

Chapter 37

Images she couldn't grab onto swam in a gray mist. An urgency tugged at Riley despite her wanting to sink deeper into the vast nothingness. It was important she didn't let go, but why?

Her senses spinning, she struggled against the encroaching darkness. Pain struck, hard and fast. It cut through the vertigo, clearing her mind of the cobwebs. She was lying on her belly with the side of her face mushed against cold concrete. Pain radiated in her head, down her neck and into her shoulders. She knew the reason why.

How could she have been so stupid? The good model citizen that she was, she pulled over at the sight of red lights and the sound of the siren behind her, only to let Mickey run up and point a gun at her head, ordering her to step out. When he tried to force her to his car, she had turned on him, striking out. The blow to her head was the last thing she remembered until she came to in the back of the squad car. Bennett had hit her again when he pulled her out of the car.

She wiggled, becoming frightfully aware her hands and feet were tied, and a blindfold covered her eyes. It was nearly her undoing. Panic knotted her lungs. She couldn't breathe. Dust tickled her nose when she gasped. Compressing her lips, she managed to stop the sneeze.

As logic reasserted itself, she forced her breathing to slow. She had to stay calm. Since she had no idea how long she'd been unconscious, did anyone know she was missing? Before Mickey clobbered her a second time, she managed to leave a clue in the squad car, a feeble attempt at best. Even if Cody found it, he wouldn't know where to find her. The terrifying reality was no one was charging to the rescue. If she was going to get out of this, she had to use her wits.

She heard a muffled voice. "Felix, get rid of her. Dump her where we dumped Jamison. No one will find her. It's the safest way out for all of us."

A second, deeper voice said, "Then you can be the one to explain to Julio why we didn't deliver her."

Felix's voice seemed familiar. With the pain affecting her thought process, Riley couldn't remember where she heard it.

A third voice, louder than the other two, entered the fray. "He's right. It's too damn dangerous to hang onto her."

She recognized this one, Mickey Bennett.

Felix answered, "You let me worry about it."

Mickey said, "Right now, Felix, your credibility with the boss is shot to hell after the fiasco at Goldmark."

"That's why Julio wants the broad, and why I'm going to make sure she gets there in one piece," Felix said. A grim chuckle erupted. "I expect he has a special treat in store for her. After all, she upset his apple cart. Once she's on her way to Mexico, I'll finish the job since the two of you couldn't manage getting rid of the dog and agent. Though their deaths will be a lot less painful than our nosy reporter."

Terror spiked at the images the man's words conjured in her mind.

A door opened, and footsteps clomped toward her. Riley let her body go lax, figuring it was better if they didn't know she was awake.

With a grunt, a man's foot pushed her body before a hand tugged her wrists and feet.

Further away, Mickey asked, "Is she still out?"

"Yeah. Why did you have to hit her twice?" Felix grumbled.

"It's not like I had a choice. She came to in the squad car."

"Well, you'd better hope she wakes up. The two of you have made too many mistakes already."

The first man's voice deepened with an ominous tone, pushing the terror even deeper into her bones. "If I were you, Felix, I'd be careful … very careful about who you accuse."

With horrifying clarity, she knew who it was. Someone they had never suspected—Billy Thatcher.

His tone less abrasive, Felix said, "You're right. No point in pointing fingers at each other. I'm going to check on the plane." The footsteps receded, and the door closed.

When Felix rolled her over, the blindfold slipped just enough that she could see under it. Across the room, she saw boots. Someone hadn't left, probably waiting to see if she was faking. Riley didn't move, making sure she breathed slowly. After several minutes, the door opened, and he walked out.

Still, Riley waited before slowly tilting her head to look under the blindfold. The pain was excruciating, though she had a glimpse of the room. It looked like a storage shed or even a garage. Dirt and dust bunnies gathered in the corner. There must be windows since rays of light danced across the concrete floor. Riley twisted her hands, feeling for what bound them. It was tape.

What happened to her backpack? A pocketknife was inside it. She rolled onto her back, then rolled again, squirming until she could see the other side of the room. A flick of jubilation shot through her. The backpack was in a corner.

She rolled until it was against her back. Her fingers fumbled for the zipper. The pressure on her shoulders as she twisted to open it sent sharp jabs of pain shooting into her brain. As she felt herself slipping away, Riley sucked in a deep breath. She couldn't pass out.

Once she got both hands inside, she cursed. Why did she always have to carry everything but the kitchen sink? The agonizing pain from poking and shoving the contents aside forced her to repeatedly stop and rest. Not finding the dang knife intensified the panic that time was running out. When her fingers finally made contact with it, her body trembled with relief.

What she hadn't felt was her cellphone. She guessed that was too much to hope for. With her fingers tightly wrapped around the knife, she pulled her hands out, laying the knife on the floor. Another round of rezipping the bag left her exhausted. Still, she couldn't stop.

Riley rolled away from the bag until she was far enough away to keep the men from getting suspicious. Using her legs for leverage, she managed to sit up. Leaning against the wall, she took a few moments to suck in deep breaths, pushing back the pain, before opening the knife.

Riley feverishly sawed at the edges of the tape, not knowing if she was cutting anything. It wasn't until she felt a slight easing of the pressure around her wrists that she knew she was making headway.

Hearing voices outside, she knew she was out of time. Desperation overloaded her senses. She'd only managed to cut part way through the tape. With a sinking feeling, she knew it wasn't enough. With a quick thrust, she shoved the knife into her back pocket where her vest would hide it. Though she did have a hysterical thought. The open blade would likely stick her in the butt, a minor detail not worth worrying about.

The door opened, and footsteps walked toward her.

Felix said, "Ah, you are awake. Excellent."

Panic wrenched her gut. What if they checked her hands? Instead, the blindfold was ripped from her head. For a moment, blurry-eyed, she blinked, then stared up at the man. Now, she knew why his voice was familiar, though she was confused. She knew him as Marlin Wetherby, but Billy called him Felix.

At the shock on her face, he said, "We haven't been formally introduced, though it really doesn't matter. You, my dear, are about to take a little trip. Someone in Mexico wants to meet you. I'm certain he has something special planned for you since you have cost us an inordinate amount of trouble and money. Now you can pay the price."

Her jaw thrust forward. She let the anger take over, repressing the terror his words galvanized. "You won't get away with it. The FBI is already onto you."

His lips twisted in a sneer. "I already have. Marlin Wetherby has ceased to exist. But then, he never did." He glanced at his watch.

Behind him, Mickey and Billy walked into the room. Mickey shot her a look of loathing.

Standing beside Mickey, Billy said, "Felix, I'm telling you this is a mistake. We have to get rid of her."

Felix turned. "Patience, El Sombra. No one knows where she is. No one knows about the airport, and the plane is on the way. Even the shadow man would have a tough time explaining why she wasn't at the airport when it arrived."

Riley gulped. The name ricocheted in her head. Billy, the friendly, outgoing deputy sheriff, was El Sombra. The man Cody said deals in death.

As Billy stared at her, the rage contorting his face never touched the dead look in his eyes. "It's still a mistake. I don't like mistakes. You and that dog should already be dead."

Riley couldn't stop the petrifying chill slithering down her back.

"She will be, but Julio wants the pleasure." From a pants pocket, Wetherby pulled out a knife. With one finger, he flipped it open. His lips twisted in a sinister smile as the tip of the knife trailed down her cheek and across her throat. "I must say I am tempted."

Abruptly, he moved the knife to her feet, slashing the tape. Felix grabbed her arm, jerking her up. Riley had only a moment to bunch the bottom of the vest with her fingers, hoping the cut ends of the tape weren't exposed. Or worse, they'd check her wrists.

He shoved her toward the door, forcing the two men to give way. "Make sure there is nothing left that someone might find, including that damn backpack," Felix told them.

As she stumbled past Billy, his malevolent gaze swept over her. "Maybe when Julio is finished with you, he'll give you to me. But then, there may not be much left to give."

Riley didn't believe the horrific fear could get worse. But then, she'd never been exposed to the evil that sparked in the eyes of the three men. Her shoulders slumped in despair. She'd never felt so alone, so helpless. Any hope of escape seemed impossible, though she clung to one thought. She still had the small pocketknife.

****

Cody pulled to a stop in front of a weather-beaten wood building. Behind him, Will parked his SUV. Everyone climbed out. Cody walked toward the runway, studying the terrain.

A red windsock at the top of a pole dipped and swayed at one end of the runway. On the roof of the building, another windsock flapped. Despite the hot, dry wind, sending dust swirling into the air, the place was eerily quiet. He walked toward the group clustered near Will's vehicle.

Janet Hancock said, "You still want me on the ridge?"

Cody's gaze scanned the rim before he said, "Yes."

After everyone tested their earbuds and mics, Janet gathered her gear, hiking up the hill, sidestepping around the heavy brush.

Cody said, "Artie, get the vehicles out of here." He tossed his truck keys to Tucker. From inside the truck, Milo howled. Cody walked over, opening the back door. "Milo, you have to stay here."

The dog's whimper stoked the fear buried deep in his gut. He'd lost men in combat. Though he mourned their loss, those feelings paled against what he felt now. This was Riley. Somehow, she had curled herself around his heart.

Cody sensed Milo knew, just as he did, that Riley's life was on the line. He also knew how iffy their plan was. It could go to hell in a heartbeat, and Riley could get caught in the crossfire.

Pushing aside his doubts and fears, he walked away, knowing Milo stared at him through the window.

Will and Grady were already at the front door to the office. Grady was working on the lock when Cody approached. When the door opened, all three trooped inside.

After a quick look, Cody said, "Way too small for all of us. And we can't use the roof. Too exposed."

Will said, "One of us needs to be in here. I'd suggest Grady and I stay outside."

Feeling the pressure that time was running out, Cody said, "Let's find a spot."

The two men picked a place lower down on the side of the ridge where Janet was positioned. Hidden within trees and bushes, their tactical camouflage clothing made them nearly invisible. Cody headed back inside.

Janet's voice said, "Plane."

In the distance, he could hear the faint drone of the engine.

"It's circling," Janet said.

Cody answered, "Checking out the airport."

Artie's voice, rising with intensity, said, "A truck is headed toward me." A few seconds later, he added, "It turned, four people inside. Riley is in the backseat behind the driver."

Cody stepped to the side of a window that overlooked the road leading into the airport. He peered out as the truck came into view.

Janet's voice echoed in his ear. "The plane is starting its approach."

"Whatever happens, make sure that plane doesn't take off."

Two clicks echoed in acknowledgment.

The slow-moving truck rolled to a stop. Cody wasn't surprised to see Wetherby behind the wheel, or Bennett in the front passenger seat. It was the third man in the backseat that took Cody aback. Until that moment, he wasn't convinced Thatcher was involved. Riley looked out the window. The bleak expression on her face ripped at his heart. No one got out.

The plan was to wait until Riley was out of the vehicle. While Will and Grady handled the men, Cody would grab Riley and get her to safety inside the building.

A four-seater Cessna Skyhawk swooped down, and its wheels bumped along the runway. The pilot slowed, turning onto the adjacent taxiway. When it reached the other end, the pilot turned again, putting the plane in position to take off.

Once the plane stopped, Bennett hopped out, loping toward it. He opened the door to talk to the pilot.

Inside the truck, a shout erupted. Bennett turned, pulling a gun. A shot rang out, and he fell. The pilot slammed the door shut and ramped up the engine. The plane rolled along the runway. More shots echoed from the ridge.

The back door of the truck shot open. Riley jumped, falling to her knees. She pushed herself up, turned and ran toward the airport entrance.

Wetherby erupted from the truck, raising his gun to shoot Riley. Cody burst out the door. At the sound of the door crashing open, the man whipped around. Rage twisted his face when he saw Cody. His hand holding the gun swung. Cody was faster. His bullet hit

Wetherby's chest dead center. He staggered, looking in disbelief at the blood spreading across his shirt, then toppled over.

Cody ignored him. Hidden on the other side of the truck, Thatcher was the real threat. Even though Will and Grady kept him pinned down, Riley was still in danger. She was running flat out away from the truck toward the road. From Thatcher's position, he wouldn't miss.

Cody darted to the front of the truck, ducking to look around the front tire. Hunched down, Thatcher had moved away from the side of the truck, looking toward the entrance. When Riley raced into view, Thatcher raised his weapon. Before Cody could react, out of nowhere, seventy pounds of maddened animal sailed through the air. The dog slammed into Thatcher, knocking him to the ground. Cody rushed toward them.

Milo had Thatcher pinned. A spine-chilling growl spewed from lips curled back from teeth inches from Thatcher's throat.

"Get him off me," Thatcher screamed as his hand groped for the gun he dropped.

Cody kicked it out of reach. Knowing the man wasn't going anywhere, he spun, frantically looking for Riley. He shouted, "Riley!"

At the sound of his voice, she stopped and turned. "Cody," she screamed as she ran toward him.

When she reached him, Cody grabbed her, wrapping his arms around her, never wanting to let go. When she pulled back, his gaze skimmed over her, looking for blood. "Did they hurt you?"

Though the terror she'd felt still lingered in her eyes, she weakly smiled. "A couple of good-sized knots on my head, that's all." At the sound of running footsteps, Riley looked behind her.

Grady and Will had sidestepped their way down the hill and were running towards them. Grady headed to Bennett, and Will stopped where Wetherby lay on the ground.

"What are you doing here? How did you know?" Riley asked.

Cody said, "It's a long story, but you can thank Will."

On the other side of the runway, a loud voice echoed. Janet hadn't missed. The plane had skidded off the tarmac. Artie and Tucker were dragging the pilot out, loudly protesting his innocence. Once they had him on the ground, Tucker slapped cuffs on him.

Cody realized he'd missed seeing his truck parked at the entrance with the doors hanging open. No wonder Milo escaped.

Grady knelt on one knee beside Bennett. He felt for a pulse. Over Thatcher's screams, he hollered, "He's dead."

From the other side of the truck, Will shouted, "So is this man."

Her rifle slung over her shoulder, Janet walked up. Cody gave her a quick nod of acknowledgment. She'd done her job with deadly accuracy.

Will came around the side of the truck. "Who's that guy?"

"Felix Lorenzo, aka Marlin Wetherby." Cody turned his attention back to Thatcher. "I guess we should get Milo off him."

Will shrugged.

"Down, Milo."

The dog ignored him as the growls deepened. Under him, the screaming stopped. Thatcher's body was motionless, his face white as he stared into the face of death. Within seconds, the dog could rip out his throat.

Then Riley repeated the command. The dog's head snapped up. Milo spun, charging toward Riley. She dropped to her knees, her arms locked around his neck and her face buried in his fur.

Grady, a set of handcuffs in his hand, said, "Hey, where'd all this blood come from?"

Cody looked down. Blood stained the side of Thatcher's neck and his shoulder.

"I did that," Riley said with a decided air of satisfaction as she stood, still keeping a hand on Milo's head. "I stabbed him in the neck with my pocketknife."

Cody exclaimed, "Where'd you get a knife?"

"From my backpack, which the idiots left where I could get to it." She held up her hands. Pieces of tape dangled. "I cut enough that I was able to rip the rest. By the way," her head nodded toward Thatcher, "Wetherby called him El Sombra."

Stunned, Will stared at the man, still cursing as he lay belly down on the concrete. "Good lord. He's at the top of the most wanted list in three states, and you stabbed him?"

Cody roared with laughter. "I'd say the women and a dog ruled the day."

Artie walked up, giving Riley a concerned look. "You okay, kiddo?"

She stepped toward him, giving him a hug and then kissing him on the cheek. "I am now."

Artie hmphed. "So, how do we clean up this mess?"

Will said, "One piece of good news. We're in a different county. We don't have to deal with Rutherford. I'll make a few calls."

Cody's phone rang. He slid it out of his vest pocket and looked at the screen. He handed it to Riley. "It's your brother."

"I guess you had to call him."

"Of course I did. I suspect he's at the newspaper office."

"Oh, my god. I'm never going to hear the end of this." She hit the answer button. "Hi, Ted."

Epilogue

A month later

Riley, seated at her desk in the newspaper office, sent the last of her articles on Goldmark and R&B Lab to Susan. Beside her feet, Milo lightly snored.

Thatcher, Braxton and numerous other personnel with Goldmark were in jail, facing a boatload of charges. Earlier, Will called to tell her the grand jury had returned all the indictments. If convicted, they probably wouldn't see the light of day, other than from a prison cell, for most of their lifetime. Braxton tried to roll over on everyone, hoping to get a lighter sentence. The district attorney wasn't willing to deal.

The evidence was overwhelming. Braxton and several of his top executives had been lining their pockets from the deal they cut with the cartel. Felix Lorenzo, aka Marlin Wetherby, was the cartel's watchdog at Goldmark.

Cody had been right about how the drugs were transported. Goldmark supplied the empty boxes, and the cartel filled them with cocaine. Planes made regular trips to the airport, dropping off the filled boxes and picking up a load of empty ones to take back to Mexico. The filled boxes were added to Goldmark's shipments of legitimate drugs. No one ever suspected a truck driver delivering drugs to a hospital, pharmacy or a doctor's office was selling boxes of cocaine to the local drug dealers. It was a sweet operation until things started to go south with overruns on Goldmark's new drug.

Then R&B Lab entered the picture with a drug that threatened the success of Goldmark's drug. Cody and Will figured Jamison was offered a tidy sum to sell out R&B Lab by creating a modified version of the drug. One meant to kill. The death of the volunteers would put R&B Lab out of business.

Billy Thatcher, El Sombra, the shadow man, controlled the distribution network while Mickey handled the local dealers. What better way for Mickey and Billy to hide than as deputies? They were certainly in a position to influence Rutherford and his investigations.

When she looked back to the first incident with the bar owner, no doubt one of them made sure there were no drugs when the place was searched, then blamed her, claiming she made up the story. It also answered who was responsible for all the events after Milo found the body. They had to act fast and likely convinced Rutherford to leave the body at the funeral home. Though who did what, Mickey or Billy, was still unknown. Billy wasn't talking.

There was another unanswered question that still had the power to send chills down her back. If she hadn't filed the story about finding the body with Susan, would Billy and Mickey have killed her and Milo? It would been easy for them to get rid of the only person who knew about the body. She and Milo would have disappeared along with Jamison. His body still hadn't been found.

Even though Rutherford denied any knowledge of his deputies' nefarious activities, he didn't escape the smear of the scandal. When it came out that he'd hired two members of a Mexican drug cartel who were operating a major distribution network for cocaine under Rutherford's nose and how he bungled the investigation of the Jamison murder, his career was finished. It didn't take long for him to pack up and leave town.

There had been one other interesting development. Julio Juarez, head of the Camargo cartel, was dead, assassinated by a rival cartel. It ended any threat of retribution.

Nicki had tied up a few other loose ends. One was the farm. She discovered Mickey Bennett was related to the Henning family that moved to Arizona after Jesse Henning sold the farm to Abel Walter.

One loose end might never get solved—the mystery of the airport. When Riley asked how they knew, Cody got a little vague. All he said was that Will had received information from ranchers in the area about late-night flights, and they believed her kidnappers planned to fly her into Mexico. That was all well and good, but it didn't explain how they knew when the plane was arriving. Riley figured there was more to the story but let it go. If Cody couldn't tell her, there was probably a good reason.

She leaned back in her chair and sighed. Riley felt Milo stir at her feet. She muttered, "It's okay, Milo." The dog still exhibited signs of nervous stress and didn't stray far from her side. Though, this time, Milo couldn't save the day. Her heart ached.

Cody had stayed long enough to help wrap up the investigation before he left, heading to Washington. She'd known all along any relationship between them was an impossibility. Fredericksburg was her home. She'd feel like a fish out of water somewhere else, especially in Washington, D.C. He was a Tracker and a dang good one. Riley didn't want him to give it up, though it wasn't surprising several people had mentioned his name as a possible candidate for the sheriff's job. He'd just laughed, saying he wasn't interested.

Even though her logical mind was convinced, her heart had hoped otherwise. Before Cody left, they became closer. She'd believed he felt the same toward her, even though he'd never said anything. Watching him drive away had been heartbreaking. Even Milo had moped around the house.

The one bright spot after Cody left was the day she received the certificate from the SAR organization. Milo was officially a Search and Rescue dog. The certificate and a picture of Milo were proudly framed and hung on her office wall. Susan had even printed a copy of it in the newspaper. Artie and the K-9 officers had thrown a dog party to celebrate.

Milo's head snapped up. He woofed, looking toward the door. His tail wagged, sweeping the floor. When the door opened, Cody walked in. Milo jumped up. Sharp barks echoed as he charged toward Cody.

Stunned, Riley just stared.

Patting Milo's head, Cody said, "I'll get to you in a minute. I've got other business. I think I still need to atone for that girlie remark."

He headed straight toward Riley, hauling her out of the chair. Holding her against his chest, he murmured in her ear. "What would you think about having me around on a permanent basis?"

She jerked her head back. Her eyes gleamed. "What the devil are you talking about?"

"You are looking at the new head of a Tracker team. One based in Texas."

Riley squealed, "Oh! My! Gosh!" Her arms wrapped around his neck as she lifted her face toward his.

Milo barked, racing around the desks.

The Story Behind the Fiction

The Iris Code does exist. It is an algorithm, a numeric representation of the unique characteristics of the iris of an eye. The Iris Code is created during the initial imaging of the eye. Once created, any subsequent scans, in reality not a scan but a photo of the iris for entry to a facility or access to a computer program, are compared to the Iris Code on file. This is very similar to using a fingerprint to access a cellphone. The imprint is compared to the fingerprint used to set up access within the phone's software.

The iris of the eye is one component of Biometrics, a technology for characteristics used to identify people. The most commonly known are fingerprints, DNA, and facial recognition.

Most fingerprint systems measure between 40 and 60 points. Iris recognition uses approximately 240 points to create the Iris Code. An iris is a stable characteristic throughout a person's life. It doesn't change with age, making it a highly reliable component of Biometrics.

What I found most interesting during my research was that using a cadaver eye is also a reality. New software has been developed to detect the difference between a cadaver and a living eye.

I hope you enjoyed The Iris Code. If you did, please leave a review.
For more information, please visit: www.anitadickason.com

Best wishes
Anita Dickason

9 781958 464052